Seared With Scars

The Second Freak House Trilogy
#2

C.J. ARCHER

Other books by C.J. Archer:

The Wrong Girl (The 1st Freak House Trilogy #1)

Playing With Fire (The 1st Freak House Trilogy #2)

Heart Burn (The 1st Freak House Trilogy #3)

The Memory Keeper (The 2nd Freak House Trilogy #1)

The Medium (Emily Chambers Spirit Medium #1)

Possession (Emily Chambers Spirit Medium #2)

Evermore (Emily Chambers Spirit Medium #3)

Her Secret Desire (Lord Hawkesbury's Players #1)

Scandal's Mistress (Lord Hawkesbury's Players #2)

To Tempt The Devil (Lord Hawkesbury's Players #3)

Honor Bound (The Witchblade Chronicles #1)

Kiss Of Ash (The Witchblade Chronicles #2)

The Charmer (Assassins Guild #1)

The Rebel (Assassins Guild #2)

The Saint (Assassins Guild #3)

Redemption

Surrender

THANK YOU

A heartfelt thanks to Karri for the beautiful cover, and to my writing pals: Chris, Freya, Keri, Mel and Robyn. As always, thank you to my family, who keep me grounded and surround me with love.

CHAPTER 1

There are moments when time seems to stand still. When watching a loved one die. Standing on a freezing street corner, hungry and homeless. Waiting for the bite of the belt on your bare back. Or hearing the words "marry me" from someone whose feelings you don't want to hurt but know will be hurt anyway.

I stared at Samuel, looking handsome and earnest on his knees in front of me on the lawn of Frakingham House. He'd just delivered every girl's ideal marriage proposal. Every girl except me. It only made my heart ache.

I couldn't fault his proposal, particularly when he offered to marry me to protect me. It was so tempting to say yes. So *very* tempting. If I had been a different woman, I would have said yes. A mere five years ago, I would have said yes. But I was no longer that naive, desperate girl. I knew better. Happiness and marriage didn't necessarily go together. Nor did love. Perhaps Samuel could take better care of me if we were married, but his name couldn't protect me from gossip. Indeed, a union between us would only expose my past to his set. I may have recently come under physical threat from the spirit of my tormentor, the master, but there were other,

5

less tangible dangers in the world. Marrying Samuel wouldn't make them magically disappear.

"Samuel," I said cautiously. "Please understand that I appreciate your offer."

The light in his swirling blue eyes faded like a dimmed lamp. He pushed himself to his feet and lowered his head. His blond hair fell across his eyes, shielding them from me, but I could read his thoughts in the stoop of his shoulders and his heavy sigh.

"I'm sorry," I murmured.

"Don't," he said quietly. "You have nothing to apologize for. I shouldn't have spoken so hastily. You're not ready."

"That's the thing, Samuel. I will never be ready. I don't want to be any man's wife. I want a life of my own, where I'm free."

His head jerked up. His sharp gaze pinned me. "I will *never* take away your freedom, Charity. I will never do anything to you that you don't want."

I pressed my hand against his chest. My instinctive move was meant to stop him from saying more—and it did—but it also filled me with a sense of longing. I'd not touched a man intimately in years, and part of me missed the closeness such touches could bring.

Samuel wore no waistcoat or jacket and I felt his heart thundering through his shirt. It reminded me that I needed to be careful with him. Since taking on my most horrible memories, he'd edged closer to the abyss of madness. That was my fault, and I would do anything to return him to the charming man he once was.

Anything except marry him or become his mistress.

All I could really do was refrain from telling him *all* the reasons I couldn't marry him. Like the fact that I feared him—feared most men—and hated the loss of self-control I felt around him. And the fact that I couldn't trust a hypnotist.

I retracted my hand and placed it against my churning stomach. "I don't mean freedom in that sense. Not in the way *he* kept me. There are other forms of freedom, particularly for a woman. I want to continue to work at the school and help the orphans in my care."

The flare of earnestness returned to his eyes, or perhaps it was the madness. "I would allow that."

"Oh, Samuel. There are other considerations. You and I are from very different worlds."

"I don't care," he said, almost begging.

"You should. The stain of my background will always follow me. Besides, I'm not sure I could live among people with so many rules." It was an attempt to lighten the tone and put the blame on me, but it didn't diminish the heat in his eyes. If anything, it fueled it. I shrank back a little. "Our differences would only compound over the years and eventually come between us, particularly if I was the reason your family disinherited you."

"I don't care what they think."

His continual disregard for them irritated me. He was lucky to have people who had an interest in his welfare and future. Then again, I suppose it's one of those things that you don't know you have until it's gone. "You should," I said. "Families are important."

"I want to make a new family. With you." He reached for me and I stepped back. His hand dropped to his side and his eyes shuttered.

"You should consider the bride they chose for you," I pressed. "Ebony Carstairs seems like someone worthy of you."

"Don't!" he snapped. "*You* are worthy. Don't let your past define you. Don't let *him* win."

"This has nothing to do with the master." Not even *I* believed that completely, and I could see from Samuel's hardened jaw that he didn't, either. The truth was, being the master's mistress—his plaything—had changed me. There was no returning to the girl I once was, the girl who believed that love conquered all. The woman I'd become after the master's death knew that true love was rare, and that it was not something I was capable of feeling.

His face softened. He lifted his hand again as if to take mine, but quickly returned it to his side. Thankfully, he stayed where he was and did not come closer. I didn't want to hurt his feelings further or alert him to my fear of him by running away.

"Will you at least take some time to consider it?" he asked.

"There is nothing to consider. My answer is no."

"But—"

"That is my final word on the matter. I'll be leaving Frakingham, soon. Hopefully we won't meet again and have to endure any awkwardness."

The muscles in his jaw corded and his body tensed. He seemed to be holding himself together very tightly; or perhaps my interpretation was colored by my own experience. A river of emotions threatened to spill out of me, but I was determined to keep them behind the dam wall. Becoming emotional would only exacerbate the difficulty of our situation.

"Goodbye, Samuel." I held out my hand. "Can we part as friends?"

"You should remain here," he said perfunctorily. "The master's spirit could still cause problems. Until we discover the other medium and stop her, you remain in danger."

It was a reasonable response, but I couldn't stay at Frakingham any longer. I just couldn't. Especially now.

I gave him a grim smile and walked off across the lawn toward the house, entering through the front door. It was like stepping into another world. The dewy, fresh morning gave way to an imposing, cool interior of stone and arches. It was how I imagined the ruined abbey on Frakingham's estate had once looked. It was just as silent too, which was odd considering four of us were preparing to leave.

I was about to go in search of someone when Tommy, the footman, came down the stairs, a valise in each hand. Neither belonged to me.

"There you are," he said. "Where have you been?"

Wrestling with my conscience. "Talking to Samuel outside."

He stopped at the base of the stairs and narrowed his gaze. "Are you all right?"

The fact he even asked the question meant he'd guessed what our conversation had been about. "Yes."

"And Gladstone?"

"Samuel is...troubled. Keep a watchful eye on him, Tommy. He needs a friend."

"*You're* his friend. *I'm* his servant."

I don't know which of us that statement stung the most. "It's possible you can cross that divide, in time, although neither of us will ever be his equal."

Mine was a much deeper divide to cross. The things I'd done in my past were inexcusable for a woman, but were perfectly acceptable for a man. I didn't push the point. Tommy seemed a little sensitive this morning. Indeed, he sounded quite snippy. What had gotten into him?

He set the bags down near the door and came back to me. He looked handsome in his footman's attire, his dark hair gleaming with Macassar oil. It was surprising he didn't have a paramour from the village. Then again, if he'd been flirting with Sylvia, he may not have given other girls a chance.

"I suppose he's going to mope about the house, moaning and groaning, now that you've rejected his suit," he said.

"You make him sound like Frakenstein's monster."

"If the shoe fits."

"Tommy," I chided. "Be kind to him. He's got a lot on his mind." A shiver trickled down my spine at the thought of what Samuel now knew about me, after using his hypnosis to delve into my memories and block them. He knew my darkest secrets, my innermost demons, my fears. How could

I be with a man who knew so much? "You will watch out for him after I leave," I said again.

He glanced past me to the arched doorway that led to the drawing room. "Are you sure you're leaving?"

I followed his gaze to see the Beauforts emerge from the drawing room. "There you are, Charity," Emily Beaufort said. She was a beautiful woman, with warm skin and even warmer eyes. She gave me a smile and kissed my cheek. "We've been looking for you."

She was backed up by her husband, Jacob Beaufort, and Sylvia. I smelled an ambush. I looked to Tommy, but he merely shrugged and headed up the stairs again. "Is everything all right?" I asked Emily.

"Yes and no." She cleared her throat. Jacob moved his hand to her arm, as if to lend her his strength. The spirit medium and her husband were going to travel back to London with the master's last victim, Wendy, and me. Or so I thought. "We have been thinking and we've decided it would be best if you remained here," she said.

I pressed my lips together to stop the retort that sprang to mind from tumbling out. The Beauforts were my school's patrons and my employers. They were good people. I didn't want to offend them with a foul word dredged up from my youth.

"Why?" I asked.

"The master's spirit is still a danger," Jacob said.

"You're vulnerable at the school," Sylvia chimed in. "Anyone can wander in off the street, and there are few able-bodied men to protect you."

"There are *no* able-bodied men," Emily said with a wry smile. "Mr. Cosgrove is the sprightliest and he's in his fifties. And he has a limp."

"Mrs. Peeble has the strength and fortitude equal to any man," I said.

"Mrs. Peeble is unique, true, but she is only one. And I cannot allow all the teachers to be armed. It's too dangerous to have weapons so near the children."

I agreed. Rules were not always followed, and some of the children had snuck into our private chambers as a lark before. We couldn't risk them discovering a loaded firearm.

"You're better off being outside London," Jacob said, looking to the window where I could see Samuel walking toward the house. "But if you cannot stay here, you're welcome to stay with us at the townhouse. The children would be delighted to have you, as would we."

I shook my head. "I won't jeopardize your family's safety." I could feel my resolve to return to London slipping away like water through my fingers. I couldn't bear to put the Beaufort family at risk. "I'll stay here."

Emily grasped my hand. "You have made the right decision," she said softly. "I know you don't truly believe that, but I do."

I tried to return her smile, but it felt strained, stretched. Rather like me, at that moment. My nerves were as taut as a violin string.

The next hour was a blur as the small party of three departed. Wendy had turned out to be an orphan, living on the streets, when the master had plucked her out of poverty and given her his unique brand of education. Her situation was so similar to mine that it gave me chills just thinking about it. At least she would be safe now. The Beauforts would house her at the school and she could train as a teacher, if she chose. *She* would be safe there—it was *me* the master wanted, not her.

We said our goodbyes at the base of the front steps, lined up formally with Tommy and Mrs. Moore, the housekeeper, joining us. Even August Langley and his assistant, Bollard, had emerged from their laboratory to say their goodbyes to the noble family. Wendy was already in the coach, eager to catch the train and return to London.

Emily took my hands and squeezed. "I promise to send word as soon as I learn anything about the master's spirit. Hopefully he will be encouraged to move on by the Waiting Area's administrators."

"These things can take time," Jacob said. "And if he wants to remain on this realm and haunt his place of death, there may be nothing the administrators can do."

"You have to make them see that a spirit like that is dangerous," Samuel urged.

"I'll do my best," Emily said. "I'll also try to discover the identity of the third medium. She must be made to see the damage she caused by summoning the master's spirit."

I nodded but said nothing. The possession and my abduction were still too recent and raw to speak of.

Emily kissed Sylvia's cheek. "Take care of each other."

"It would be easier to do that if the supernatural would leave us alone," Sylvia muttered. "I doubt that will happen, though." She sighed. "This house seems to attract it."

I looked past the coach toward the ruins, just visible near the lake. Perhaps it wasn't the house that attracted the supernatural, but the old abbey. It certainly seemed to have an otherworldly energy about it.

"What do you expect from a place called Freak House?" Langley said. It was difficult to tell if he was trying to make us laugh or being quite serious. He didn't smile. The genius recluse rarely did.

The coach departed and the rest of us returned inside. Samuel disappeared upstairs with Langley and Bollard, probably to work on their experiments in the laboratory. I wondered if he would allow himself to be strapped to that throne-like contraption again. The hideous thing looked like something out of a horror novel, complete with wires and pipes that I suspected were somehow attached to the test subject. I would certainly never sit in it.

It was a relief not to have him near, however. I couldn't bear any awkwardness between us, and there most certainly would be awkwardness now. How could there not be?

"It's just us again," Sylvia said, sitting daintily on the sofa so that her bustle didn't get in the way. "I will miss the Beauforts. They're such charming company, and very grand, don't you think, Charity? Mrs. Beaufort is a true lady," she went on before I could get a word in. "She may not be a great beauty in the traditional sense, but she is very elegant. She comes from a rather dubious background. Did you know that?"

"I wouldn't say dubious," I said, feeling a need to defend her.

"Her family is far beneath the Beauforts."

"Only somewhat," I said hotly. "It's not like she's been outcast from society completely." *Not like me*, I wanted to say. I bit my lip, wishing I hadn't risen to the bait, but then I began to wonder if it *was* bait. Sylvia didn't seem to notice my irritation. Indeed, she seemed absorbed by thoughts of her own. She cast more than one longing glance at the door.

I knew whom she wanted to see walk through it. Tommy. They'd been conducting a flirtation, something I'd recently warned him to cease. It wasn't fair on Sylvia. She was an innocent when it came to men. Besides which, her uncle would forbid it and perhaps even end Tommy's employment. By buying the Frakingham estate, August Langley had dragged himself up from mere scientist to landowner. He wouldn't want to rise so high only to have his niece marry so low. Nothing good could come of a liaison between Tommy and Sylvia, only heartache. Tommy should have known better than to encourage her.

Their situation was uncannily similar to mine and drove home the fact that I'd done the right thing in refusing Samuel's proposal. Starry-eyed lovers may think that a grand *affaire de coeur* could conquer all problems but, in truth, it could not. There were some divides that were too wide to cross.

"I think I'll ring for tea," Sylvia said, rising.

It was probably a ruse to see Tommy. I didn't say anything, and thank goodness I didn't have to. He arrived a few minutes later and performed his duties with formal indifference, just as a footman should.

"We'll have some cake, too," she told him. "Or do you think it's a little early for cake?"

"Whatever you wish, Miss Langley."

"I was asking your opinion, Tommy."

"I have no opinion on the matter."

"Oh. I see." She frowned. "Just tea, then. We should watch our figures anyway."

"Very good, Miss." He bowed and backed out of the room. Even I thought his demeanor too formal; the silly fool had taken my advice to the extreme.

Sylvia watched him depart, her doe-like eyes blinking rapidly. "Whatever is the matter with him?"

"I'm sure it's nothing," I said. "Just ignore him."

"Do you think I've said something to upset him?"

"Why are you worried about what the servants think?"

She sighed. "You're right. I'm being overly sensitive. It's probably an insignificant squabble he's having with one of the other servants below stairs." She bit her lower lip and shot another glance in the direction of the door. "I do hope it's nothing I've done."

"I'm sure it isn't." If I didn't distract her, she would mope about and make the situation worse. "I was thinking of going for a walk later. Would you like to come?"

"What a grand idea! We could go into the village and browse the shops."

"Oh, no, I don't think so. I have no need to buy anything."

"But you said yourself, only a few days ago, that you might like a new dress in a color that is neither black nor gray."

I had indeed, but that was before the memory block had worn off and before the master had abducted me again. Now, the very thought of abandoning my dull clothes made me shrink inside. Wearing something colorful would only draw attention to myself. I'd had enough attention from lusty men and jealous women to last me a lifetime.

Sylvia touched my knee. "If money is a problem, I'm sure we can come to an arrangement. Jack has entrusted the estate's finances to Samuel while he's away and I'm sure he

can be persuaded to give you something for a new outfit."
She winked. "Indeed, he'd probably pay from his own
pocket."

"It's not that."

"A loan then, rather than a gift."

"I have enough money of my own," I said through a
tight-lipped smile.

"I know how proud you are," she prattled on, oblivious
to my rising temper. "But there's really no need. A lady
should be showered with gifts by gentlemen."

"You forget that I'm no lady. Besides, gentlemen have
showered me with gifts for much of my adult life and look
where it's gotten me." I rose and left the room without so
much as a glance back to see how my words had affected
her. She knew my situation and how men, including the
master, had kept me as their paid mistress. Even he had
given me trinkets and baubles, from time to time. He'd
bought me pretty things but had demanded absolute
obedience and favors in return. The cost had been too high
then, and it was too high now, even with Samuel.

Perhaps I was being too harsh on Sylvia when she only
meant well, but I was frustrated at having to remain at
Frakingham and not being able to return to the school and
children.

I decided to go in search of Tommy and see if I could be
of use somewhere in the house. I hated being idle and I
wasn't above doing servant's work, although I suspected the
other staff might think me unconventional at best and
disrespectful to my hosts at worst. So be it. I had to do
something and I couldn't walk around the estate all day.

I was passing by a window when I caught sight of a
coach rumbling up the long drive. It was probably Langley's
coach, returning from taking the Beauforts and Wendy to
the station. But it didn't continue on to the stables at the rear
of the house. The driver wasn't Fray, either, and the horses
were a dark brown instead of light. Tommy strode out to
open the door. He bowed as a lady emerged from the cabin,

the bright green feathers decorating her hat brushing against the doorframe. I recognized her, and the gentleman behind her.

Mr. and Mrs. Gladstone. Samuel's parents.

CHAPTER 2

Tommy was sent to fetch Samuel while Sylvia and I sat in strained silence in the drawing room with his parents and brother. Before I could flee, she had grabbed my hand and dragged me with her to meet our uninvited guests. I thought it a little unfair, since she knew Mr. Gladstone had called me a whore on his last visit. However, she seemed more uncomfortable than me, and *I* was positively wretched with anxiety. Our nerves weren't helped by the fact that both Mr. and Mrs. Gladstone refused to meet our gazes. He stared at the doorway as if he could make Samuel appear if he glared hard enough, and she sat meekly on the sofa, with her head bowed and her hands folded in her lap.

Only their eldest son, Albert, spoke to us. Samuel had told me that the heir to the Gladstone fortune was a sickly man, and he did indeed look ill. He was an insipid version of Samuel. His hair was lighter and lanker, his skin paler, his stature smaller. It must have been difficult for him having a younger, healthier brother with a vibrant nature. Not that Samuel was vibrant of late, but he had been before he became privy to my memories.

"We do apologize for not writing in advance of our visit," he said to Sylvia. "I hope it's not too much of an inconvenience."

Sylvia stopped biting her lip long enough to say, "Oh, uh, no."

It was hardly convincing. Albert blushed and adjusted his stance. He must have known what had transpired on his parents' last visit, and no doubt he knew of their fear that Samuel had formed an attachment to me. I admired him for trying to keep the meeting on a polite footing, despite the coolness of both his parents and our anxiety.

He glanced at his mother then at me, but when he saw me watching him, he quickly looked away. His blush deepened.

I elbowed Sylvia to force her to say something to ease his awkwardness. She cleared her throat. "We're delighted to meet you, Mr. Gladstone," she said. "Samuel has spoken about you."

"Call me Bert, since you call my little brother by his first name. Besides, Mr. Gladstone is my father." He pulled a face. "Wouldn't want to get us confused, eh?"

She gave the elder Mr. Gladstone a nervous glance, but if he heard his son he made no sign of it. Not even his mother chided him. She sat on the chair, as impassive as a porcelain doll.

"Tommy will bring tea shortly," Sylvia said. "I'm sure you need some refreshments after your journey. Have you come directly from London?"

Bert nodded. "We drove most of yesterday and stayed overnight a few miles away. After an early start this morning, here we are."

Movement at the door drew everyone's attention to Samuel standing there. He stood like a wronged god, beautiful and strong yet seething with fury. I half expected a tempest to follow in his wake.

"What are you doing here?" he growled at his father.

His mother sprang up. "Samuel!" She ran to him and embraced him. He rested his hand on her shoulder and looked at me over her head. The anger in his eyes dimmed, but it was still there, lurking at the corners.

He pulled away from her and greeted his brother with a friendly handshake.

"It's good to see you looking well," Bert said.

"And you," Samuel said.

Bert gave him a lopsided grin that reminded me of Samuel's. "You need to have your eyes checked, little brother."

"Don't joke about it."

Bert's response was a simple shrug. "As to your question about what we're doing here, Mother thought it would be a good idea to bring me along to help convince you to return home."

Samuel's gaze slid to his mother, still hovering in the doorway, looking like she would burst into tears at any moment. He ignored his father altogether. "And you agreed?"

"I wanted to see you again. It's been too long." Bert coughed with such violence that his whole body shook with the effort.

"You should sit," Samuel said, steering his brother to a chair.

Bert pulled his arm free. "I'm all right," he snapped. "Stop treating me like an old maid." He suddenly glanced at Sylvia and me as if he'd just remembered our presence.

Samuel didn't pressure him to sit, but remained at his brother's elbow. "I'm not coming home," he told Bert. "Your journey is wasted."

"Nonsense," Bert said with a sudden smile. "Not only do I get to see my brother again after a long absence, but I have the pleasure of meeting these two delightful ladies."

Delightful? I'd not spoken two words to him. Clearly he was cut from the same charming cloth as his brother.

Tommy entered, carrying a tray filled with tea things. He poured and served while nobody spoke. It was a strange atmosphere that had me on edge; I didn't belong there and I wanted to leave, but Sylvia still held my hand clamped between both of hers.

The silence stretched and stretched. The sounds of sipping filled the room. Only Samuel didn't have tea. He stood near his brother, his shuttered gaze slipping to me, from time to time. His father had not said a word, and I realized it was his response everyone was waiting to hear.

Eventually, Sylvia's bubbly nature got the better of her and she broke the silence. "Will you be heading home today?"

"That depends," Bert said with a glance at his brother.

"On what?" she asked, oblivious.

"On when I agree to return with them," Samuel drawled. "You'll be waiting a long time, Brother. I told you, I'm not going back."

"Then it seems we're in need of a place to stay."

"The village inn is comfortable enough."

Mrs. Gladstone sighed heavily. "We stayed there last time. The rooms were terribly small." She appealed to Sylvia. "And I'm quite sure I spied a mouse."

Sylvia pulled a face. "I hate mice. You must stay here, Mrs. Gladstone. I insist."

"No," Samuel said.

"Agreed," his father said, shooting an arched look at his wife, which she ignored. "The village inn will do us—"

"We accept you offer," Mrs. Gladstone cut in. "Thank you, Miss Langley. That's most kind."

I blinked. The exchange had happened so quickly and the response was quite unexpected. I thought the Gladstones wouldn't *want* to stay at Frakingham. Indeed, Mr. Gladstone seemed put out that his wife had ignored him. He huffed and puffed his displeasure, but did not overrule her. Even Sylvia seemed taken aback by the acceptance. No doubt she threw out the offer from politeness and assumed it would be refused.

"Bloody hell," Samuel muttered.

"Samuel," his mother chided. "Mind your language around Miss Langley."

It wouldn't have been lost on anyone that she didn't include me. It would seem she didn't think me worthy of good manners. I set down the teacup and pulled my hand free of Sylvia's. My presence wasn't welcome and I had the feeling they wanted to talk about me, anyway. They'd get it over with faster if I left.

"Excuse me," I said, rising. "I have a matter to attend to."

"Stay here," Samuel said. "Please," he added as an afterthought. "I'm sure my brother would like to get to know you better."

"Indeed," Bert said, beaming. "Both of the ladies."

"Thank you, but I do have something I must do." Run and hide. I scampered out of the drawing room. Once in the corridor, I pressed my hand to my churning stomach and drew in a deep breath. It would seem I was about to catch up on the books I'd selected from the library. I had a feeling I would be spending the rest of the day and most of the evening in my room.

I retreated upstairs and settled onto the chaise by the window with a book. My peace didn't last long. A door slammed somewhere below and then came Samuel's raised voice. "I will not marry her!"

It would seem the topic of Ebony had arisen again. I didn't understand his reluctance. She was a viscount's daughter, a beauty, and seemed nice enough, although I'd only met her once, briefly. Samuel had told me she was politically ambitious and would be unhappy with him, but I couldn't quite see how. She already knew he didn't want a life in politics and she still wanted to marry him anyway. The poor girl was in love with him and he wanted nothing to do with her.

Because of me? I couldn't be sure if I was his reason for rejecting her, or if he'd already made his stance clear before we met. I hoped the latter was the case. I didn't need the extra guilt on my shoulders.

There was something else that struck me about Samuel's heated protest. I'd had no visions. In the past we'd had visions when one or both of us grew emotional, but this time there was nothing. We were cured. Thank goodness! I suspected the unblocking of my memories was responsible for that.

A knock on my door had my heart leaping into my throat. "It's me," came Sylvia's voice.

I opened the door and she breezed inside. "Are you all right?" I asked her. "You look pale."

"I'm exhausted from the worry." She plopped down on my bed and lay back against the pillows. "The Gladstones are terribly hard work and Samuel isn't making matters easier. Did you hear him shout at them just now?"

"Please don't tell me any more. I don't want to get involved in their squabbles."

"You *are* involved, whether you want to be or not. Your name was mentioned."

"Sylvia," I warned. "I know what they argued about, but I don't wish to know the details."

She sighed. "Very well. But I will say this. Samuel used to be such a pleasant gentleman. He never snapped at anybody, and now all he does is bite everybody's head off when they speak to him."

"Has he been rude to you?"

"No-o," she hedged, sitting up. "Not rude, just short. He certainly didn't hold back with his parents, though. I can't say I like his father, but at least he seemed to be trying to control his temper, whereas Samuel didn't even care. Poor Bert had a devil of a time keeping him from saying anything that could irreparably damage their relationship, but in the end, he stood no chance. Samuel has become quite the force."

"Amen," I muttered, sitting beside her. "Was his mother very upset at his storming off?"

"She was in tears. His father looked like he would have an apoplexy, his face was so red. Bert didn't seem to know what to do or who to side with."

"I'm sure he can see his parents' point."

"And yet I think he sees Samuel's perspective too." She sighed and we fell into silence.

A few minutes passed before I realized she was staring at me. "You want to ask me something," I said.

"I know it's none of my affair, but…Charity, are you and Samuel…you know?"

"No, we are not! I'm not like that anymore."

She bit her lip. "I'm sorry. I didn't think you were, but there is certainly *something* going on between you."

"The only thing going on between us is that he asked me to marry him."

Her eyes widened so much I worried she might strain them. "He did?"

"I said no."

"Whatever for? Charity, your future would be secured if you married him."

"Not quite. His father would disinherit him if he wed me."

"There is that. He seems quite set on Samuel marrying that viscount's daughter. But…" She shook her head slowly. "He might have changed his mind in years to come and re-instated him."

"There will never be enough years for Mr. Gladstone to come to terms with Samuel marrying me. Anyway, that is not why I rejected him."

She heaved another sigh. "I know how you feel about marriage, Charity, but it doesn't have to be a trap. Not with the right man, one with your best interests at heart. Samuel cares for you deeply. He's willing to become estranged from his family for you."

"I don't want that!" I shot to my feet and strode to the window. "I wish he'd see sense, but he seems to be growing more and more unreasonable of late."

"Perhaps he's falling deeper and deeper in love with you."

I looked out the window and spied Samuel striding down to the lake and ruins. His back was rigid, his fists closed at his sides. "It'll pass," I murmured.

"I'm not so sure."

There was another knock on the door and I went to answer it.

"I'm sorry to disturb you," Bert said, hands behind his back and a small smile on his lips.

"Not at all," I said. I couldn't invite him into my bedroom so I stood awkwardly at the door, waiting for him to say his piece.

"Would you care to take a walk with me?" he asked. "I'd like to see those ruins. They look interesting."

"Perhaps we should stay nearer the house," I suggested. For one thing, Samuel had ventured toward the ruins and, for another, we should remain in clear view. I wouldn't want his parents accusing me of corrupting their eldest son as well.

Sylvia came up behind me, startling Bert. He bowed. "I'm sorry, Miss Langley, I didn't see you there."

"It's quite all right." She slipped past us, her lashes lowered. "Enjoy your walk. Luncheon won't be long."

"I'll be taking it in my room," I told her.

She opened her mouth to speak, but caught herself with a glance in Bert's direction. "I'll have Maud bring up a tray."

Fortunately we didn't run into Mr. or Mrs. Gladstone on our way out of the house. Bert and I set off on an amble around the formal part of the garden. The squares of clipped hedges only reached to knee height and roses in the center did not hide us from view. I wasn't taking any chances, particularly since I had the prickly sensation that we were being watched.

"I suspect you know why we're here," Bert began.

"I do. I heard Samuel's response, too."

"Ah. Yes. My brother has quite the temper and doesn't hide it." He frowned. "It's most unlike him. He's usually so amiable. Do you know why he has become more argumentative and morose?"

While he knew about Samuel's hypnotism, I didn't want him knowing that his brother had been affected by the dark memories I'd asked him to block. That would only lead to questions about the events from my past and I didn't want to talk about them with anyone, let alone a stranger.

"No," I said.

"The change has come as quite a shock. We haven't seen much of each other in recent years, you see. After he left for University College, we drifted apart."

I lifted my face to the sunshine and drew strength from its warmth. "I want to assure you and your parents that Samuel's disinterest in Miss Carstairs has nothing to do with me."

"Doesn't it?" he said, idly.

"No, it does not. There is nothing between he and I except friendship. Indeed, I'm not sure there's even that."

He stopped and stared at me. "Is that so?"

"I'm not interested in securing Samuel for myself." I swallowed hard and hoped he hadn't noticed my hesitation.

"Well. That's curious. My parents are adamant that you're the reason he won't marry Miss Carstairs."

"Is that based on the time I met them at Claridge's?"

"No, it's based on the time he told us he was going to marry you, not her."

My breath caught in my throat. My chest constricted. "When did he say that?"

His eyes sparkled, but there was no tilt of his lips into a smile. I couldn't tell what he was thinking. "Just now, in the drawing room."

"Oh."

"You do know it's futile, don't you? A union between you and he isn't possible. It would ruin his life."

I bit the inside of my cheek to stop my retort, but it didn't stop a flash of red exploding in front of my eyes. What a cruel thing to say! I wanted to shout at him and call him every crude name in my extensive cant vocabulary. It was either that or give in to tears of self-pity.

I managed not to cry or show my anger. I fought to regain composure, on the outside at least. I told myself that my anger was unfounded. Of course, he was right; a reasonable woman couldn't argue with that. Yet I hated hearing it stated so baldly.

I continued on at a leisurely pace, as if his words hadn't just slapped me across the face. "It would ruin mine, too." A little note of petulance escaped, but that was the only sign I gave that he'd hurt me. "I have a nice life at the school where I teach. I answer to no husband or father. I can choose what I do and when I do it."

"Then you are indeed fortunate."

"You know that I lived on the streets for many years," I said, watching him out of the corner of my eye.

He clasped his hands behind his back. "I do."

"Do you see that it would be difficult for me to go from the life of freedom that I had then to one where I was beholden to a husband?"

"Samuel would be kind." He was testing me. I knew it, and he probably knew that I knew it, yet we danced the little dance because he wanted answers and I suddenly wanted to give them.

"He's a good man," I said. "But he's not for me. You're right. We would be wrong for one another." I looked to where the ruins and lake lay in the distance. I couldn't see Samuel, but I knew he was there. "He'll understand that, one day."

"Good," he said cheerfully. "Then there is nothing standing in his way of marrying Ebony except a broken heart. I have it on good authority that they mend in time."

I said nothing. His jauntiness seemed out of place and didn't sit well with me.

"As long as it doesn't take too long." His tone had turned serious.

I frowned at him. "Why the urgency?"

"My health," he said on a breath. "It worsens."

I should have said something uplifting or tell him that he looked healthy enough to me, but I suspected he would see through the lies. "Is there nothing that can be done?" I asked.

"Various medical practitioners have been consulted and they all say it will finish me. It's the when that they can't agree on. But I suspect it's probably months rather than years."

"Oh," I whispered. "I'm sorry."

"Our parents would like one of us settled in a good marriage with children. It cannot be me so it's up to Samuel to continue the Gladstone line," he quipped.

I said nothing. Indeed, there was not much to say to such grave news.

"It's also why we want him to come home. It's time he learned estate business."

"Then why send him away to university at all?"

"Because he caused too much trouble. He was too idle, too mischievous, and too well liked by…well, by everyone." He cleared his throat, but that only led to a coughing fit that had him doubling over to suppress it. I stood politely by and waited until it ended.

"He went to prison," I said, hoping to get some answers out of him.

"You know about that?"

I nodded.

"Do you know what for?" he asked.

"No."

He started walking again. "Good. It's better that you don't. Better for everyone."

Damnation. It would seem I would forever be in the dark on Samuel's secrets. It was quite unfair, since he knew mine.

"Miss Evans," Bert said, stopping once more beside a deliciously scented rose.

"Call me Charity."

"Charity." He smiled weakly. "I'm glad we met. If nothing else, I now understand my brother's infatuation with you." His eyes dipped. His gaze slipped down my length then up again, feverishly hot.

I took a step back, startled. I wasn't sure how to take his words or stare. Was he being vulgar or paying me a compliment? I didn't know him well enough to understand his meaning.

"I hope you won't be keeping to your room for the duration of our visit," he said. "I'd like to speak to you again."

"I doubt we'll see much of each other. It's too uncomfortable for everyone."

He gave a small bow then headed back to the house. I followed a few minutes later and returned to my room without running into anyone.

***

I ate luncheon and dinner in my room. No one questioned whether my excuse of a headache was genuine. I read a book and wrote letters to the children at the school, and watched the world go by outside. Mr. Gladstone rode off on a horse and returned late in the afternoon looking somber and distracted. His wife went for a walk to the ruins. My only visitor was Sylvia and that was to ask my opinion on which dress she ought to wear to dinner. Not even Samuel came to see me. He'd been avoiding me ever since I'd turned down his marriage proposal. I couldn't blame him for that.

Sylvia peeped in again later as she headed to her room. "I'm going to bed," she said. "The party has dispersed for the evening."

"How was it?" I asked. "Did Samuel make another scene?"

"He refused to eat with us. It would seem you both have headaches tonight."

I wish he'd been more civil. I couldn't bear to be the cause of his estrangement from his family any longer. I should speak to him again and reiterate my position. This time I would be more forceful and direct. He had to be made to see that pursuing me was futile.

"Good night," she said. "See you in the morning. Let's hope they leave before luncheon."

"Indeed."

I got ready for bed and went to close the curtains. A light knock on my door had me halting before I reached them. It could only be Sylvia again, or perhaps Samuel being a little too bold.

"Who is it?" I said through the closed door.

"Bert."

I blinked. What was he doing here so late?

"Can I come in?" he asked. "I wish to speak to you about Samuel. Something's come up. Something troubling."

I fetched my wrap and flung it around my shoulders then opened the door. Bert looked handsome, dressed in his dinner suit. His skin didn't look quite so awful in the poor light.

"I'm sorry to bother you so late." He glanced past me, clearly wanting to be invited in.

I hesitated. My old fears resurfaced, sending heat prickling my skin. I shouldn't be afraid. This was not the master. Bert was an ill man and the brother of a friend. Yet still I hesitated.

"I spoke to Samuel before dinner," he went on. "I want to tell you what he said, but not out here." He glanced left and right along the corridor.

I stepped aside and he entered. I left the door open, but he shut it. I moved back toward the window, away from the bed, keeping him in sight. Being with the master had taught me that. Keep him in view, watch for subtle movements and there will be no surprises when he came for you.

Bert didn't come for me. He remained near the door and smiled. It didn't touch his lackluster eyes. "I know this is awkward and I'll be brief."

"Is Samuel all right?"

"Hmmm? Oh, I suppose so. I haven't seen him this evening." He held up his hands. "I confess. That was a ruse to get you to let me in."

My heart struck up a wild rhythm. My limbs felt as limp as jelly. I put my hand to the windowsill to steady myself. It was happening all over again.

"Don't be afraid," he said. "I'm not going to hurt you. I probably couldn't, anyway. I'm not as strong as I used to be." He chuckled, but I didn't see how it was amusing. He'd tricked his way into my room. No gentleman did that.

"Don't come near me or I'll scream," I snapped.

"I just told you I won't hurt you. There's no need for hysterics. Besides, I doubt anyone will believe that *you* were being led astray by *me*."

I bit my lip and tasted blood. I hated to acknowledge it, but he was right. Not even Sylvia or Tommy would think me innocent of seducing Bert. Only Samuel might, since he knew from my memories that the very idea abhorred and frightened me. How ironic that the man I'd rejected was the one who could defend me. It would have been laughable if it weren't so sad.

"Now," he said, stepping closer. "I have a proposal for you." Another step closer, and another.

"Please stop," I whispered. I felt sick. I couldn't breathe, could barely hold myself upright. I gripped the window frame so hard that my fingers hurt.

He didn't seem to hear me. He came right up to me. I could smell his hair wax and the stale, dank scent of a sick man. "We both know you're in this for the money."

I couldn't respond, even though I wanted to tell him he was wrong. My tongue was too tied up to form words.

"I like you," he went on. "You're a beautiful thing." His gaze raked down my body, like it had done that afternoon.

Why hadn't I realized then what he wanted? "My current mistress is a sweet girl, but she's nothing like you." He touched my cheek, my throat. "You can take her place. I'm not very demanding, what with this bloody pathetic body and all, and I pay damned well. So what do you say?"

I somehow managed to shake my head. I only hoped it was convincing enough.

"There's no fear of complications." He stretched his neck as if his collar rubbed the skin. "The doctors say I cannot have children." His face colored, and I wondered how humiliating it had been for him to tell me that.

"Nevertheless, my answer is no." I'd almost added "no thank you," but stopped myself. Old habits were hard to break, but I would *not* thank him for his offer.

He clicked his tongue. "Stop being difficult. If it's Samuel you're holding out for, then you're wasting your time. Despite what he says, he won't marry you. Father won't allow it and Samuel can't afford to be cut off. Besides, he knows what being saddled to a woman like you could do to his reputation. He's no romantic fool."

I let him prattle on. He said nothing that I didn't already know, but it still hurt to hear him confirm it. Although I'd rejected Samuel, a part of me liked being his love interest. A very big part. A part I must deny.

"Bloody hell, Charity!" It would seem all pretense of gentlemanly behavior had been dropped. He huffed out a long, frustrated breath. "Stop holding out for him. He won't pay you. He's much too used to getting women for free. Did you know that?" His eyes brightened as he latched onto a new tactic. "He's had many women. Dozens upon dozens, is my guess. Many of them a better class of girl than you, my dear, although none so pretty."

"I don't want his money," I muttered. "I don't want anything from him."

"Nonsense. I know your type. You want it all—marriage, money, the estate. You know he'll inherit after I'm gone so you got your claws into him early."

"I only discovered you were ill recently, whereas I've known Samuel for months. Now, please leave my room."

His nostrils flared. "Stupid girl. You're a mere dalliance for him. A trifle."

"I want nothing from your brother. I want nothing from your family. Now go. Please," I added, my voice trembling.

Perhaps it was that tremble which made him step back. Or perhaps he simply remembered himself. Despite his apparent retreat, I did not relax. I couldn't. I was wound up too tight.

"He'll discard you just like he discarded the others." When I didn't respond, he shook his head, sadly. "My offer will remain standing until I no longer have need of a mistress. Good evening."

He left. As soon as the door clicked shut, I slid to the floor and held my shawl tighter at my chest. As determined as I was not to cry, a few tears of relief escaped. I sat huddled against the wall, wondering why I'd been cursed. What had I done to attract the advances of men like the master and, on a lesser scale, Bert? Years ago, I'd enjoyed the notice of gentlemen. Not anymore. Now I abhorred it.

I got to my feet and went to draw the curtains. Two figures below caught my eye. The moonlight glinted off one blond head and one gray. As my eyes adjusted to the darkness, I could make out Samuel's athletic build and his father's sturdier one. They stood a little apart on the gravel path cutting through the formal garden. While Samuel paced up and down, occasionally throwing his hands in the air or dragging them through his hair, his father kept his back to his son and stood as solid as an oak tree.

Then, after a few more excruciating moments of being snubbed by his son, Mr. Gladstone turned and said something to Samuel over his shoulder. Samuel shook his head then stormed off, away from the house. I lost sight of him in the darkness. His father remained where he was.

I closed the curtains and climbed into bed. The events of the evening had unsettled me and I couldn't sleep. The sooner the Gladstones left, the better. It would seem Samuel was the only likeable one among them.

All the more reason that I couldn't accept his proposal and drag him down to my level.

***

I first realized something was amiss when the maid arrived with my breakfast. Her hands shook as she set the tray down on the table by the window and glanced nervously at me.

I sat up in bed and blinked gritty, tired eyes. "Is everything all right, Maud?"

She glanced at the window, piquing my curiosity further. What was happening outside that made her nervous? "It's so awful," she whispered, approaching the bed.

I sat up straighter and held out my hand to her. She seemed in need of comfort. When she took it, I knew something was terribly wrong. Other than Tommy, the staff had been wary of me. They didn't treat me with the same formality as they treated the regular residents, but they didn't talk to me like I was one of them, either. In their eyes, I was neither worthy of a higher status nor an equal one, yet they couldn't treat me lower to my face.

Maud seemed to forget all of that as she sat on the edge of my bed and clutched my hand as if it were a lifeline. "It's Mr. Gladstone," she whispered.

"What about him?"

She swallowed and blinked back tears. "He's dead."

CHAPTER 3

I felt like I would slide off the bed and onto the floor. I let go of Maud's hand and bunched the bed linen in my fist to steady myself. "Which Mr. Gladstone are you referring to?" I croaked. Oh God, please don't let it be Samuel.

"Senior."

I fell back against the pillows and shut my eyes. Relief clogged my throat and upset my stomach.

"Are you all right, Miss?" Maud asked.

I nodded. "Just...shocked. How did he die?"

"That's the awful thing. He was mauled by a wild dog."

"Good lord!"

"It's happened before. Freak House is plagued by the creatures. Or cursed, more like. We all thought it was behind us though." She shivered violently. "I can't believe it's happening again."

An urgent knock on the door preceded Sylvia bursting in. "Get up, Charity. Something's— Maud! You're here." Her gaze switched from the maid to me. "You already know?"

I nodded.

Maud rose, bobbed a curtsy then hurried out.

"I wish she'd waited for me to break the news," Sylvia said, sitting on the spot Maud had vacated. "Isn't it awful? I didn't like the man, but I didn't want this to happen to him."

"So it's true? He was mauled by a wild dog?"

"We-ell." She bit her lower lip and frowned hard at me. She was the easiest person in the world to read. Going by her expression, I didn't have the full story and she was reluctant to tell it to me. "That's not quite true. Perhaps."

"Perhaps?"

"He was certainly mauled, but we don't know what by."

"Maud said you've had trouble with wild dogs before. You don't think it could be them again?"

"Actually, it wasn't wild dogs last time. That was the story we gave everyone for the damage done by the demon."

I gasped. "Oh! I see." I'd heard about the demon, of course, but since the estate had been peaceful for some time—other than the master's interruption—I'd put it from my mind. "That one died, didn't it? Is this a new one?"

She clutched my hand. "I don't know. Samuel and Tommy are investigating."

"Is it safe for them to be out there?"

"They're staying together and they have Jack's knife. It's a special one that can kill demons."

A single knife didn't sound like much protection, no matter how special it was. We both cast worried glances at the window.

"Where was his body found?" I asked.

"Between the woods and the ruins."

I shivered. The woods looked dense. The ancient canopies tangled together high above, cutting out most of the light. It was a large area and easy to hide in. "Have the police been alerted?"

"They just arrived. If the last time is any indication, they'll do a rudimentary search of the estate then leave. I hope they don't stay long. It's too dangerous for them out there now. They're completely unaware of what they're dealing with."

"How did Samuel take the news?"

"Stoically. I suppose he was shocked at first. The stable boy found the body and told Tommy. Tommy told Samuel while he sent Maud to wake me. By the time I saw Samuel, he was as composed as always. If it had been Uncle's body out there, I don't think I would be so calm about it all."

"We show our grief in different ways," I murmured half-heartedly. I tended to agree that calmness was unusual. It was his father, for goodness' sake. Surely he ought to feel *some*thing.

"Will you come downstairs with me?" she asked. "I must comfort Mrs. Gladstone and I can't do it alone."

"My presence won't be welcome."

"I think she's too upset to worry about that now. Come with me, please. I *need* you, Charity." Her lip began to tremble.

I gripped her hand harder. "Very well. If you insist. Help me dress."

I nibbled a slice of toast as she laced my corset. Once my dress was on and hair done, we ventured downstairs together, only to find Mrs. Gladstone had retreated to her room to lie down.

"She's taken a powder," Bert said. He stood at the drawing room window, where he could see most of the front lawn and formal garden. He glanced at me from beneath damp lashes. His face had some color, but there were deep grooves around his eyes and mouth.

"I'm sorry for your loss, Bert," I said. I meant it. He wasn't a bad man, just not a gentlemanly one, as far as I was concerned. I felt the same about his father. He certainly didn't deserve to die so horribly.

"Thank you." He leaned against the window frame as if he didn't have the strength to stand unassisted. "We shouldn't have come here," he murmured.

Sylvia tucked her hand into my arm and urged me further into the room. I didn't want to stay, not near this man. He made me feel base and self-conscious. I wished Samuel were there to grieve with him.

Clearly Sylvia didn't know what to do either. We sat together on the sofa and waited. The silence grew thin, but it didn't break until Samuel finally entered.

"Where's Tommy?" Sylvia asked before he'd barely stepped into the room.

"Kitchen," Samuel said. His gaze slid to mine, and I was a little surprised he didn't look as upset as Bert. Troubled, yes, but not distraught.

"You have my heartfelt sympathies, Samuel," I said.

He gave me a nod of thanks and went to his brother, but didn't touch him. I don't know what I expected them to do. Embrace? I wasn't sure if the upper classes ever held one another for comfort.

"How's Mother?" Samuel asked.

"Upset," Bert said. "She's resting, now. She was in quite a state after you left. Did you find the animal that did it?"

Samuel clasped his brother's arm. "There's something I need to tell you about that. Something you're going to find quite unbelievable, at first."

Beside me, Sylvia stiffened. "Samuel," she warned. "Is that wise?"

"I don't know, but I have to tell him."

I agreed. With a brother who could hypnotize people, Bert must surely be open to the possibility of the supernatural. Besides, he had a right to know the truth.

"Have to tell me what?" Bert asked.

By the time Samuel finished expounding about demons and what had transpired at Christmas on the estate, Bert needed to sit. He was looking gray again and sweat dampened his hairline. He stared at Samuel, his mouth slightly ajar.

"Do you believe this, Sylvia?" he asked.

It would seem *my* opinion didn't matter to him, only theirs. "It's all quite true," she said, somewhat morbidly. "I've seen strange things happen here myself. Anyway, why would we lie about such a horrible thing like that?"

Bert continued to stare at Samuel, perhaps wondering if he were being hypnotized into believing him. That would have been *my* first instinct. "Let's say I believe you," he said. "Let's say a demon took our father's life. Why him?"

"Wrong place at the wrong time, perhaps," Samuel said. "A newly summoned demon is hungry. It devours everything in its path until it's satisfied."

"Apparently they're quite dumb creatures," Sylvia added. "They're not capable of independent thought, except when it comes to eating. They need directing on our realm by their summoner."

"Unless they've been sent here by their own people," Samuel said. "However, that seems to be so rare that the experts agree no demon has been purposely sent here for years."

Bert rubbed his forehead and slumped forward a little, as if the weight of the new knowledge was too heavy for his frail body. "This is all so…exhausting. I'm not sure what to think."

Samuel clasped Bert's shoulder. "I know. I'll do whatever I can to help you and Mother as you come to terms with it."

"Come home."

Samuel hesitated before nodding slowly. "I need to stay for a few more days to secure the estate here. I won't leave while that thing is out there." He spoke to his brother, but he looked at me. His heated gaze on my face was as intense as ever; even now he thought about protecting me. It was a heady thing, but it made me squirm under his scrutiny. I didn't want it. I looked away, but not before I saw the way Bert glared at him with dark, consuming envy.

"Where is Jack's knife?" Sylvia asked.

"I have it," Samuel said.

"Then you must use it to send that thing back."

"It won't solve the other problem."

"And what is that?"

"We must find out who summoned it. If we don't, they may simply summon another."

"Bloody hell," Bert muttered. "How will you go about finding the responsible party? Any suspects?"

"One," Samuel said. "The man who summoned the last one here has the knowledge and an unhealthy interest in the supernatural."

"Myer," I muttered.

Sylvia wrinkled her nose. "Horrid man."

"To summon the demon, he would have to be in the area," I said. "But I thought he went back to London."

"I'll go into the village and ask the Butterworths if he has returned," Samuel said.

"You can't go out now!" Sylvia cried. "It's too dangerous. And you must grieve with your family."

"I have to go. We need to know if he's here or not."

"And if he isn't?" I said quietly.

His gaze locked with mine. "Then we must look for another suspect."

I swallowed. Sylvia whimpered and I worried that she might faint. Thinking about who else might be responsible had me equally fretful. There couldn't be too many people in the vicinity of Frakingham who not only knew how to summon a demon, but possessed the necessary amulet.

"I wonder," Bert murmured. "Who do you think was the last person to see him alive?"

"All of us, at dinner," Sylvia said with a shrug. "Well, everyone except Charity and Samuel."

Samuel had met him after that, late in the evening. I'd seen him and his father from my window. Indeed, he could have been the last person to see his father alive. How awful that their final words to one another had been harsh ones. Despite his calm demeanor, he must be horrified as well as sad; his father had been mauled. The sight would have been gruesome. I wanted to go to him and comfort him, but did not. I suspected I was the reason he had argued with his father last night.

***

Samuel returned, grim-faced, from the village some time later. "Myer is in residence in Harborough," he told Sylvia, Tommy and me.

We'd watched the coach drive around the back to the stables and waited for him at the rear door that led to the courtyard. Samuel had then ordered the coachman and stable boy to shelter inside the house for safety. No one was to go outside unless armed and accompanied by a group of men.

"Then he did it!" Sylvia cried.

"He claims not," Samuel said.

"We are not fool enough to believe *that*. Are we?"

"Why would he summon a demon here again?" Tommy said. "Jack threatened him."

"And doesn't his access to the ruins depend on Mr. Langley's good will?" I asked. "Surely he wouldn't jeopardize that."

"He wouldn't," Samuel agreed.

Sylvia sniffed. "True. But he's mad and likes to experiment with the supernatural. He doesn't care who he harms in the meantime."

"I hate to think that of anyone," Tommy said, "but you may be right."

She looked surprised to have someone agree with her and almost smiled, despite the horrible nature of the conversation.

"There is another possibility," I said.

They all looked to me. Samuel took a step closer, but stopped before getting too near.

"The master may somehow be responsible."

Samuel dragged his hand through his hair and lowered his head. It was all the confirmation I needed that he agreed with my suspicions.

"But why?" Sylvia asked. "I don't understand. If the master's ghost wishes to have you back, Charity, why not just possess someone again and abduct you, like last time?"

"Perhaps his spirit medium won't do it again," I said, hopeful. I hated to think that a medium had deliberately summoned an evil spirit into a body. Perhaps the first time had been a mistake, or she'd not been old enough to know what she was doing. To do it a second time was heinous indeed.

"Or perhaps she can't," Samuel said quietly. "She may have moved on or died herself."

"We can only hope," Sylvia murmured. We all blinked at her, but she seemed oblivious to how callous she sounded. I supposed she meant well, in her own way.

"I don't think it's the master," Tommy said with an emphatic shake of his head. "Mrs. Beaufort is connected to the spirit realm and assured us the administrators would alert her of any changes to the master's spirit form. She would have sent a telegram."

I sighed. "That brings us back to Myer again."

We walked through the warren of rooms and corridors to the main part of the house. Tommy peeled off to double-check that all external doors and windows were still locked. Samuel was about to go upstairs to see his mother when we met her coming down.

She wore a gray day dress. Mrs. Moore must have found a black cap and a veil of black crepe in the attic and loaned them to her. The veil was so thick that Mrs. Gladstone's face was obscured almost completely. She stepped slowly down the stairs, leaning heavily on Bert at her side. Samuel joined them and took her other hand. I was pleased to see that he'd resumed his family responsibilities. It was a shame it had taken the death of his father to rally him.

"Come into the drawing room, Mrs. Gladstone," Sylvia said. "We'll have some tea brought in."

Mrs. Gladstone allowed her sons to steer her. She walked slowly, as if she were about to succumb to a fit of the vapors at any moment. My heart went out to her. She'd not only unexpectedly lost her lifelong companion, but her own future was now shrouded in uncertainty. With her eldest son inheriting the fortune and estate, she should be secure. But his illness put everything in doubt. If he died, and Samuel wed me, I could have her thrown out of her own home. Of course, I had no intention of marrying Samuel, but she thought I did.

I followed them, unsure if I was doing the right thing. I wanted to show Mrs. Gladstone that I was sympathetic, but I didn't want my presence to remind her of why she and her husband had come to Frakingham in the first place.

We sat in the drawing room and waited in silence for the tea to arrive. There was an unnerving air about our little party. Nobody seemed to know what to say. The silence was punctuated by Mrs. Gladstone's occasional sobs and the eventual arrival of tea.

"Thank goodness," Sylvia blurted out, upon seeing Tommy holding the tray in the doorway. "Er, I mean, tea is just what we need right now. Thank you, Tommy."

He bowed and was about to retreat when Samuel called him back. "I've had a thought about the situation we spoke of earlier. Can you ask the other staff if they've seen anyone on the estate recently? Anyone who shouldn't be here, that is."

He nodded. "I'll do it right away."

"Why?" Mrs. Gladstone asked.

Samuel seemed caught out by her question. "I, uh, it's an estate matter."

"Has something been stolen?"

Samuel shook his head. "It's probably nothing."

"I saw someone," she announced.

"Go on," Bert urged.

She dabbed her handkerchief to her nose beneath her veil. "From my window. It was late last night, after I retired. There was a light bobbing in the distance. It came closer to the house and I saw it was someone holding a lamp. The moon was bright and I could make out his silhouette, but not his face. He was quite tall and thin."

Samuel's gaze connected with mine. We both must have thought the same thing—Myer was tall and thin.

Mrs. Gladstone began to cry into her handkerchief. "What if he'd been taken too?"

Bert put his arm around her shoulders. "He wasn't," he assured her. "They would have found his remains."

"This is so awful," she sobbed. "I hate this place. *Hate* it."

I didn't need to look at Sylvia to know that Mrs. Gladstone's words would have been a stab to her heart. She may not like Frakingham's reputation, but it was her home. I dared a glance at her, but she sat primly, her face impassive. Too impassive for a rather excitable girl. Tommy watched her too, his brow deeply furrowed.

"We'll be gone soon," Bert soothed. "As soon as the undertaker releases Father's body into our care, we'll take him home."

"When?" she pressed. "When will that be?"

"A day or two," Samuel said. "No more."

She suddenly twisted in her seat and grasped his shoulders. "You will come back with us, won't you?"

Samuel removed her hands and held one of them in his own. He nodded.

She patted his cheek. "My beautiful boy. I'm so glad you'll soon be home where you belong."

Her words were meant to sting me. Everybody seemed to know it. Sylvia and Tommy watched me, a mixture of sympathy and curiosity on their faces. Bert gave me a somewhat triumphant arch of his eyebrows. Only Samuel didn't look my way. He sat rigidly beside his mother on the sofa.

"Be good boys and pack your father's things for me," she said. "I don't want the servants to do it."

"We'll do it later."

"Now, if you don't mind," she added, softening the hammer blow of her direct order with another pat of Samuel's cheek.

"Of course," Bert said, rising. "Would you like us to escort you to your room?"

"No, I'll stay and have my tea."

Bert walked off, but stopped at the door when he realized Samuel hadn't followed. "Coming?" he asked his brother.

Samuel hesitated then finally nodded, but only after I gave him a small, encouraging smile. A smile I hoped would tell him not to worry about me. I didn't know what his mother thought of our intimate exchange, shielded as she was by the veil, but I suspected she wouldn't have liked it.

They left, as did Tommy, leaving Sylvia and I on our own with Widow Gladstone. I was about to announce that I needed to also leave, when Mrs. Gladstone spoke.

"Miss Langley, could you direct your maid to pack my bags so we're ready for an immediate departure, if necessary."

Sylvia shifted uncomfortably on the chair. She might have been about to protest for my benefit, but Mrs. Gladstone spoke again.

"Now, please." Her tone did not invite disagreement.

Sylvia shot me an apologetic wince then hurried out of the drawing room.

"If you wanted to speak to me alone, you only had to ask," I said once she was gone. "I wouldn't have objected."

Mrs. Gladstone raised her veil and pinned me with a cool, gray stare. Her eyes and nose were swollen from crying, but that didn't diminish her ferocity. "You're a rather forward girl, considering."

"Considering my position as a sewer rat, you mean?"

Her gaze didn't falter. "I wouldn't have put it quite so baldly."

"I have nothing to fear from you, Mrs. Gladstone. Indeed, I'm glad we're alone. There are some things I wanted to say to you and now that you've set the tone with plain-speaking, I'll do likewise."

"You should at least allow me the courtesy of going first. That's the respectable thing to do."

I gave a nod. "Given the circumstances, I agree."

She gave a small grunt and narrowed her eyes at me. I suspected she thought I'd be more uncouth and disagree with her. "Once my son leaves here, you're not to contact him."

"I can't agree to that."

"Why not?"

"Because I'm staying at Frakingham for the time being. If he returns here—"

"He won't."

I bit back my retort and simply gave another nod. She didn't want to think about Samuel leaving her, and it wasn't up to me to shatter her illusions. That was Samuel's battle to win. That's if he did indeed wish to return to Frakingham, as I suspected.

"In that case, we're of like mind," I said. "I don't wish to see Samuel anymore, after this." My heart tumbled to the rhythm of *traitor*.

Mrs. Gladstone's lips pinched. "You're lying."

Convincing her wasn't going to be easy. "I know you don't understand, considering my past, but it's true. A previous…paramour cured me of any tender feelings toward men."

"Paramour? Is that what you call them?" It would seem she didn't know that Bert kept a mistress. Or if she did, she didn't include him in her snide assessment of the type that did. "Samuel isn't like other men," she went on. "He's far more charming, for one thing. If he has his heart set on you, it would take a very determined woman to resist."

"You don't think I have that determination?"

"I think you don't *want* to resist."

My heart sank. It was useless. She wouldn't be swayed from her assumptions. "Then I'm sorry for you, but it's not up to me to persuade you. You can believe what you want to believe." I rose to go, just as Mr. Langley and Bollard entered.

"Ah, Mrs. Gladstone, I'm glad I found you," Langley said. Bollard pushed the wheelchair into the room. He was breathing heavily, as if he'd been walking very fast. "Samuel said you were in here with Charity."

He looked at me and I frowned back. Had Samuel asked him to check in on me and ensure I wasn't trapped with his mother for too long? How curious if it were true and Langley had agreed. I'd not known the old scientist was so thoughtful.

Mrs. Gladstone lowered her veil and turned her head away. "She was just leaving."

"Indeed," I said. "Please accept my condolences on your loss, Mrs. Gladstone. I know you don't believe me to be sincere, but I am."

She didn't acknowledge me in any way, so I walked off. Bollard briefly touched my shoulder as I passed and offered a small smile. I smiled back. I was beginning to like the big mute.

I headed up to the room in one of the towers and lounged in the chaise by the window. The day was dull and wet so I didn't miss being outside. The only movement came from the raindrops sliding down the glass.

My conversation with Mrs. Gladstone troubled me, not because I resented her thinking of me as a gold-digger, but more because of what it meant for Samuel. It was obvious that his mother didn't understand him. She didn't see that he only wanted to be given space to make his own choices, even if those choices were mistakes. If only she trusted me, we could work together to steer Samuel into Ebony's arms.

My heart beat harder in protest, but I ignored it. I wasn't the right woman for Samuel, and he wasn't right for me. No man was. In time, my heart would come to realize it too.

"I thought I might find you here." Samuel's voice startled me. It was as if my thinking about him had conjured him from thin air. He stood in the doorway, his shirt sleeves rolled to the elbows, revealing his muscular forearms.

I suddenly felt ill at ease. I went to get off the chaise, but he put his hands up.

"Please, stay. You look comfortable."

I remained, but sat instead of lounging. "Did you and your brother finish packing already?"

He lifted one shoulder. "Not yet, but there's no rush. He had to lie down and I took the opportunity to search for you."

My face heated. "Oh. Thank you for sending Mr. Langley down to rescue me. It wasn't necessary. Your mother and I were having a perfectly civil conversation."

If he saw through my lie, he gave no indication. "You guessed." The corner of his mouth twitched. "I thought you might."

"I assured her that I have no intention of marrying you."

The twitching stopped. He looked down at the floor. "I'm sure she was happy to hear that."

"I don't think she believed me, but I'm glad I made my feelings known regardless."

"You did," he mumbled. "As clear as day."

"Oh, Samuel. Please, let's be friends again. Just friends."

He looked up and I was startled by the deep shadows in his eyes, the sad turn of his mouth. "I'm sorry. You're right. I don't want there to be any awkwardness between us."

"It's inevitable that there will be, for a little while." I didn't mention not wanting to see him again. There was no need to rub salt into the wound, especially since he would soon be leaving with his mother and brother anyway. By the time he was able to return to Frakingham, I might be home in London.

"There's something I wanted to show you," he said, reaching into the pocket of his waistcoat. He pulled out a small square of paper and handed it to me. It was blackened at the edges from burning. "I found this in the fireplace of Father's room. Read it."

The note consisted of a single sentence written in a nearly illegible scrawl: *I know what you did.*

CHAPTER 4

I know what you did. The five words scribbled on the piece of singed paper sent a chill rippling down my spine.

"What does this mean?" I asked Samuel.

He shook his head slowly. "I don't know. There's no indication of who it's from. There was a waste basket near the writing desk," he added.

"So why burn it?" I muttered.

He took the paper back. "It wasn't burned completely."

Curious. "Have you shown it to your mother?"

"Not yet."

"Perhaps you shouldn't. It might upset her more."

"You're very kind to think of her, Charity. Particularly when she hasn't been so kind to you in return."

"She hasn't said anything I haven't heard before."

He closed his eyes. His chest expanded with his deep breath. "That's precisely why I think we should marry. I can protect you from such cruelty."

"Oh, Samuel. That's noble of you, but you can't. Marriage will only make it worse, and not just for me, but for you and your family. Can you imagine what your mother's friends will say behind her back? Or perhaps even to her face?"

"If they do, then they're not true friends," he spat. "She'd be better off without them."

I wanted to chide him for not understanding his mother's position, but didn't. Our relationship wasn't like that. In the brief few days in which my memory had been blocked, perhaps I could have. I had more courage then. Now, just the thought of speaking my mind to a man—any man—had my insides twisting into knots.

He suddenly sat on the chaise beside me and grabbed my hand. He held it firmly. Too firmly. I did not try to pull away. Resisting had only ever made the master's grip harder.

But Samuel was not the master. I needed to remember that.

"Will you not reconsider, Charity?" he urged. "I can make you happy, and I know you will make me happy."

Given our circumstances, I doubted that very much. "I've said my piece. Please let's not discuss it again." I tugged and he let go.

He paced to the window and back, twice, before standing before me once more. "Everything has changed now that Father has gone," he said, fixing me with a steady gaze.

"Has it?"

"I won't be cut off, for one thing."

"Bert wouldn't follow through on your father's wishes?"

"No. He's too fond of me."

If he were so fond of his brother, why would he try to buy the woman Samuel loved?

"Nothing has changed, as far as I'm concerned," I told him. "Now please, let's end this discussion. It's too upsetting for both of us."

He stared at me. Really stared. "If you didn't care, how could it upset you?"

"I never said I don't care!" My outburst startled me. I bit my lip and watched him closely for signs of backlash for my impertinence. "I'm sorry," I mumbled.

"Don't apologize." The corner of his mouth lifted. "I like to see you fire up, on occasion. I know you say what you're thinking when you speak so vehemently, and I want to know what you're thinking, Charity. I want to know everything about you."

"You already do."

He shook his head. "I know your memories and the emotions associated with them—joy, fear, hope. But I don't know what you want for the future, or what you're thinking *now*."

I said nothing. I couldn't. My nerves were too raw, my heart sore, not only for him, but for me, too. For what might have been if my past had been different and I'd never succumbed to the master's charms.

"Damnation," he muttered. He scrubbed his hands down his face. When he removed them, there seemed to be more creases around his eyes and deeper shadows within. "Why is it I never know what to say to you? I admit to being at a loss, here. That's not something I'm used to where women are concerned. There, now you know more about my current state of mind than I do about yours."

I smiled at his candid admission. It was more charming than any form of flattery.

Samuel leaned against the window frame with a sigh and stared out at the solid expanse of gray sky. His face was in profile, but I could see it fully in the reflection. His lips pinched together and his nostrils flared. He was trying hard not to let his emotions get the better of him.

I considered going to him, but decided to remain seated. A simple gesture such as a hand on his arm could too easily lead to a comforting embrace. I couldn't risk that.

"I know you didn't get along with your father, of late," I said, "but it's still a terrible thing to lose him. I can't imagine what you're going through."

"You lost both your parents."

"I never knew my father and hardly knew my mother. Her death wasn't a big loss. You have my utmost sympathies, Samuel."

He gave me a flat smile in the window's reflection. "Thank you. I'll be all right. It's Mother I'm worried about, and Bert. His health worsens."

"He told me he's dying."

He jerked around to face me fully. "He did? When?"

"We spoke yesterday." I smoothed my skirts over my lap, but my hands trembled, so I dug my fingernails into my palms. "He said you have to return home so you can learn to manage the estate. It's even more urgent now."

"I wish he wouldn't speak as if his death were close. The doctors don't know how long he has left."

The doctors may not know, but Bert might have some notion. He knew himself better than anyone. But I didn't tell Samuel that. He had enough burdens and loss to bear for the time being.

"Nevertheless, you'll need to take on a greater responsibility," I said.

"I'll cross that bridge when the time comes."

I didn't push it further. He seemed to be in denial about the gravity of Bert's illness. Perhaps after the shock of his father's death wore off, he could come to terms with it better.

"I have to return home, for now," he said. "But I won't stay more than a few days. I can't leave you and the others alone here for long while there's a demon on the loose."

The mention of the demon set my mind bending in that direction again. Essentially, the person who'd summoned the demon was a murderer. If it turned out to somehow be the master's doing, I wouldn't be surprised. He was a cruel man with no morals. Myer didn't seem quite so ruthless, just selfish and single-minded in pursuit of the supernatural.

"Your family must come first," I said. "We have Tommy and Bollard to protect us, and Jack's knife."

"It's not enough!"

His growled words startled me. The wildness of his eyes hammered home how fragile his mind had become since becoming privy to my memories.

"You need to take some time away from here," I said firmly. "Be with your family and friends."

"*This* is my family now. *You* are my friends. All of you."

"You don't really think that. I've seen how close you and Bert are. Your mother loves you too. Don't throw that away."

He heaved a ragged sigh. "I need to be here, Charity. I *need* to protect you." He tapped his chest. "It hurts me in here to know that I can't."

I sprang to my feet before I knew what I was doing. I couldn't listen anymore. Couldn't hear his sweet words or look into the whirlpools of his eyes. His tender sentiments were hammering against the wall around my heart. One more blow might shatter it.

I couldn't afford that. Not after I'd tried so hard to build it.

"Go home, Samuel," I said, my voice trembling. "We'll be fine without you." I turned and left, not daring to look back. I couldn't bear to see the damage *my* words caused.

***

I ate luncheon in my room. I intended to remain there, alone, for the rest of the day, but Tommy disturbed my peace mid-afternoon.

"Sylvia sent me to tell you that the Butterworths are here," he said. "They've brought Myer with them."

I groaned. "Is she with them now?"

"Yes, as is Samuel. Mrs. Gladstone and Mr. Albert remain in their rooms."

"Then why am I needed?"

"They thought you might like to hear what Myer has to say about summoning the demon. They haven't asked him yet."

"Sylvia can relay anything pertinent from the interview."

He rolled his eyes. "For God's sake, Charity, stop hiding away up here. It's cowardly."

I blinked back hot tears. It was one thing to be called a coward by someone I didn't know well, as August Langley had once done, but from a long-time friend such as Tommy, it hurt.

He sighed and came further into the room. "I only meant it's not like you to cower in your room. You've always been one to confront matters."

I shook my head and dabbed at my eyes. "The old me did. But you don't know me anymore, Tommy. I've changed in recent years. You're right. I *have* become cowardly."

His gaze lowered. "I wish Jack were here."

"So do I."

"He'd be straight with you. He'd tell you direct what he thought of your behavior. But it looks like it's up to me and I know you're going to hate me for it."

"I could never hate you or Jack. We've been friends too long to let a few words come between us."

"You haven't heard what I'm going to say yet."

"I thought calling me cowardly was the extent of it."

That almost produced a smile, but it would seem the task he'd set himself was too grave to allow it to flourish. "You've become a shadow of the girl you once were."

He paused, perhaps waiting for my response. I said nothing. There was nothing to say.

"You used to be lively, happy. You had strength of spirit and a quick wit. You used to laugh all the time, and make us laugh. But you've lost all of your vitality. It's like you've given up since...since that man did what he did. It's like he took the essence of what made up Charity Evans, and never gave it back after you escaped."

My throat burned with the tears clogging it. He was right. The master had stolen my spirit and not even his death had seen its return to me. He'd crushed it beneath his boot until it was nothing but dust. There was no getting it back now, after all this time and all that he'd done. It was lost forever.

"What do you expect of me?" A whisper was all I could manage without breaking the bank that held back my tears.

"I expect you to fight to take back that essence. I want to see you enjoy what you *do* have, not what you lost."

"The girl I once was is gone, never to return."

He clicked his tongue and bobbed down in front of me. I didn't meet his gaze. Couldn't. "That's what I'm trying to tell you. Fight for her. Fight to get her back. You have to try, Charity, and I'm not seeing you try anything stuck away in here." He touched my hand, but I snatched it away and buried it, scar and all, under my skirts.

"You don't know anything," I snapped. "You weren't there. Now, kindly keep your opinions to yourself. Besides, I don't see what any of this has to do with me staying in here. I'm avoiding Mrs. Gladstone." Bert too, but I didn't tell him that. "It has nothing to do with me having changed, or turning into a shadow, as you put it."

"Doesn't it?"

"Of course not. Mrs. Gladstone is grieving. She doesn't need to meet me around every corner, reminding her that her son has sunk so low as to want to marry a scarlet woman. I don't consider myself cowardly at all in this instance. I'm simply being considerate of her feelings."

"Nonsense. You could be there for her son, or even for her. See this as an opportunity to show her the real Charity Evans, the kind-hearted and capable woman. Given time, she will grow to like you. The real you."

"Now is not the time for grasping at opportunities to inveigle myself."

"I don't mean inveigle—"

"Besides, having her like me only applies if I want to marry Samuel. I don't. And since I don't, the Gladstones mean nothing to me. They can think what they wish. I simply don't care."

"You don't mean that."

"I do. And since you can't see it, then you don't know me anymore, Tommy. Now, kindly leave me alone."

"Not until you come downstairs and listen to what Myer has to say. And hurry up about it. They're waiting for you."

I did so want to hear Myer's response, but I'd dug my heels in so deep I wasn't sure I could dig them out again. "Sylvia can relay the conversation."

"She'll forget something important."

"You, then."

"I'll refuse."

I sighed. "You're the most stubborn, pig-headed man I know. Besides Jack."

He suddenly grinned and I was grateful beyond words to see it. It meant we were still friends, despite everything we'd said to one another.

"Are you sure Mrs. Gladstone isn't there?" I asked.

"She isn't. Neither is Mr. Albert. Come on, or I'll have to send Sylvia up to fetch you. She'll be far more insistent."

I sighed. "Very well."

We went downstairs together, but parted at the bottom of the staircase. He headed to the service area and I made my way to the drawing room, but avoided looking directly at Samuel. Our last conversation had been upsetting for me. I didn't want to see how it had affected him.

Mr. Myer sat in an armchair near the unlit fireplace, and the Butterworths sat together on one of the sofas. It was quite a shock seeing the dough-faced Harborough mayor again. The last time I'd seen Mr. Butterworth, he'd been possessed by the spirit of the master. Fortunately he knew nothing about that time and gave me an open smile. I smiled back politely, but took a seat as far away from him as possible.

Mrs. Butterworth peered down her equine nose and appraised my outfit. From the look on her face, she thought it as dreary as the sky outside. She dismissed me with a casual glance in Sylvia's direction. That suited me. I didn't want her notice.

Sylvia handed me a cup of tea. "Samuel was just telling the Butterworths and Mr. Myer that they shouldn't have come," she said with a wink. "Because of the wild dog."

So it would seem the Butterworths weren't to know about the demon. A wise decision. The fewer people who knew about the supernatural, the better. Besides, I wasn't so sure either of the Butterworths were the sort to keep such information to themselves. Mrs. Butterworth was quite the chatterbox.

Myer remained silent and still. Of the three of them, he alone knew the wild dog story was simply that—a story.

"We're well armed," Mr. Butterworth said. "Nothing could—"

"How large is it?" Mrs. Butterworth interrupted. Mr. Butterworth narrowed his gaze at his wife, but did not try to wrestle the conversation back.

"Huge," Sylvia told her. "Quite the monster."

"You've seen it, Miss Langley?"

"Uh, no. Samuel has."

I found my gaze automatically wandering to Samuel, sitting in an armchair off to the side. Thankfully, he wasn't looking at me, but at Myer. He inclined his head. "It was foolish of you to come."

"We wanted to see if there's anything we can do," Myer said.

"Not unless you've brought some device with you to defeat it."

"I told you," Mr. Butterworth cut in. "We're armed."

"Are *you* armed, Mr. Myer?" Samuel asked.

"I have a gun, but no other weapons," Myer said. Meaning he had no amulet to send the creature back.

It was a conversation inside another conversation with the inner one being the real one. It was all so strange to listen to, watching for a reaction from the Butterworths. They were the only ones not privy to what we were really talking about. So far, they seemed oblivious to the strained undercurrents and the double meanings.

"Everett wants to know how long it will be before you kill the creature," Mrs. Butterworth said. "He wants to resume his research. He does find those abbey ruins fascinating, what with his interest in the supernatural. Don't you, Everett?"

Her mention of Myer's given name reminded me of their adultery. It would seem Mr. Butterworth was quite unaware of the liaison, although his acceptance of Myer as a frequent guest in his home could have meant he knew of it and didn't care. Of course, there was always the possibility that Myer had coerced Mrs. Butterworth through hypnosis and then wiped her memory of it afterwards. According to Sylvia, they'd discovered that Myer had hypnotized Mrs. Butteworth at least once to instigate the liaison, but only at her request. Apparently it was to calm her nerves.

The entire affair seemed much too sordid for such well-to-do people. It lowered them in my eyes, and yet it was not lost on me that they considered me baser still, despite me never having been with a married man.

"Are you quite sure your father's death was a result of a...wild dog attack?" Myer asked Samuel. "Were the wounds similar in nature to the last victims?"

"Come now, Myer," Mr. Butterworth scolded. "There are ladies present and Mr. Gladstone is in mourning."

"These things should be discussed," Samuel told him. "I'm very interested to hear Mr. Myer's opinion."

The folds on Mr. Butterworth's face scrunched. He opened his mouth to speak, but his wife got in first. "Why?" she asked. "What has it got to do with Everett?"

"Nothing," Sylvia said with a wave of her hand. "Nothing at all. Isn't that right, Samuel?"

Samuel smiled tightly. He hadn't taken his gaze off Myer the entire time. Myer stared straight back.

"Well?" Myer asked. "Were they the same?"

Samuel nodded. "There's no doubt in my mind they were caused by the same sort of animal."

"But you caught and killed the last one," Mr. Butterworth said.

"This one may have come from the same pack."

"This is awful," Mrs. Butterworth whimpered. "I do hope it stays in your woods and doesn't venture into the village."

"We all hope that," Sylvia agreed.

"Poor Mr. Gladstone," Mrs. Butterworth muttered. "Poor, poor man. What an awful thing to happen. Yet I am glad you got to see your father again, Mr. Gladstone. He said he'd not seen you for some time."

That got everyone's attention. Sylvia, Samuel and I stared at her. "You met him? When?" Samuel asked.

"Oh, I've never met him. Have you, dear?" She didn't wait for her husband's response before continuing on. "At least I don't think I have." She frowned as if trying to recall a distant memory. "Anyhow, he wrote to us. He wanted to know the history of Frakingham House."

"Whatever for?" Sylvia blurted out.

Mrs. Butterworth shrugged her large shoulders. "He didn't say. I suspect he chose us because we're the most important family in the village." She puffed out her considerable chest, testing the seams of her jacket. "He asked if we knew of any strange goings-on up here in the past."

"And what did you say in your response?" Samuel asked.

"That we only knew about the wild dog attack of last Christmas. But that wasn't really *strange* now, was it. Simply…unfortunate. As it is again, this time. Poor man. Poor, poor man."

Samuel's jaw hardened. He was being very stoic, considering he'd just discovered his father had some suspicions about the estate. Did he know about the ruins and their supernatural energy? Or about the demons and the little ghosts in the old dungeon? All of those things had come to light before I'd visited, but I'd been informed.

"Did he write to *you*, Myer?" Samuel asked.

"No," Myer shot back. Oddly, he glanced at the doorway. "Why would he?"

"Perhaps he heard of your interest in the abbey ruins. Since he wanted to know about strange goings-on, who better to ask?"

"Well he didn't."

"Have you ever spoken to him about supernatural matters?"

"Again, why would I?" It was neither a yes nor a no.

"But you've met my parents before?"

Myer shrugged one shoulder and once more his gaze flicked to the doorway. "I think so. At a ball or my club, perhaps. I can't recall. I meet a lot of people."

Samuel looked like he would persist, but it was obvious Myer wasn't going to give him a direct answer. "What brings you back here to Harborough, Mr. Myer?" I asked. It was the first I'd spoken since exchanging greetings, and my voice seemed to startle everyone. "Do you have more research to conduct?"

He nodded. "There's still much to be done."

Mr. Butterworth snorted. "You're wasting your time, Myer. If that place were full of supernatural energy as you think it is, the air would be thick with ghosts."

"Do you believe in the spirit world?" Sylvia asked him.

"No."

How ironic that he'd been possessed. I smiled into my teacup and caught Samuel smirking too, out of the corner of my eye.

"They're a figment of the imagination of some very greedy women who purport to be able to communicate with them," Mr. Butterworth said. "Liars and swindlers, the lot of them."

I'd like to see him say that to Emily Beaufort's face. She might laugh him off, but I doubted her husband would. Mr. Butterworth had better keep his opinions to himself near Jacob Beaufort or risk getting a bloody nose.

"*I* believe," Mrs. Butterworth said cheerfully. "Indeed, I find the whole thing fascinating. Mr. Myer has been sharing his findings with me. I thought we might write a book together."

Her husband grunted and sipped his tea.

"Did my father say anything else in his letter?" Samuel asked.

Mr. and Mrs. Butterworth both studied their teacups as if they could see a polite answer in them. Clearly the answer they wanted to give wasn't the one we needed to hear.

"Go on," Samuel urged. "He's gone now. You won't be breaking a confidence by telling me."

Mr. Butterworth gave the game away first by glancing at me. It would seem *I* had been a topic in Mr. Gladstone's letter. Heat crept up my throat to my cheeks, burning and shameful.

"He told you about me, didn't he?" It was more statement than question. I wasn't sure I wanted to hear the answer.

Mr. Butterworth sipped his tea and took great pains to savor it. Ever the politician not wanting to upset anyone, he left the difficult explanation to his wife.

Samuel, however, got in first. "Forget it. Forget I asked."

"No," I cut in.

"Perhaps he's right," Mrs. Butterworth said. "It's not important, anyway."

"It is important," I snapped. "I should have the opportunity to defend myself, shouldn't I? Or is my position indefensible?" I wasn't sure whom I was addressing, but it was too late to back down now. The blood gushed through my veins, sending my pulse racing and making my tongue loose. Everybody in that room knew what I was. There was no secret. I might as well have my say on the matter.

"Charity." Samuel was standing beside me. I hadn't noticed him move. His voice soothed me a little, but not to the point of being hypnotic.

"Don't," I warned him. "Your father would have told the Butterworths that I lived in the alleys of London as a child. He probably said terrible things about me." I turned away from him. The pain etched into the grooves of his face had the power to keep me quiet, and I didn't want to be quiet. Not this time. "He's right," I told the Butterworths and

Myer. Only the latter met my gaze fully, his own eyes filled with curiosity. The Butterworths sipped their tea as if nothing were amiss and nobody was even talking. Perhaps they thought if they pretended not to hear me they could go on as if nothing had changed. But I'd had enough of burying my head in the sand. It was time to own up to my past. Or some of it, at least. There was no need for all the sordid details to emerge. I didn't want to sicken them.

"I never knew my father," I told them. "My mother was a drunkard and worse. She died when I was nine and I lived on the streets thereafter with a group of other orphans." I didn't know if they knew about Jack's past, so I didn't mention that he was one of those orphans. His story wasn't mine to tell. "We did what we could to survive and lived by few rules. When I grew up, I was invited to be the companion of a gentleman. He was kind and taught me how to read and write."

Mrs. Butterworth blushed. Her husband flicked a glance at me, but quickly returned to studying his teacup again. Myer stared openly, his eyes wide.

"There," I said. "That's my entire story. If Mr. Gladstone didn't inform you in his letter, you no longer have to wonder. I'm sure you were curious."

Myer sat back in his chair and sighed. He knew more than that, of course, after being involved in my escape from the master's spirit, but it would seem he'd hoped for some details. The man sank further and further in my opinion.

Mr. Butterworth set his teacup on the table and cleared his throat. "Time to—"

"Depart," his wife said, also setting down her teacup. "Yes, I think so." She avoided looking in my direction, but cast a polite smile at Sylvia. "Thank you, Miss Langley. You must come to visit my girls soon. They could do with some good company, since there is so little of it in the village. After your guests have left you, of course. All of them."

Meaning me. She didn't want *me* anywhere near her children. She was worried I would corrupt them. It would seem Mrs. Butterworth was never going to be my friend. So be it. I didn't care, not a whit. I only hoped Sylvia wouldn't be overcome with misguided loyalty and defend me.

Fortunately, she did not. She gave a polite smile that I knew to be quite false and agreed to pay them a call. Beside me, Samuel shifted his stance and his hand rested on my shoulder, reassuring and solid. It instantly had the effect of calming my nerves, much in the way his hypnotic voice could, at times. I knew I should be unsettled by that, but I wasn't. I only wanted to touch my own hand to his in thanks.

The Butterworths and Myer were about to exit when Mrs. Gladstone entered the drawing room. She seemed to float across the floor, her dark gray skirts like a somber cloud carrying her. She stopped short, however, and lifted her veil. She stared, wide-eyed, at Myer.

"Everett!" she cried, pressing a hand to her chest.

Everett? She must know him quite well to address him by his first name. How interesting that he'd just denied knowing the Gladstones except as passing acquaintances.

CHAPTER 5

"Mrs. Gladstone," Myer said smoothly. "Let me offer my condolences on the death of your husband."

The Butterworths also gave their condolences, but Mrs. Gladstone hardly noticed them. She was still staring at Myer as if she were in a daze.

"Mother?" Samuel asked. "Do you know Mr. Myer?"

His voice seemed to rouse her from her stupor. She waved away his question. "A little. Your father too. Indeed, I believe they spoke recently."

We all turned to Myer. He fiddled with his tie as if to straighten it, but ended up making it crooked. "I, uh, yes. Now that I think about it, I do know Gladstone. Did," he corrected himself with a wince. "Poor fellow. Terrible business."

"My husband's death has come as a shock," Mrs. Gladstone said, dabbing at the corner of her eye with her handkerchief. "I'm quite overcome. My sons have been a great support to me, however. I'm so happy to have them both back in the family fold."

Her attempts at distracting us from the intimacy of her greeting of Myer weren't lost on me, and most likely not on Samuel either. His face was a picture of brooding contemplation. He must itch to question his mother further in private.

"Did you and my father discuss Frakingham in your recent conversation?" he asked Myer instead.

"Something like that," Myer said.

"Could you be more precise?"

"Alas, my memory is not what it used to be."

Samuel snorted. "I doubt that very much. Tell us what you spoke about, Mr. Myer."

Myer swallowed heavily. "Now that you mention it, I do recall some of our discussion. Your father was curious about the ruins. I told him they have an energy that intrigues me. I also told him of my suspicions that this place was once the center for supernatural activity, but is no longer, for reasons unknown."

"Did he ask you about Lord Frakingham?" Mr. Butterworth said. "Only that's what was in his letter to me. He was quite interested in his lordship's time here."

"He did, but I wasn't able to help him on that score. I know nothing of Lord Frakingham."

I turned to Samuel to see his reaction, but he was looking at his mother. She stood quite still and seemed unaware of the turmoil her arrival had created.

The Butterworths once more attempted to leave and this time they made it out of the drawing room. Myer followed, first glancing at Mrs. Gladstone. She nodded politely then lowered her veil. Sylvia followed them out and I could see that Samuel wished to as well, but didn't want to leave me alone with his mother. I followed Sylvia to alleviate his uncertainty.

We waited in the entrance hall as the Butterworth coach was brought around. An alert Tommy sat alongside the driver, his hands resting on the shotgun across his lap. Apparently weapons from our realm couldn't kill demons, but they could stun them long enough for someone to run away.

"Do be careful," Sylvia said to the Butterworths as Maud handed them their coats. "The wild dog is very fast and can come from seemingly nowhere."

We watched as the Butterworths hurried to the coach and stuffed themselves into the cabin. Myer went to follow, but Samuel held him roughly by the arm.

"If I find you've lied to me about your friendship with my parents, I'll be sure to pay you a visit." He bared his teeth in a grimace. "And I can assure you, I'm not the pleasantly polite fool I once was."

Myer swallowed hard. "I can see that. Let me assure you, there is no friendship between us and there never has been." He tried to pull away, but Samuel didn't let go.

"One more question. Did you write a note to my father with the words 'I know what you did' on it?"

"Your father?" Myer shook his head with vigor. "No! I've never written to him. Now, kindly let go. You're crumpling my sleeve."

Samuel released him and we kept watch as he descended the steps and climbed into the cabin. Tommy said something to the driver then jumped down and joined us. We watched and waited until the coach was out of sight.

"They'll be safe once they're off the estate," Sylvia said, folding her arms around her body. "Won't they?"

"Of course," Tommy said. "Quite safe. The last rogue demon kept to the woods. I'm sure this one will, too."

Sylvia seemed satisfied with that answer. She breathed a sigh and headed to the drawing room. Tommy gave us a flat-lipped smile and followed her.

"I'm retiring to my room for the rest of the day," I told Samuel.

"Charity." He rubbed his hand over his jaw and neck. "About what happened in there...I'm sorry. I wanted to stop it. You shouldn't have to listen to people like that."

He could be so endearing sometimes and he looked quite lost at that moment. His face was once more a boyish one, with big blue eyes and smooth jaw. Lately, he'd seemed older than his twenty-two years, and not the handsome, charming youth I remembered from our earlier encounters. He'd become a rougher, harder version, the sort of man who never laughed. I shouldn't miss that charming youth with the disarming manner who could get a woman like me into trouble—who could hurt a woman like me in so many ways—but God help me, I did.

I had the silly urge to caress my thumb along his cheek to see if I could rub away the steely mask, but I managed to keep my hands by my sides. He would only see it as encouragement, and encouraging him now would be cruel.

"I brought it on myself," I said.

"I disagree."

"Don't be so obstinate, Samuel. Of course I did. I knew that at the time, and I know it now. Your loyalty is sweet, if somewhat misguided."

He made a choking sound. "It bloody well is not!"

A lady would have protested at his language. It was time to remind him that I wasn't one. "It bloody well is!"

He gave me a withering glare. "If you're trying to prove a point, don't. It's the wrong point."

"It's not to me. The Butterworths knew about me, or at least suspected. Your father's letter to them confirmed it. I brought it up because I wanted to clear the air and, in a way, it did. I'm only sorry that it has put Sylvia in an awkward position, now. At least they don't *seem* to hold it against her and Mr. Langley for having me as their guest."

"Why in God's name should they?" he shouted. "They're sanctimonious hypocrites and I've a good mind to tell Butterworth what his wife has been doing with Myer behind his back."

I shrank away, startled by his vehemence. He was so *angry*. I picked up my skirts and brushed past him.

"Charity!" he called as I ran up the stairs. "Charity, I'm sorry. I didn't mean to speak so harshly."

I paused on the landing. "It's not your fault," I tossed over my shoulder. "None of this is. I wish...I wish you wouldn't feel as if you have to protect me all the time. You don't."

I continued up the stairs. I thought he might try to follow me, but he didn't. Indeed, he didn't come to see me until the next morning, after breakfast.

***

"I'm leaving shortly," Samuel said. He leaned against my doorframe, his arms and ankles crossed like he belonged right there. I'd grown used to him not wearing a waistcoat or jacket, yet seeing him in just his crisp white shirt and trousers took my breath away. He wore no tie either, revealing a triangle of smooth skin at his throat that I could have stared at all day. If angels were real, they would resemble Samuel at that moment. Or perhaps he was a fallen angel, since an air of brooding darkness clung to him.

"Father's body has been released," he went on. "We'll take it home for burial, then I'll come back as soon as I can. In the meantime, be careful. Stay indoors. Let Tommy take care of you."

I let him think I would still be here when he returned. He seemed to have set aside our argument from the day before. Perhaps he didn't want our last moments together to be awkward or unkind. I was glad. I didn't want to part like that either. Besides, I wasn't even sure if it was an argument. Nobody was at fault. He'd frightened me with his strong words, but I shouldn't have been so anxious. It was something I needed to remind myself of constantly.

"Safe travels," I said. "You must be careful as you leave the estate too."

He inclined his head in a nod. He shifted his stance, lowering his arms to his sides. "I questioned my mother about her acquaintance with Myer."

Of all the things I expected him to say, that wasn't one of them. "Oh?"

"She told me she doesn't know him well, but knows Mrs. Myer a little better."

That didn't seem right to me. She'd called Myer by his first name. Mere acquaintances didn't do that. Indeed, it spoke of a close association. Uncomfortably close. "Do you believe her?"

He shook his head. "I told her so."

"Was that wise?"

"Probably not, considering what she's been through." He massaged the deep grooves scoring his forehead with his thumb and forefinger. "I wasn't thinking. I'm not doing a lot of it, lately." His eyes briefly flared with heat as his gaze connected with mine. "It gets worse. I asked her if Myer was my father."

The thought had occurred to me too, but I'd not thought him foolish enough to ask his mother yet. He truly wasn't thinking clearly. The old Samuel wouldn't have been so blunt.

"And?" I urged.

"And she said he wasn't. To say she was horrified and offended by my question is not doing justice to her reaction."

"I'm not surprised," I murmured.

He looked pained. "I apologized immediately, but the damage was done."

"You have time to repair your relationship now that you're returning home."

"I'll try."

"Do you believe her?"

"I don't know. I suppose I have to. I do think she's lying about not knowing Myer well, though. What are your thoughts, Charity?"

"Mine? Why do you want to know what I think?"

"Because I value your judgment. Heaven knows it's better than mine, of late."

I felt honored by his faith in me, although I couldn't say why. It simply felt nice to have him think well of me. "I think you're right and that they know each other better than she's letting on, but I do believe her when she says Myer isn't your father. You have the same eyes as Mr. Gladstone, and the same complexion. There's nothing of Myer in you."

He blew out a measured breath. His face softened. "I'm glad. Thank you, Charity. You've eased my mind greatly."

"I imagine the mere thought of Myer being your father would be unsettling."

"More like nauseating." He gave me a crooked smile. I returned it. The smile vanished and the heat returned to his eyes. He took a step toward me and, suddenly, I felt awkward again. He was in my room uninvited and he wanted something I wasn't willing to give. He wanted me. It was clear as day in the intensity of his gaze.

I held up my hand, warding him off. "Samuel," I began.

I didn't need to go on. He stepped back. "Sorry," he mumbled. "I forget, sometimes."

Forget that I'm afraid of him? Of charming men? Forget that I've become a coward again? I wanted very much to ease his conscience and tell him that I knew he would never hurt me, but something deep inside stopped me from saying it.

Samuel didn't seem to know where to look and, after a moment of strained silence, he gave a hasty bow. "Goodbye, Charity. I'll see you in a few days. Be careful and…and, well, just be careful."

"I will be. Don't worry about us while you're gone."

"I can't not worry," he said simply.

I watched him walk away from me along the corridor. His broad shoulders and back strained his shirt seams, but it was lower down that caught my attention. No other man had quite such an enticing rear.

I blushed fiercely and hurriedly closed my door. Good lord! What was I doing staring at Samuel? What sort of woman did that?

My sort. The base sort.

I tried to settle into a book, but found myself constantly staring out the window, looking for the demon. There was no sign of it, thank goodness, but that didn't settle my jangling nerves. They jangled more when someone knocked on my door.

"Bert!" I said, upon seeing him standing there, just as his brother had done a few minutes earlier. He too had shed his jacket and waistcoat, however he still wore his tie. I wondered if he were trying to imitate Samuel. If so, he'd failed. He was limper, his presence somehow less. Despite having a similar appearance, Bert's face didn't make me want to gaze upon it for hours and study every contour. His eyes didn't draw me in like Samuel's, or tempt me with suppressed desire.

"I just came to say goodbye," he said, echoing his brother's words. Everything about Bert was an echo of Samuel, from his appearance to his manner. I wondered if he realized it.

"Goodbye," I said. "Safe journey." The sooner I could get him out of my doorway, the better. I didn't want to be alone with this man. I went to shut the door, but he blocked it.

"I'm going to miss seeing your beautiful face," he said, his voice breathy.

"Thank you. It's been a pleasure to meet you." What else could I say?

"I hope this isn't the last time we meet."

"Our paths are unlikely to cross again."

"Does that mean you haven't changed your mind?"

"I haven't," I said stiffly.

His lips pinched together. "My offer remains. I'll install you as my mistress—"

"Don't. Speak of it no more, please."

He arched a brow, an imperial gesture that I couldn't imagine Samuel using. "I don't think you're in a position to be so selective, Charity."

"There is nothing selective about my decision. I do not wish to be your mistress, or anyone's. I believe I've made my position clear enough. Kindly remove yourself from my doorway."

"You're quite the shrewd businesswoman, I see." He chuckled. It made my insides clench and my muscles tighten, ready to spring out of his way. "Very well. Tell me what you want in return and I'll match it."

There would be no reasoning with him. He simply didn't hear me no matter how loudly I spoke or how many times I reiterated my position. "Goodbye, Bert."

I tried to push on the door, but he pushed back. "Let's not play games," he said darkly.

Don't back away, Charity. Don't back down. I gritted my teeth and forced my rising fear aside. I could put a man like Bert back in his place. I had done it before. Admittedly that had been years ago, when men like him didn't frighten me and I'd been bolder, yet still innocent in the ways of men.

I thrust my hands on my hips. "How dare you insult our hosts by approaching their guest with such a vulgar proposal."

He snorted. "I don't particularly care what the people in this backwater think." A smile touched his lips. I didn't trust it. He was going to make his move. "You'll never see my brother again. You know that, don't you? Mother will keep him tied to the estate now that she's getting him home."

"That's the way it should be. I've told you before, there's nothing between Samuel and me, nor do I want there to be."

He grunted. The smile turned into a cruel twist. "You're a terrible liar."

"Move, sir. I want to close my door."

He didn't move. Indeed, he took a step inside. His eyes turned flinty, flat. Cold. I'd seen Samuel's eyes change like that too, when he was suffering from his maddening thoughts.

I backed away and swallowed the ball of fear in my throat. Bert was a weak man, in mind and body. I needed to remember that. I could conquer my fear, and I could conquer him, if necessary. Nobody need know about this meeting or his offer. Samuel need never find out.

"Do you know what my brother did to land himself in prison?" he asked.

My step faltered, earning me a sneering grin. It was not a question I had expected.

"Ah. So you do want to know. Hmmm, should I tell you or not?"

"Leave," I croaked.

"I don't think so. Indeed, I think I will tell you. It might serve to open your eyes to his true nature."

I should have blocked my ears. I should have pushed past him and run away. But heaven help me, I wanted to know what Samuel had done. My curiosity conquered my fears in the end. I let him tell me.

"He hurt a woman." The triumph in his voice sickened me. His words sickened me. Surely it must be a lie. "Indeed, it's worse than that."

A shiver wracked me and I folded my arms around myself to suppress it. There would be no shutting out Bert's sneering tone, however, and his sanctimonious grin. "How could it be worse?" I asked.

"He raped her."

CHAPTER 6

No. No, no, no. The words pounded a rhythm against my skull, drowning out all else.

Not Samuel. Please God, not him.

"I don't believe you." The words were out before I could decipher the tangled emotions and thoughts tying themselves into knots inside me.

"You should," Bert said. "You know that he can make people do whatever he wants, even when they don't want to do it. He has a power, my brother. He hasn't always used it wisely."

"I don't believe it because I see the way women look at him without being hypnotized. He doesn't *need* to hypnotize them."

The muscles in his jaw trembled, as if he were working hard to control his emotions. His fists closed at his sides. I eyed them warily. "Why would I make this up?" he snarled.

"Because you're jealous of him." The words were out before I could stop them. If I'd had more control, I wouldn't have dared utter such a cutting remark.

His trembling grew worse. His nose twitched and he blinked rapidly back at me. I recognized the signs of madness and anger, so I was prepared. He swung his fist, but

I dodged out of the way. The momentum sent him reeling forward, allowing me to slip past him.

"You *whore*. You filthy, disgusting creature. You're not worth my time."

"Go home before you do something you'll regret."

I didn't wait for his response. I ran along the corridor and down the stairs to the main part of the house where he wouldn't dare pursue me. Since I didn't want to see either Samuel or Mrs. Gladstone, I made my way to the service area and found a quiet corner in the servants' dining room to sit and wait for my limbs to stop shaking.

It was some time before I ceased eyeing the door and could set aside my fear. The servants left me alone. They were too busy preparing for the Gladstones' departure to worry about the strange guest who preferred hiding to being with her hosts. Tommy was nowhere to be seen, probably helping the Gladstone's driver prepare the horses and coach, or looking out for the demon.

My body may have stopped trembling, but my thoughts were still in turmoil. I'd been wrong about Bert. I had been sure he wouldn't be a physical threat. I expected him to be more chivalrous, like his brother, but he and Samuel were not cut from the same cloth. Samuel was strong where his brother was weak, both physically and morally. They were, however, both troubled men, in different ways.

He raped her.

Bert's insidious words burrowed into my mind again, and I couldn't dislodge them. Surely he'd said it out of frustration, built up over years of feeling inferior. Samuel wouldn't do something so despicable. He didn't need to.

And yet he was hiding something. He *had* gone to prison and he wouldn't tell me why.

Tommy entered, disrupting my thoughts. "The Gladstones are gone," he announced. "You can come out of hiding now."

74

I almost retorted that I wasn't hiding, but of course he was right. I blew out a measured breath. "Any sign of the demon?"

"None. All's quiet." He flopped onto a chair opposite me and rubbed his hand over his face.

"You're exhausted," I said. "Watching for the demon has done you in. Go and rest for an hour or so. The Langleys will understand."

"I can't. With Gladstone gone, there's just me to look out for everyone."

"Nonsense. We're not invalids. There's Bollard, Sylvia and me, plus the servants. We can all take turns watching. It doesn't have to be only you."

"It's not just that. I have to go into the village."

"Why?"

"Gladstone asked me to fetch the letter his father sent to Butterworth. I'm to send it on to him. He wants to see its contents for himself."

"Go tomorrow."

"Why put it off?"

"Because that way you can drive me to the station. I'm catching the London train."

"Bloody hell," he muttered. "You kept that quiet. Didn't want Gladstone to know, eh?"

"I thought he might try to stop me."

"And you don't think I will?" He leaned back in the chair and crossed his arms over his chest, daring me to test him.

"I expect you to try. I also expect Sylvia will protest. But I have an answer for both of you."

He waited, his brows raised.

"My answer is..." I leaned forward. "I can do what I want. Either you drive me to the station or I'll walk. It's not too far."

He looked like he'd argue with me, but in the end he gave a frustrated grunt. "Very well. I'll drive you. But I'm not informing Sylvia. She'll somehow think it's my fault. She thinks everything is my fault lately," he muttered.

I didn't have the strength to ask him what he meant by that. My thoughts were too occupied with my own problems. "I'll resume demon watch from the tower room," I said. "You go and rest. I'll fetch you if I spot it."

I made my way up to the top of the house and stretched out on the chaise by the tower room's window. Time passed slowly. Demon watching was terribly boring yet oddly exhausting. It was difficult to keep my eyes open, and even more difficult not to let my mind wander back to the events of the morning.

I wondered if I could have behaved differently when faced with Bert's attentions. Perhaps I should have told Samuel. No, that would have been beyond awkward. They were brothers. I didn't want to come between them. That led me to wonder if Bert had indeed lied about the reason for Samuel's stint in prison. He must have. It had been so cruelly said. Yet the idea ate at me and ate at me.

Thankfully distraction arrived in the form of Sylvia. "There you are!" she cried. "I've been looking for you everywhere."

"I'm on demon watch," I said, nodding at the window. "No sign of it so far."

"Where's Tommy?"

"Resting. He's been working very hard lately and it's likely he'll need to stay alert tonight."

"Yes, of course." She bit her lip and eyed the door as if contemplating going to check on him. I had to think fast to keep her with me. Those two could not be allowed to spend time alone together.

"Sylvia, do you think Samuel is capable of hurting anyone?"

She looked startled by my question. "Of course not. He's a gentleman." Her face darkened and her brow furrowed. "Although now that I think of it, he proved to be quite capable of harm during our Christmas troubles. He claims he used to box at university. What an odd question though. Why do you ask?"

"No reason," I said lightly.

"Tell me, Charity. You've piqued my curiosity."

"It was just something Bert alluded to. He mentioned that Samuel once hurt someone, but he gave me no details. Do you think he spoke the truth or was he trying to disparage his brother's good reputation?"

"Good lord, you want me to answer that? I don't usually get asked such serious questions."

I smiled. "Then perhaps it's time you were."

"I suppose so. Although it hurts my head a little to think about it. I much prefer questions about clothes and hats."

"Sylvia," I prompted.

"Oh yes, Samuel. Let me see." She chewed on her lip and I was worried I'd never get an answer out of her at all. Not a sensible one, anyway. Then finally she spoke. "Is he supposed to have hurt anyone recently or some time ago? Only, a change seems to have come over him of late. He's certainly angry enough to *want* to hurt someone who has wronged him or the people he cares about."

"A year or two ago."

"Then I think Bert is lying. Samuel was ever the gentleman before...well, before..."

"Before I came here."

She flounced onto the chaise beside me and fussed with her skirts, settling them around her. "Besides, I've seen the way everyone treated him at the Beauforts' ball. He was immensely popular. Everyone spoke to him as if he were a long lost friend. They wouldn't be like that if he'd done something terrible. Believe me, that set knows every little sin everyone has committed. The gossip mill is constantly in operation." She sighed. "I do wish I could be part of it."

"You want them to gossip about you?"

Another sigh. "No, but to attend the balls and soirees every night would be so thrilling! And to wear beautiful gowns and jewels. There would never be a dull moment."

I imagined it would grow dull after a while, but I didn't say so. Hearing her speak of boredom and balls made me even more certain that I'd done the right thing and directed Tommy to stay away from her. He could never give her what she craved and she would quickly grow bored of *him*.

"I am right though, don't you think?" she said. At my blank look she added, "About Samuel being popular. Surely London society would shun him if he'd done something awful."

"You're probably right."

Unless his father had covered up the crime.

***

I didn't tell Sylvia I was leaving until later in the day for fear that she would be angry with me. Judging by the scowl on her face when I did finally tell her, I'd been right. Although I tried explaining my need to return to the school and my life in London, she refused to agree, claiming I was putting myself in danger. I'd had enough of her lectures by dinnertime, and told her in no uncertain terms that what I did was none of her affair.

"You're doing this because Samuel's gone, aren't you?" she said the following morning as we watched Tommy carry my valise down the stairs.

"No. I'm doing this because I want to see the children again."

"They'll be fine on their own. They've got other adults to care for them."

"That's not the point."

She threw her hands in the air. "Then what is?"

My lip began to wobble against my will. I bit it and stared down at my boots until I could be sure my tears wouldn't spill. "I miss them. And...and I don't want them to forget me." There. I'd said it. Let her call me silly or pathetic and then we'd be done with it and I could go.

She hugged me instead, unbalancing me. "Oh, Charity. You're such a goose. Of course they won't forget you. How could they! You're quite unforgettable."

I wasn't sure how to take that, so I simply thanked her. She pulled away, but kept hold of both my hands. Her thumbs rubbed the scarred skin there. She was aware of the scars, of course, and knew how I'd gotten them. She was not aware of the ones on my back. Only Samuel was.

Thinking about him and what he knew had tears stinging my eyes again. What would he do when he discovered I'd left the relative safety of Frakingham and returned to London?

"You won't write to him and tell him, will you?" I said to both Sylvia and Tommy. "At least not for a week or more. I don't want him rushing off from his family to lecture me. They need him, now."

"They need to learn to live without him," Tommy said, setting the valise down on the tiles.

"Why do you say that?" Sylvia asked.

"Because he's not going to stay there long. He told me so, and I believe him."

"And when his brother becomes too ill to manage the estate?" I said. "Or dies? What will he do then?"

"He's not dead yet."

"Why are you so certain Samuel will return soon anyway? What did he tell you?"

He didn't get a chance to answer me. Langley and Bollard came down the stairs to see me off. The servant carried his master in his arms, proving just how strong he was; August Langley was not a small man. It was a devoted act if ever I saw one. The couple constantly surprised me, in one way or another. I'd not expected to like them, but I did. Very much. I only wished I could trust them, but the gruesome nature of Langley's scientific experiments set my nerves on edge.

"You will take care, Charity," Langley said, clasping my hand.

"Of course."

"Go to the Beauforts if there is any danger. Immediately."

"I will. I won't do anything to endanger the children."

His lips flattened, telling me exactly what he thought of that—I was endangering them simply by returning. Perhaps it was true. Perhaps I should change my mind and find rooms elsewhere in London. I'd think about it on the journey home.

Tommy removed my coat from the stand by the door and handed it to me, then picked up my valise. "It's time to go."

"Thank you, Mr. Langley," I said. "You've been most tolerant having me here. I know I'm not the sort of guest you would want in your home."

"That's not true."

The mute servant cocked his head to the side and regarded his master sternly.

Langley blew out a breath. "I admit to not being quite so enthusiastic at first. You're not the sort of girl Sylvia should be associating with."

"Uncle!" she cried.

"It's all right," I said. "I understand." Somehow it hurt less when he said it. Perhaps because there was no malice in his tone, just the truth.

"But then it was explained to me that she needed female companionship after Hannah left. She seemed to like you, so it was an easy decision."

Sylvia leaned over and pecked her uncle's cheek. "That was almost a nice thing to say."

I smiled. "Thank you, Mr. Langley. And thank you too, Mr. Bollard."

The big man lowered his head, but not before I saw him blush. I knew then that it was probably he who'd talked his master into letting me stay. Either him or Samuel.

The coach came around and Tommy escorted me out, my valise in one hand and Jack's knife in the other. Fray, the coachman, had a shotgun across his lap.

I climbed into the cabin and waved to the others through the window. Tommy shut the door and we drove off. A small lump unexpectedly lodged in my throat. I'd not thought I'd be quite so saddened to leave Freak House. My stay hadn't been particularly pleasant, but it had been easy compared to the bustle of my London life.

The coach rolled swiftly through the great iron gates and I breathed a sigh of relief as we joined the main road into the village. There was no sign of the demon.

The Harborough railway station was positioned a few streets behind the High Street row of shops. They were a mixture of tired old buildings in need of a lick of paint and well-kept ones with clean windows. Brass lamps hanging above doors gleamed in the morning sunshine and shopkeepers hovered outside, trying to entice customers in. We had to drive along High Street to get to the station, but instead of going straight on, the coach stopped outside a butcher's shop. I opened the window and peered out to see if there was an obstruction up ahead. There was none.

What I did see was Mr. and Mrs. Butterworth, strolling toward us on the footpath, their twin daughters trailing behind and their third, much younger one, hopping along on one foot, her hat in her hand, the ribbons trailing in the dirt. Neither of the elder Butterworths looked our way, but they must have seen us. Our coach was the grandest in the street and it belonged to the infamous Freak House. Everybody else, including the Butterworth children, stared as if they were waiting for us to do something gossip worthy.

It was a piece of luck for Tommy to come across them now. He could get his request over with quickly and take me on to the station before my train departed. He climbed down from the driver's seat and approached the Butterworths as they came within earshot. They stopped, rather reluctantly in Mrs. Butterworth's case. She shot a glance at me, but gave me no greeting. I expected none.

"Good morning," Tommy said, removing his hat. "I'm sorry to trouble you sir, ma'am. Mr. Samuel Gladstone has sent me on an errand to ask something of you."

"Oh?" Mrs. Butterworth said, angling her rather prominent chin. "I thought he left."

"He did. He delivered his instructions to me yesterday."

The three Butterworth girls crowded behind their parents. I couldn't tell the twins apart. They even wore the same outfits, striped crimson and canary yellow dresses with matching jackets. Their broad-brimmed hats sheltered their fair skin from the sun, but I could just make out the direction of their gazes. They fell on Tommy. In contrast, the youngest girl watched me. I smiled at her. She waved back.

"Get on with it, man," Mr. Butterworth snapped. "We haven't got all day."

"Mr. Gladstone would like to see his father's letter to you, sir," Tommy said.

"Whatever for?"

"For personal reasons, sir."

"Personal reasons?" Mrs. Butterworth echoed. "What does that mean?"

I, er..." Poor Tommy. It would seem he hadn't expected to have Samuel's motives questioned.

"For sentimentality," I cut in.

That earned me a withering glare from Mrs. Butterworth. Clearly she didn't think it my place to speak. To Tommy, she said, "Unfortunately, that's no longer possible."

"Why?" I asked.

Again, to Tommy, she said, "The letter has been destroyed."

"Destroyed?" I poked my head further out of the coach window. "How?"

"I accidentally dropped it in the fireplace. So there you have it. We're very sorry, but the letter no longer exists."

"Ah," her husband said. "That explains why I couldn't find it when I searched my study last night. I wanted to check the exact wording of certain paragraphs since I could no longer recall its contents. Never mind."

"What do you mean you could no longer recall it?" Tommy asked. He seemed as curious about that statement as I was. Mr. Butterworth's memory had been perfectly all right the day before.

He shrugged. "I cannot recall specifics, that's all. Obviously the contents of the letter weren't important or I would. No matter. Now, if you don't mind."

The couple walked off as Tommy hastily thanked them. The twins trotted after their parents, but glanced back at Tommy at precisely the same time. One blushed. The other hooked her arm through her sister's and hurried away.

The youngest girl did not follow her sisters. She came up to the coach door. "He's been at it again," she whispered.

"Who has been at what again?" Tommy asked, bending down to her level.

"Mr. Myer," she said matter-of-factly, as if she thought Tommy a dolt for not knowing. "He's been making my head dizzy."

"Dizzy?"

"Do you find you've forgotten things after the dizziness goes away?" I asked.

"Forget things?" The girl looked positively indignant. "I never forget. I'm a spy for Her Majesty the queen! I remember everything."

I bit back my smile. She was an adorable thing, and reminded me of one of the girls in my care at the school. I wanted to give her a hug and thank her for brightening my day. "Of course," I said. "How silly of me."

"Time does seem to go really fast when he's near," she went on. "But only sometimes. Do you think that's peculiar? I think that's peculiar," she said before either Tommy or I could answer. "I'd better put that in my report."

"Jane!" Mrs. Butterworth called. They'd stopped two doors away, at the draper's shop. "Stop dawdling!"

"I have to go," Jane said to us.

"You'd better," I said. "Oh, and Jane. Be careful. Make sure nobody sees your report except the queen herself."

"Yes, miss." She took a step away, but retraced her steps. "And miss?"

"Yes, Jane?"

"You're very pretty." She blushed and skipped off to join her parents, her curls bouncing. Mrs. Butterworth grabbed Jane by her thin little arm and dragged her into the shop. Jane just had enough time to turn and wave before the door banged shut behind her.

Instead of returning to sit alongside the driver, Tommy climbed into the cabin with me. "The station, Fray," he ordered before closing the door. He settled on the seat opposite me, angling his long legs away from mine. "Is it right to let that girl think she really is a spy?"

"She's just a child. A little fantasy here and there isn't going to land her in the asylum."

"I don't think I ever made up stories like that when I was a child."

"That's because you and I never had a childhood. Hard work and hunger aged us prematurely."

"I suppose," he murmured. We passed by the draper's shop. Jane Butterworth stood in the bay window beside a dressmaker's mannequin. She was in the process of removing the peacock blue fabric arranged around the mannequin and draping it around herself. I smiled.

"Do you believe Mrs. Butterworth destroyed the letter?" Tommy asked.

"I do. The question is, why?"

"And why won't Mr. Butterworth tell us what was in it, when he's already given us some details yesterday?"

"That is not the real question, Tommy. You should be asking whether Myer has wiped Mr. Butterworth's memory of the letter's contents."

"Bloody hell," he muttered. "You think he would hypnotize Butterworth to make him forget? Why would he?"

"Perhaps there was something in the letter that mentioned him, or implicated him in something deeper. But there's another question we ought to ponder, too."

"What?"

"Whether Mrs. Butterworth destroyed the letter at her lover's insistence. Or whether he made her do it while under hypnosis."

CHAPTER 7

The countryside was beautiful, but it lacked the energy of London. There was always something new and different to see in the city, no matter the time of day. Everyone had something to do, somewhere to go, or something to say. The surging, rumbling tide of traffic and the masses of pedestrians rushing to and fro outside King's Cross station would have been alarming for a country girl, fresh off the train, but I was used to it. The constant yet familiar sounds were a comfort. I knew this city like a lover knows her mate. I knew where to find food at midnight, or a bed at midday. I knew where to look when someone disappeared, and I knew which lanes to avoid, no matter the hour. London was a thrilling place to live, but a dangerous one, too.

At least I was far from the place where the master had died and his spirit now haunted, but there were still other dangers in a city riddled with crime. I remained vigilant as I walked away from the station into the narrower streets nearby. The one I wanted was lined with a mixture of old and new buildings, some housing disreputable businesses while others were occupied by respectable families. It would be safe enough for me to walk during the day, but not at night. I didn't plan on leaving the hotel after dark, however. That would be foolish.

The hotel itself was one I'd known for years, although I'd not stayed there since my time with the master. It was a slender building, squeezed between squat ones. A faded sign announcing vacancies hung from chains above the door.

I enquired after a room and received a curious look from the desk clerk. He was perhaps in his forties and was shaped like the hotel itself, slender-boned with long fingers. He looked down his pointy nose at me and offered no smile of greeting and exchanged no pleasantries.

"Payment in advance," he said, holding out his hand, palm up. "Two shilling for a night."

I handed him the coins and accepted the key in return.

He nodded at the stairs. "Third floor, first door on the right."

"Is there no one who can take up my valise?" I asked, glancing around for a porter.

"Aye, there is," he said, sitting back in his chair by the office door. It creaked under his weight. "I'm looking at her."

I sighed and headed for the stairs. A chivalrous man would offer to carry it for me, but I got the feeling he was enjoying watching me haul it up. It wasn't particularly heavy, but my arm quickly grew tired and I needed to use both hands up the last flight.

Once in the room, I removed my boots and collapsed onto the bed. Paint peeled off the ceiling and a water stain the length of my forearm discolored one corner. The wallpaper had faded to a dull pink shade, and cobwebs provided the only decorations in an otherwise bare room. A maid probably hadn't been through it in some time.

My little room at the school was looking better and better. At least that was clean. But I was determined not to go back there yet except for a few short visits to ensure everyone was well. Then there was the other matter to attend to. My real reason for returning to London.

I sighed and stared at a black spot on the wall opposite. The black spot moved and I saw it was a beetle. I jumped off the bed with a yelp and picked up my boot. The creature died instantly, but it got me wondering about other things that could have gotten into the room. Or into the bed.

I stripped back the covers and shook out each blanket and the linen. Then I beat the mattress with my fist. Nothing crawled out of it, but I jumped several times on the mattress to make sure. I picked up the pillow and thumped it against the wall. If there had been anything alive in there, it wouldn't be anymore. I did the same with each blanket until I was certain it was free of lice or beetles, then I checked it over again just to make sure.

I hated lice and other creatures small enough to crawl into orifices. They'd been the bane of my childhood and once I'd dragged myself out of the gutter and into the homes of gentlemen, I vowed never to sleep in a bed with lice again. If only the master had known my terror of them, he would have had another tool to frighten me into obedience with. As it was, he had used violence instead.

It grew late and I didn't want to be walking around the city in the dark, so I left after remaking the bed. I bought a beef pie from a pie shop, and ate it standing nearby, clear of the counter, along with several others. Afterward I hurried back to the hotel. Dusk came early to a city where the sun struggled to break through the blanket of smoke and I didn't want to linger.

The desk clerk glanced up from the newspaper spread out on the counter, but didn't even acknowledge me. He returned to his paper without flickering an eyelash.

I went to bed early, since there were no candles to read by and only a pathetic lamp that hissed and faded in and out. To my surprise I slept soundly and awoke a little after dawn, feeling refreshed. Already the city was awake. A cart rolled past my window on the street below and bottles rattled. Someone called out a cheerful "Good morning!" and was answered with a morose "Is it?"

I washed in the bathroom at the end of the corridor. The pipes protested with a groan and spat cold water into the stained bath. I quickly completed my ablutions and dressed.

It was too early for one of my errands, but not for the other. I walked to Clerkenwell instead of riding the omnibus, partly to fill in time, but also because I needed to connect with the city again. I'd been too long away in the soft, gentle countryside, with nothing to do but read and stare out of windows. Walking briskly through the noisy, dirty streets of London reminded me how much I'd missed the vibrancy of the place. With so much to look at, my mind was constantly occupied and my thoughts hardly ever ventured to Samuel. It was of utmost relief. I *could* think of other things. I *could* set aside the memory of his proposal. And I could live a full life at the school with the children to keep me company.

My feelings were confirmed when they greeted me with smiles and hugs. I patted their shoulders and tugged on their hair, but I did not hug them back. Such intimacy, even with children, left a lump in my throat that made swallowing difficult. I had been that way since escaping from the master, except for the too-brief days when Samuel had blocked those horrid memories.

"Miss Charity!" cried Mrs. Peeble from the top of the staircase. I'd gotten no further than the entrance hall. The sea of children calling my name and asking me where I'd been was too thick to wade through. "We weren't expecting you back so soon! Mrs. Beaufort informed us that you could be away for quite some time yet."

"I'm just visiting," I said.

She flapped her arms at the children and they parted for her like the Biblical sea. "Shoo! Off to classes with you all."

Some ran off, others lingered a little longer, eyeing me carefully, as if they expected me to leave while they weren't looking.

"I'll come and see you all again soon," I told them. "Now off you go."

Reassured, they trotted away. I smiled as I watched them go. "I've missed them," I told Mrs. Peeble.

"They've missed you. We all have."

I was taken aback. It was the most sentimental thing she'd ever said to me. Mrs. Peeble had once told me that kind words led to weakness and laziness, and that I should treat the children firmly. I had disagreed with her, but my opinion had been met with a smug "You'll see."

"Enough foolish talk," she said.

I smiled, reassured that nothing had changed in my absence.

"Have you eaten breakfast?" she asked.

"Not yet."

"Then come into the drawing room." Tilly the maid walked past and welcomed me home. "Fetch Miss Charity something to eat," Mrs. Peeble directed her.

Tilly rushed off and I strolled through the hall to the adjoining drawing room.

"Where are you staying?" Mrs. Peeble asked.

"A hotel near King's Cross."

"A hotel! Whatever for? Come back to your room here."

I shook my head. "I can't. You know why."

Her round features scrunched into a frown. "The danger is still present?"

"It has lessened somewhat, but I wish to remain cautious."

She clicked her tongue. "How long will this continue?"

It wasn't a question I could answer. I only hoped it ended soon, and I told her as much. "But I couldn't stay away from the children any longer. I had to see them."

She lowered herself into a chair, slowly at first, then falling the last few inches as if her knees could no longer maintain the steady pace under the pressure. "They've asked after you every day."

"I've missed them, and my life here. Being away has given me a fresh appreciation for it."

I asked after the children individually and was given a thorough, if somewhat military, account of their health, education and a list of their naughty deeds. I listened as I ate the breakfast of toast and sausages that Tilly brought in.

Afterwards, I toured the classrooms and spoke to the children. They were full of questions which I fielded as best as I could without mentioning anything that might frighten them. I spent the rest of the morning talking to each student about what they'd learned in my absence.

I finally tore myself away from them after luncheon. Mrs. Peeble encouraged me to stay and eat with them, and I was grateful for it. Afterward, I said my goodbyes and tried not to shed the tears welling inside me as my students hugged me one by one.

"I'll be back soon," I told Mrs. Peeble at the door. "I can't stay away from them for long, but I can't live here, for now."

"I do hope this business is sorted soon. The police still don't know who tried to kidnap you?"

I shook my head. "It's not their fault."

"Be careful, Miss Charity."

"I will." I headed down the front steps to the street. Some of the local children crowded around, hoping for money or scraps. I handed out bread left over from our lunch to grasping, dirty fingers. Most thanked me and ran off to a recessed doorway or a lane to eat their fill before passing the rest on to other family members. All except one, a boy of about ten with dark, darting eyes and a pinched face that spoke of hunger and desperation. I didn't recognize him. He shoved the bread down his shirt and pulled the edges of his jacket closer over his chest. It was too small, the cuffs riding to his mid-forearm, but he covered the lump of bread well enough that no one would know it was there and rob him for it. I expected him to scamper off, back to wherever it was he lived, but he remained standing at the corner, those clever eyes watching me.

"Do you know that lad?" I asked one of the girls still hovering nearby.

"Nope," she said between mouthfuls. "He's new. Been 'ere a few days, just standin' 'round. Me brother asked 'im what 'e wants, but 'e wouldn't say."

This part of Clerkenwell didn't get many strangers wandering in, particularly children. If he were an orphan hoping to get into the school then he should have knocked on the door and asked for help. He would have been given a bed, food and clothing without hesitation and with no questions asked.

So if he wasn't there for the school, what did he want?

I stared at him and he stared back, those piercing eyes boring into me. Then he suddenly lowered his head and began to stroll away. I started toward him.

"Excuse me!" I called out.

He sprinted off and was long gone before I even reached the corner. There wasn't a sign of him anywhere. It was as if the rookery had swallowed him up. Orphan children had ways of disappearing into thin air. When I'd been his age, I could crawl into the tightest of spaces where adults wouldn't think to look. I decided not to pursue the child. If he were indeed an orphan in need of the school, he would return. Hunger would encourage him to knock on the door eventually. If he wasn't there for the school but to spy on me, then it was best that I didn't follow him. He might lead me to the master's ghost and a trap. There was even a chance that he was possessed by the master's spirit himself.

I hurried off and made my way to the busier, safer, main road. I caught an omnibus to the Home Office on Whitehall. It was housed in one of those gray, imposing buildings that dominate the street in much the same way Mrs. Peeble looks down at her students in cookery class. I was directed to a bald, bespectacled man sitting behind one of the gleaming polished desks arranged around the hall.

"What can I do for you?" he asked without looking up from his paperwork.

"I need to know what crime a particular person committed," I said.

Perhaps he wasn't expecting a female. His head jerked up at the sound of my voice and he blinked owlishly at me. "Why?"

I sighed. I had a feeling this was going to be a long and fruitless conversation. "Can you just tell me if that sort of information is on public record?"

"If he went to trial, yes."

"I'm not sure if there was a trial."

He set his pen down in the wooden ink stand at the edge of the desk and steepled his fingers. "Then how do you know he committed a crime?"

"I suppose I don't. All I do know is that he was arrested and sent to Newgate for a few days before being released."

"Why was he released?"

"I don't know," I said with a tight smile. "That's what I'd like to find out."

He opened one of the desk drawers and pulled out a piece of paper. "Fill this out."

"Is this a form to make an inquiry?"

"That's right."

"But I thought I could make the inquiry here, with you, and *you* would look up the records while I waited."

He laughed and picked up his pen. "Fill out the form and someone upstairs will answer it. The response will be sent to the address you put down here." He pointed to a space near the bottom with the end of his pen.

"How long will that take?"

"Four weeks."

"Four!"

"Or five." His glasses slipped down his nose and he regarded me over the rim. I thought he'd laugh again, but he did not.

"Why so long? It's just a simple thing to look up the records. I can give you approximate dates to make it faster."

He pointed to another space on the form. "Make a note of them here."

I could have screamed. The old me might have tried flattery and a flirtatious wink. Instead I simply gritted my teeth and asked, "Is there no way to circumvent this process and get an answer sooner?"

He shoved his glasses back up his nose and resumed checking his paperwork. "Not officially."

"What about unofficially?"

He looked up again. "I suppose you could try, but it involves visiting the prison itself. And then it will only work if the governor remembers your criminal."

It was not an appealing thought. Prisons had terrified me from a young age. My mother had told me stories of friends and family who'd been caught stealing and sent to prison, only to die in a dank, crowded cell from starvation or disease. Jack, Tommy and I had been lucky to escape capture on several occasions, thanks in large part to Jack's talent. He'd set more than one copper's trousers alight so that we could slip away in the resulting chaos.

I handed the form back to the clerk. "Thank you. I won't be needing this."

I set my frustration aside and headed to Newgate. The formidable, solid walls of the prison ran alongside the street, but passersby seemed unperturbed at having dangerous criminals housed a few feet away on the other side. It took me several deep breaths before I could summon the courage to enter the adjoining governor's house. I'd never been inside a prison before and I wasn't sure what to expect. Certainly not the office where a servant directed me. It was a normal office with two clerks pouring over almanacs and ledgers at their desks. Books bound in greens and browns lined the shelves behind them and a dresser, housing dozens of small drawers in rows of eight, was pushed into a corner. I waited for one of them to speak to me, but they continued to study their books and ignore me. Fortunately, the governor finally appeared.

He too wasn't what I expected. He was a small man with soft hands and the most magnificent gray whiskers that reached past his chest in wiry coils. He smiled gently at me. At least, I think it was a gentle smile. It was difficult to see his lips amongst all that hair. The corners of his eyes crinkled, confirming my suspicions. He introduced himself as Governor Draycott.

"What's a pretty young girl like you doing in a filthy den like this then, eh?" he asked, sitting back in his chair and regarding me.

"I'm on an errand to find out some information for a friend," I said.

"What sort of information?"

"It's to do with a gentleman who was here for a brief stay, perhaps a year or more ago."

"Gentleman, eh? Don't get too many of those in here. But that sort of information is kept with the other records at the Home Office. The bureaucratic bobs over there can help you." He folded his hands over his paunch and interlinked his fingers. He was waiting for me to say something. Testing me?

"I haven't got time for them to shuffle papers from one pile to the next and back again," I said.

He chuckled and leaned forward. His eyes sparkled amid all the crinkles. "Nobody has, and yet it's the way things are done."

"The proper way," I said carefully.

"Aye, the proper way. But you're here to go the improper way, am I right?"

I smiled. "I don't have the luxury of time. I'll be leaving London soon and I'd like to be in possession of the information by then. I thought you could help me. Going straight to the source is always better than second-hand knowledge, and since the information is public anyway, I hoped you could spare a few moments of your valuable time."

"Valuable, eh? Not too many in the Home Office would think my time worth a penny. I'm just another prison guard to them, only my whiskers are grayer." He chuckled again and stroked his beard. "But since I can't resist a pretty face, I'll try to help you. Tell me about this gentleman and I'll see if I can remember him. I've been here long enough to have seen most gents who've passed through in the last ten years or so and my memory's as strong as ever."

"His name is Samuel Gladstone. He's the son of Mr. Henry Gladstone of Oxfordshire. The younger Mr. Gladstone wasn't incarcerated here for long, so I suspect his case didn't make it to trial and he was released without charge."

The governor held up his hands for me to stop. "I'm sorry, miss, but I can't help you." He opened up a large ledger on his desk and studied it. I'd been dismissed.

"Why not?"

"That information is confidential," he said without looking up.

"What do you mean?"

"Confidential means I can't tell you."

"I know what it means. I don't understand *why* it's confidential."

"You should try the Home Office. That's the proper course of action for these sorts of inquiries."

"I have tried them!" My frustration was boiling over. I'd wasted a lot of time between the Home Office and now Newgate, and I'd gotten precisely nowhere. I threw up my hands and let them slap down on the desk. The ink in the well rippled. "A moment ago you were eager to help, but as soon as I mentioned the Gladstones, you closed up. Why? What is it you're not telling me?"

"Nothing. Now, kindly see yourself out. I'm very busy." He licked his finger and flipped a page of the ledger.

"But—"

"Don't make me call the guard, miss. He's rough and I'd hate to see a pretty lady like yourself manhandled to the street for all to see."

I clenched my teeth and somehow managed to keep my temper from erupting. I stalked out of his office, past the guard and out to the street. Screaming would have been cathartic at that moment, but there were too many people around. So I walked all the way back to the hotel very fast, so that by the time I reached my room my anger had dissolved.

I flopped down on the bed, the fight having gone out of me. The fog that had descended upon me cleared and I was able to think clearly again. The governor had known about Samuel's case, that much was obvious. He'd been keen enough to help me until I'd mentioned the Gladstone name. There was only one explanation for it: Mr. Gladstone had paid him to destroy all records of Samuel's stay at Newgate.

I had no doubt I would have struck a wall at the Home Office too, or perhaps a *well* down which certain inquiries were tossed, never to be seen again. Whether Mr. Gladstone had paid the police to drop the charges or not I couldn't be sure, but my guess would be that he had. He didn't want any whiff of the scandal to reach the members of the upper classes.

I sighed. In a way, it confirmed that Samuel had indeed been to Newgate, but I was still in the dark as to why. All I had to go on was Bert's accusation. I didn't want to believe Samuel capable of *that* crime, yet I had to be sure.

There was really only one course of action for me to take next. I couldn't remain in London, but I didn't want to return to Frakingham and idly wait for the master's spirit to be whisked away. I would learn nothing there, and I desperately wanted to know whether Bert spoke the truth. I *had* to know. It consumed me now that I saw the extent of Mr. Gladstone's cover-up. It had to be something terrible, something that could ruin Samuel's future and the Gladstone name.

Although I had never quite trusted Samuel and his hypnosis, I did think him a good man overall. I couldn't bear to be wrong. I didn't want to be even more afraid of him than I already was. Yet it was looking like Bert was right.

I must go to Samuel's home and somehow make inquiries without him seeing me.

CHAPTER 8

I paid the school one more visit on the morning of my departure. To my surprise, a magnificent coach waited out the front. The driver was having a devil of a time keeping the children away from the gleaming black paintwork and horses. I was afraid he'd use his whip on them, so I ordered them to stand back.

"Perhaps let them take turns patting the animals," I advised him. "That's if you'd like fewer finger marks on your doors."

He thanked me and tugged on his cap. By the time I reached the top of the stairs, he'd hopped down and was organizing the children into two rows.

The coach didn't belong to the Beauforts and I was curious to see who had ventured into Clerkenwell. Few toffs would dare.

"Miss Charity!" Tilly said, upon seeing me setting my valise down in the hall. "What luck. There's a fine lady here asking after you. Mrs. Peeble was about to send her on her way, but now you're here, there's no need. She's in the drawing room, miss."

"Who is the fine lady?" I asked.

She didn't get a chance to answer me. Mrs. Peeble appeared with a lovely dark haired woman dressed in green silk. I recognized her as Ebony Carstairs, the woman who wanted to marry Samuel.

"Miss Evans," Ebony said smoothly. "Mrs. Peeble has just finished telling me that you weren't in the city. How fortunate that you're here after all." Her tone was icy, her smile false.

"Mrs. Peeble wasn't aware that I'd returned," I lied. Mrs. Peeble had only been protecting me, and I saw no reason to tell Ebony the truth.

"Now that you have, perhaps we could speak." She was already in the drawing room by the time she finished her sentence.

Mrs. Peeble rolled her eyes at me. "Want me to come in with you?" she whispered as I passed.

"I'll be all right."

"Very well, but I'll remain out here."

I entered the drawing room after Ebony. "Would you like some tea, Miss Carstairs?"

"No, thank you. I won't be staying long." She sat primly on the edge of the sofa, her body twisted to the side to give her bustle ample space. "We must talk about Samuel."

"There is nothing to discuss," I said. "As I told you last time, there is nothing between Samuel and me. We're friends. I've explained as much to his family, too."

"Friends? Come now, Miss Evans, we both know that's not possible."

I bristled. "Why not?"

"A gentleman and a woman of..." She eyed me up and down, not bothering to hide her disdain, "...a woman cannot be friends. It's unthinkable."

"To you, perhaps."

She gave me a pointed look and another false smile. I'd been prepared to like this woman. She'd been demure and polite upon our first meeting at Claridge's, when I'd also met Samuel's parents for the first time. But now that we were alone, she was proving that first impressions could be misleading. Like most of her class, she thought herself above me in every way, not only by birth but by *right*. No matter what I said or did, I would never change her opinion.

"I am not entirely unsympathetic," she went on.

"Do tell."

She pressed her lips together, no longer bothering with the smile. "I know what you want from him—"

"No, I'm not sure that you do."

"Stop interrupting," she snapped.

"Stop saying things that require an interruption."

"I don't know what he sees in you." Her gaze focused squarely on my chest. "On second thoughts, perhaps I do. I'm not blind and nor is he."

My face heated, much to my horror, not in embarrassment but in pent-up frustration. This beautiful woman must know how irritating it was to be seen as nothing more than a useless ornament, there to decorate a gentleman's arm. She wouldn't know the dangers of such beauty like I did, protected as she was by her father's title. I prayed she never would. No matter how much I disliked her, I didn't wish that kind of misfortune on anyone.

"I feel I must defend Samuel," I said. "He does have a little more depth than the average gentleman. He's quite capable of intelligent conversation with a woman without staring at her...bodice."

"Intelligent?" She laughed. "My dear, you may have perfected the accent, and I admit that you probably have a rudimentary grasp of reading, but do you honestly think that *your* education can compare to mine? I've been tutored from a very young age on all manner of subjects."

"Dear Miss Carstairs," I said, matching her supercilious tone. "Didn't your vast array of governesses and tutors tell you that education and intelligence are not the same thing?"

Her lips stretched into a sneer, but it was fleeting and replaced with the false smile again. She smoothed her hands over her lap, slowly, deliberately, and pinned me with that green stare. No matter how much I wanted to think otherwise, there was intelligence in her eyes.

"Let me be perfectly clear with you, Miss Evans."

"You mean you haven't already?"

Her gaze narrowed. "Samuel is a good man. If you marry him, he'll be brought so low as to be inconsequential."

I thought it an odd thing to say, yet I supposed being someone of consequence was of the utmost importance to Ebony and her ilk. I doubted Samuel cared very much, although I didn't know him well enough to be sure. Perhaps hiding at Frakingham had been forced on him, and what he really wanted was exactly what Ebony wanted too—to be important.

"I'm not going to marry him," I told her as directly as I could. I didn't tell her that I'd already turned him down. That particular arrow wasn't mine to shoot. Besides, it might lower Samuel in her eyes. I couldn't do that to him when there was a chance he might still wed her. The upper classes did things that went against their heart's desire all the time. Now that Samuel's father was dead, he might see the sense in marrying Lord Mellor's daughter.

"He doesn't pay for mistresses." She wrinkled her nose, as if the very word disgusted her. "He doesn't need to."

"Have you been speaking to his brother lately?"

"Why?"

"No reason." I blew out a breath and forged on. "Listen to me, Miss Carstairs. I sympathize with your position. I do. I can see how it must look, but I am not Samuel's mistress, nor do I wish to be, nor does *he* wish me to be."

"Untie Samuel from your apron strings, Miss Evans. Let him go."

"Believe me, he is very much untied. Indeed, he left Frakingham House for his own home. I suspect he won't be able to leave there for some time, if at all."

"Let's hope the death of poor Mr. Gladstone has shown Samuel the need to remain there. He will inherit, one day."

"His brother is not dead yet," I said.

Her eyes sharpened. "Of course. He may live for years. Let's hope so, if only to give Samuel time to settle into a more fitting role first."

"More fitting?"

"Didn't you know? He's going into politics?"

"Samuel? A politician?" I laughed at the absurdity of it. Samuel's interest in politics reached no further than mine. Of course we both had a passing interest, but that was it. I'd learned some time ago that I was quite powerless at influencing the government and so paid it little attention. Since Samuel never once mentioned politics or government policy, I'd assumed he shared my opinions.

I may not have known Samuel particularly well, but I did think I was right on that score. He had far more interest in August Langley's research than attending political meetings. But it was not my place to tell Ebony that. Indeed, she suddenly stood, her chin tilted defiantly. I suspected my laughter had finally undermined her confidence.

"I love Samuel," she said, her voice shaky. "And I will not give him up easily."

Of all the things she'd said to me, her declaration rattled me the most. I'd pegged her as an unfeeling, ambitious toff. It was clear from the shine in her eyes and the flare of her nostrils that I'd been unfair. She had a heart after all, and that heart wanted Samuel.

"I'll see myself out," she said.

"Wait!" I rushed to block her exit. "I have something to ask you."

"About Samuel?" She gave an inelegant huff. "And you said you had no interest in him."

"I do have an interest in him, but only as a friend. I know you don't believe that, but please, hear me." I squared up to her and she straightened too. Although we were of a height, her hat was taller. I suspected she would consider that a point won. "Was there a time when Samuel was absent from the London social scene? It would have been a year ago or more."

"Samuel was never one for social events. He only ever attended when his mother made him. Why?"

I shook my head. "It's nothing."

"I don't believe you. Tell me."

I should have known she'd leave propriety behind and try to get an answer out of me. "It was simply something he alluded to. A time in his life when something happened. He wouldn't tell me what," I added quickly. "I wondered if you knew."

"If I did, I wouldn't tell you. Knowing your type, you would use the knowledge of it against him, in some way."

I smiled sweetly. "I didn't say he'd done anything scandalous. Thank you for confirming it."

"Come now, Miss Evans, even somebody like you must know that a gentleman or lady only drops out of society when there is scandal afoot."

I arched my eyebrow at her. "And if Samuel did do something scandalous, something unforgiveable? Would that change how you feel about him?"

"Don't be absurd. I never said that Samuel did anything wrong, and certainly nothing unforgiveable. He's a good man. That's why we would be a perfect match. Formidable, as they say." She did not smile, but she didn't need to for me to see the triumph in her eyes or hear it in her voice. "Step aside, please. I must go. I'm on my way to the Gladstones' country seat for the funeral tomorrow."

I shifted out of the way and watched her stride off, her head high. I heard the front door open and close while I stood rooted to the spot, and wondered why I ever thought she'd be a good match for Samuel.

***

The Gladstone family home was in Oxfordshire, near a sizeable village with a good inn. I rented a room from the innkeeper whose friendly, chatty nature proved to be useful. It seemed the Gladstones were the most prominent family in the area. Their estate employed a considerable number of staff and their tenant farms were prosperous. The conversation naturally steered toward poor Mr. Gladstone's gruesome demise and the subsequent return of the prodigal son.

"Of course we're all glad to see Mr. Samuel home again," the innkeeper said as we walked slowly up the stairs to the room I had rented. "It's only a shame it took his father's death for him to return."

"Is the funeral going to be a public or private affair?"

"A public service will be held at St. Catherine's. That's the church on the hill you would have seen after you left the station. A private one will be held just for the family and guests too, I expect, then he'll be buried in St. Catherine's graveyard. Are you going, miss?"

"I'll attend the public funeral. I'm an acquaintance of the family."

He arched a brow. "Acquaintance, eh?"

"I work at Claridge's. The Galdstones stay at the hotel whenever they're in the city and I've gotten to know them well. I wanted to pay my respects to poor Mr. Gladstone." It was a terrible lie and I suspected he saw right through it, but he had the decency not to say so. He probably pegged me to be the mistress of one of the Gladstone men. No respectable young woman traveled unaccompanied.

"How is the family holding up?" I asked.

He paused outside one of the doors along the corridor and set down my valise. "They're as well as can be expected, considering the blow. He was a healthy man, Mr. Gladstone. He could have lived for years."

"So unlike Mr. Albert," I said with a sad shake of my head.

"Aye."

"Has his health always been poor?"

"Aye, ever since he was born he's been sickly. Not like his brother. Strapping lad is Mr. Samuel. Full of life."

"He is," I agreed. "It's as if he has compensated for his brother's lack of vitality and is determined always to be happy."

"Now, I wouldn't go saying that." He unlocked the door and handed me the key. "Mr. Samuel's had his darker moments."

"Yes, of course." I frowned. "There was that difficult time when he was banished from London. We did miss him at Claridge's. He'd been such a frequent visitor before that."

"Your loss was our gain," he said, smiling.

"Do you know why he was banished?" I leaned closer, conspiratorial. "The hotel staff said it was something to do with a woman."

"I wouldn't know anything about Mr. Samuel's women," he said with a laugh that made his jowls wobble.

I took a chance and pressed a florin into his palm. He pocketed it.

"All I do know is the family weren't the same afterwards," he said, glancing back the way we came. "They retreated into the big house and had few visitors. Not even other family members came to visit."

"It sounds very lonely, particularly for someone like Mr. Samuel. There were no visitors at all, you say?"

"Aunts, uncles, cousins—they used to visit all the time beforehand, but that stopped when Mr. Samuel came home in shame. It wasn't until he was sent off to University College that they returned for hunting and parties. It's like...it's like they were afraid of him," he murmured, frowning. "Strange, really. He's the most likeable one of the lot. Can't think what he could have done to make them fearful."

"Did any relatives visit at all while he was home?"

He pursed his lips in thought. "Only a cousin or two."

"Oh yes, those ladies? What are their names again?"

"Not ladies, miss. Gentlemen, both of them." He indicated the room. "You'll find it comfortable enough. Dinner is served in the dining room downstairs until eight and breakfast is from six. Let me or the wife know if there's something you need."

I thanked him, even though I was hardly aware of speaking. My mind still reeled with what he'd just inadvertently told me. Not only had Samuel indeed been banished from London for a period of time, he'd also done something that frightened women only. The pattern fit with Bert's accusation.

I spent much of the evening sewing black crepe to the cuffs and collar of my dress and hat. It could be removed easily enough afterwards and set aside until needed again.

The following morning I headed up to the church early and found a seat at the back, in the corner. The congregation trickled in over the next hour. The church was full by the time the family arrived. It was easy to pick them out with their elegant, well-cut clothes and tall hats. There were quite a few of them, elderly and young alike. They watched as Mrs. Gladstone, Samuel and Bert slowly made their way to the front. I didn't watch them throughout the service, or afterwards as we filed out of the little old stone church into the drizzling rain. I kept my gaze on the cousins, aunts and uncles. What I learned from simple observation worried me further.

The young females, probably cousins, chatted with Samuel and, occasionally with Bert. Some flirted shamelessly, being overtly friendly when offering their sympathies. There was simply no need to press oneself against him at his father's funeral. All were quickly whisked away by hovering mothers and fathers as soon as the parents noticed. The young gentlemen were not.

It would seem the elder members of the family knew the details of the scandal, the younger ones didn't. My observations strengthened Bert's claim. But how could Samuel have done...that? He wasn't violent. He wasn't desperate for female attention, either. Yet clearly he'd done something that made the family want to keep the young ladies at a distance. Surely he wouldn't hypnotize a girl against her will and then...

No. Not Samuel. I didn't trust him, but—

Wait. *I didn't trust him.*

I blinked through my veil and stared at him as he held an umbrella over his mother and accepted condolences from the villagers. There were two reasons why I didn't trust him. Firstly, I was naturally distrustful of charming men. Secondly, I didn't trust him because *he was capable of hypnotizing accidentally;* I'd almost been a victim myself. And when a woman was hypnotized by Samuel, she took an even greater liking to him. He could do whatever he wanted with her and she'd be willing while she was hypnotized. Afterwards, she might regret her actions. Afterwards, she could claim he coerced her.

The world tilted. My mind reeled. I pressed my hand against the cool, damp stones of the church wall to steady myself. Samuel may have been guilty of rape after all. I wasn't sure if it would have been considered that in his eyes at the time, but I think even he would have realized the crime he'd committed later on.

I lifted my gaze to him and was surprised to see him staring at me, a frown drawing his brows together. He couldn't have known it was me, thanks to the heavy veil covering my face, but I hurried off anyway. I didn't want to see him. Didn't want him to approach me and lift the veil and see the horror and fear in my eyes. I'd always been cautious of him, but now real fear clutched my insides. Samuel may not intentionally have hurt anyone, but he had great capacity to unintentionally cause injury. And I had the scars to prove that I'd borne enough injury in my life.

I reached the churchyard gate before Samuel intercepted me. "Charity." His voice startled me, even though I'd heard him approach. He came up alongside me. He didn't touch me, didn't take my arm and force me to look at him.

I kept walking.

He maintained the same pace. "Charity, I know it's you. Please, stop. If you don't, I'll have to follow you and leave my own father's funeral."

I stopped. "That was unfair," I said, rounding on him. The sight of him made my heart hammer harder and brought my fears rushing back again. I edged away.

He shrugged one shoulder. "I think I've forgotten how to play by the rules."

Despite my fear, the sight of him tugged at my heart. The profound change in him was marked. He may have been clean shaved and wearing a suit, but he somehow looked even more ragged than usual. The lines around his eyes were made darker and deeper by the shadows circling them. The inner corners were blood red, the whites duller. He shifted his weight from foot to foot, and the muscles in his jaw jumped. He seemed not to know what to do with his arms, either. He folded them over his chest then let them hang loosely at his sides before putting them behind him. If I didn't know him, I'd have thought him mad or well on the way to it.

A madman was capable of doing terrible things.

I dampened my rising fear. We were in a public place. Nothing would happen. I glanced past him to see his mother, brother, Ebony and several others staring back at us, curious frowns on their brows. They wanted to know who was the mysterious woman beneath the veil.

"How did you know it was me?" I asked.

"I'd know you anywhere even if you wore a sack over your head." Despite the madness in his eyes, his voice was perfectly smooth and rich.

A little thrill of tingles washed through me at the sound of it. I shook them off and forced myself to concentrate. "You ought to get back," I said. "It's best if they don't know it's me you're talking to."

He moved, blocking my line of sight to his family. "You're right," he said quickly. "You should go. Don't let them see you." He gave my shoulder a little shove.

I blinked at him. Why the sudden change of heart? He'd asked me to marry him mere days ago, so why did he not want me near now? I'd been dreading being discovered because I was afraid he'd try to force me into the family fold where I was neither wanted nor wanted to be. It seemed I had nothing to fear on that score.

"I'll come see you later," he said, glancing over his shoulder at his family. "Are you staying at the Stag and Huntsman?"

"I'll be gone later," I lied. My train didn't leave until the following day. "Stay with your family. They need you."

"And *I* need *you*." He didn't shout, but his voice slammed into me as if he had. It was dark, desperate and edged with steel. "Charity, please, don't leave without seeing me."

"I'm seeing you now," I said, trying hard to ignore my twin fears—fear for his sanity and fear of him hypnotizing me.

"It's not enough. Christ." He removed his hat and dragged his hand through his hair. The ends were damp from the rain. "You're right. You have to go. Leave the village as soon as possible. Go back to Frakingham where you're safe."

"Safe? There's a demon there!"

"Go!"

He shifted again, impatient to get away, or more precisely, for me to leave. I didn't understand it, but I was dealing with a man on the edge of madness. I wasn't sure anyone could understand him while he was in this state.

I was about to move off when a figure caught my eye. A tall, thin man bent over Mrs. Gladstone's hand. "What's Myer doing here?" I said before I could check myself.

Samuel turned to look just as his mother snapped her hand out of Myer's. Her face wrinkled in what looked like disgust or perhaps hatred. She turned her cheek to him, dismissing him. He bowed and walked off. She did not spare him another glance.

"Why indeed?" Samuel said quietly. "He must want to pass on his sympathies. He did say he was an acquaintance of my father's."

And probably of his mother's, too. "But the nerve of him being here when his demon killed your father."

"He didn't summon the demon."

I frowned. "How can you know that for sure?"

His pupils dilated. He ground the heel of his hand into his temple as if trying to push away a thought. "Go, Charity. Please, get yourself far away from here. I'll see you at Frakingham."

I left. I didn't want to stay anyway. As curious as I was about Myer's presence, I wanted to get away from Samuel and every other Gladstone. I hurried back to the Stag and Huntsman and looked out the window at St. Catherine's on the hill.

What had happened in just a few shorts days to push Samuel closer to the abyss of madness? Did it have anything to do with why he wanted me to leave quickly? Or did it have something to do with what he'd done in his past?

Perhaps it was both. Perhaps he knew he couldn't trust himself not to hypnotize me and control himself while I was under that hypnosis.

I didn't get a chance to explore those thoughts further. A knock on my door announced a visitor. It must be him. He was the only one who knew I was in the village.

"Who is it?" I called through the door.

"Open up at once," came the clipped tones of Mrs. Gladstone. "Or I'll have the innkeeper open the door for me."

CHAPTER 9

Mrs. Gladstone charged into my room like an ominous cloud as soon as I'd opened the door a crack. She still wore her widow's weeds, a stiff little veil skimming her chin. She was alone.

"How did you know I was here?" I asked, shutting the door and rounding on her. I refused to be intimidated by this woman. I had nothing to fear from her.

She seated herself on the chair by the window and raised the veil. The glare she fixed on me could have frozen a desert in summer. "I'm no fool. My son runs off to speak to a tall, willowy woman and returns with madness in his eyes. It could only be you."

So she considered me the one responsible for his state of mind. I couldn't argue with that. "I came to express my sympathies. I hoped to remain anonymous."

She made a miffed sound through her nose. "You are not the sort of woman who can go about unnoticed, Miss Evans, even with your face covered."

I wasn't sure how to take that, so I said nothing. I remained standing by the door. There were no other chairs in the small room and I didn't want to sit on the bed. It seemed inappropriate somehow.

"Let's be frank with one another, Miss Evans. I want you to leave the village in the morning."

"I am. My train ticket is in my reticule."

She blinked rapidly. "Very well. Good. I admit to being surprised. I thought you'd remain to torment us."

"Mrs. Gladstone, I have no reason to torment you. I want only what you want—for Samuel to have a happy life."

The tiny lines around her mouth pinched together. "Then why come at all?"

I couldn't answer that truthfully without giving away my curiosity over Samuel's stint in Newgate. What I could do was try to inadvertently get some answers out of her now that she was here. "I hoped to observe Samuel's family, as it turns out."

"Observe us? Are you a scientist, Miss Evans? Are we an experiment?"

"I'm no scientist, but I do have an interest in the unexplained. Strange phenomena pique my curiosity to a point that I cannot sleep until I know how and why something happens."

Her face changed as I spoke my little lie. She seemed to age several years. Her cheeks and jowls sagged, her eyes drooped. The superior manner vanished. "You belong to the society?" she whispered.

"No."

That seemed to relieve her a little. Once again she looked me in the eye. "You're curious about Samuel."

"Yes. His ability to hypnotize is not something I've come across before, although I now know that Mr. Myer also possesses the talent."

"It's not a talent," she said, curling her lip upon the final word.

"My interest in Samuel is purely that. Curiosity."

"Why didn't you tell me earlier?"

Because I hadn't thought of it then. "I wasn't sure if you or your husband were prepared to admit that Samuel could hypnotize. I rather thought it was something you wanted to sweep under the rug."

She dabbed at the corner of her eye with her handkerchief despite it being dry. "The inexplicable might be a curiosity to you, Miss Evans. To us, it's a cross to bear. I don't expect you to understand how traumatic Samuel's hypnosis is for us."

"Perhaps if you didn't view it as a cross to bear, but rather a gift to harness, you might be more accepting of it."

She scoffed. "Don't be absurd. You don't tell a blind man that he's lucky not to be able to see. Do you think Mr. Langley considers himself fortunate that he can't walk?"

"Those disabilities are not the same as Samuel's condition."

Another scoff. She rose from the chair and lowered her veil again. She was about to leave and I'd not yet discovered answers to my questions. Her unexpected visit might as well be put to good use.

"Do you feel that way because of what Samuel did?" I asked.

She went very still. "What are you talking about?"

"He told me why he was sent to Newgate."

Lie upon lie upon lie. I was digging myself into such a deep hole that I might never be able to climb back out.

She sniffed. "I don't believe he told you anything. He would never speak of that to anyone, let alone you."

"Why not?"

She swept past me. "Good day, Miss Evans. We have nothing further to say to one another."

I wasn't quite so prepared to let her go now that I had her alone. She might not tell me why Samuel was in prison, but she could tell me other things about him. "I find it curious that you still want him to marry Miss Carstairs," I said before she opened the door. "Aren't you afraid that her political ambitions for him will expose his scandalous past?"

"Is that your way of disparaging your opponent and promoting yourself?" She barked a harsh laugh. "Pathetic."

"We aren't opponents because I have no interest in marrying Samuel. I simply want to know why you think marrying him off to an ambitious woman is a good idea when he has no similar ambition and a vulnerable past."

"Something can be done to dampen her enthusiasm, and once it is, there'll be no impediment to them marrying."

"Samuel says he doesn't love her. I would have thought that impediment enough."

"Marriage isn't about love, but I don't expect someone of your ilk to understand that. Marriage is about unions and strengthening what you already have. Samuel needs Ebony. As the second son, he can do no better. As the second son with an ill older brother, it's important that Samuel marries well."

"I agree. He isn't in a position to marry where he wishes, but I do think you're making a mistake in forcing him to wed Ebony. Find a different wife for him, Mrs. Gladstone. One with less ambition and a sweeter personality. That is my advice to you, as a woman with Samuel's best interests at heart."

It was difficult to tell how she took my words with the veil covering her face. She didn't immediately leave, however, and appeared to be peering back at me through the black crepe. I took advantage of her stunned silence to ask another question.

"How do you and Mr. Myer know one another?"

"I…" She pressed her hand to her temple and I thought perhaps our meeting had been too much for her. She was, after all, genuinely grieving. "We're old acquaintances."

"You don't find it curious that he and Samuel are the only ones capable of hypnosis?"

"No," she snapped. "Why should I? What are you implying?"

"I'm implying that there must be something linking them. Have you never asked yourself what that might be? Or asked Mr. Myer?"

Her shoulders stiffened. Her back straightened. "I don't like your tone, Miss Evans."

"I would consider telling Samuel what that link is, if I were you. It might go some way to mending your relationship with him."

"Our relationship does not need mending. It is also none of your affair. Instead of poking your nose into Samuel's life, you ought to project some of that curiosity onto the Langleys. Tell me, Miss Evans, do you know what Samuel and Myer have been working on in Mr. Langley's laboratory?"

"No-o," I hedged. "Do you?"

"I believe it has something to do with reading minds."

I blew out a measured breath, unsure whether to be relieved that she spouted such nonsense or not. "Nobody can read another's mind."

"Not yet," she quipped. I couldn't see her smiling, but I got the feeling she was enjoying herself immensely at my expense. "With the help of two hypnotists, I suspect it's only a matter of time. Perhaps, Miss Evans, you ought to be more concerned about that. The consequences of such a device would be rather…interesting."

"Device?" I echoed.

"The chair in the laboratory. Haven't you seen it?"

"Yes. Yes, I have. But surely Mr. Langley wouldn't create something so…wicked."

"You have far more faith in him than me. Far more faith in all of them."

I watched her sail out of my room and down the corridor to the stairs. I shut the door and leaned against it. Her final words tumbled around my head, over and over. Had she told the truth about that chair and Langley's experiments? If so, why was Samuel willingly involved? It was shocking to think him eager to be able to read minds as well as hypnotize.

Yet Mrs. Gladstone hadn't been shocked. Clearly she didn't think her son possessed good moral fiber. And who knew a man better than his own mother?

***

I didn't catch the train to London. I returned to Harborough, instead. There was little I could do in the city, wary as I was of returning to the school. Besides, speaking with Mrs. Gladstone had sparked my curiosity about Langley's experiment. I wanted to get to the bottom of it. I needed to know for certain whether she was right and Langley was indeed hoping to create a contraption that could read minds, and whether Samuel was involved. It was bad enough knowing he could hypnotize; it was worse thinking he wanted to read minds as well.

I was beginning to think I didn't know him at all.

Tommy met me as the wagon I'd ridden upon came to a stop near the front steps of Frakingham House. He did not greet me with an open smile, as he usually did when I arrived, but with a rifle and a scolding.

"You ought not to have come," he said, glancing at the wagon driver who'd brought me. "Especially unarmed. Not with the...wild dog still loose."

"The driver said he had to deliver supplies to Frakingham," I said. "He is also armed."

The driver showed Tommy his rifle. "Now get them crates from out back," he said. "I want to be on my way. You ain't paying me enough to do this."

Tommy unloaded the crates and my valise then sent the driver on his way. He ushered me inside, leaving the crates behind. "You shouldn't have come," he said again.

"I had to. Has the demon showed up?"

"It came once to the house."

I gasped. "Is everyone all right?"

He pinched the bridge of his nose and nodded. "It prowled around for a while then left. It hasn't been seen since."

"You look tired. It's taking its toll on you, isn't it?"

"Don't worry about me." His tone was curt, his manner aloof and somewhat miserable. I didn't think it was entirely attributable to exhaustion.

"What's wrong?" I asked as he closed and bolted the front door.

"Nothing. I thought you were in London."

"I decided to return after all."

I got the feeling he wanted to say something to me, and I was about to ask him again if anything was wrong, when Sylvia called out from the doorway leading to the drawing room.

"Charity! It *is* you!"

"It's a pleasure to see you again, Sylvia," I said, approaching her. "I'm sorry I gave no notice of my arrival. I do hope you can forgive me for the inconvenience."

I expected her to take my hand and tell me I was welcome, but she did not. Her mouth flattened. Her gaze darted from Tommy to me. "Yes. Well. You're here now." She spun around and returned to the drawing room.

"Is everything all right?" I asked Tommy. "Have I upset her in some way?"

"Don't mind her."

"But I must mind her! If I've done or said something—"

"How could you? You've not even been here."

There was truth in that at least, but still, I must have done something. She was usually so pert and bright, not this sullen, ill-mannered girl.

"You can have your own room again," he said as he climbed the stairs. "I'm sure Miss Langley will send Maud up soon to prepare it for you. She's not completely forgotten herself."

By the time we reached the door to my bedroom, I was quite out of breath attempting to keep up with his fast pace. "Tommy? Something is wrong. Speak to me."

He swung open the door and dumped my valise on the bed. "There's nothing to say."

"The mood of this place has changed since I was last here. You and Sylvia have changed. Why?"

He shoved the curtains aside and the weak afternoon sunlight filtered into the room. "It's not for me to say."

I threw up my hands. The conversation had quickly become exasperating. "Nonsense. I am your old friend. You can tell me everything."

He rounded on me, his eyes flashing. He towered over me, and if it had been anyone else, I would have been afraid. But it was only Tommy, one of the few men I trusted. Indeed, one of only two. "Very well," he growled. "Let's just say that you were right and I came to realize it too late."

"Right about what?"

"About me and Sylvia. Miss Langley. She's not for the likes of me. I took your advice and have been nothing but a good footman in her presence. She asked me why the change and I told her it was the way it had to be between us, from now on. She hasn't spoken to me since, except to give me an order to do this or do that."

I pressed my lips together to stop my smile from breaking out. "Isn't that what a mistress is supposed to say to her servant?"

He grunted. "It's not *what* she asks me to do, it's how she tells me to do it. She lords it over me, turns her nose up and such."

I clasped his hands in mine. "Oh, Tommy. I know it troubles you to be treated like a footman. Despite what you claim, I know how hard it is for free spirits like us to take orders. But she's only treating you the way most servants are treated." I hugged him. "You did the right thing. She'll feel a little bruised for a while, but she'll be better off in the long run. You both will, once you find someone more appropriate."

"If you say so," he muttered into his chest.

"I'm proud of you, Tommy. You did what was best."

Poor Tommy. He looked miserable. I believed what I'd told him, however. He would be better off and so would Sylvia. They just needed time for their hearts to recover.

A gasp from behind us had me pulling away. "Sylvia!" I cried. "We didn't hear you."

"Clearly." Her gaze focused on Tommy's arm where I gripped it. Her jaw hardened. "I see that Dawson has looked after you."

Tommy bowed to her then left the room. I watched him go. Sylvia did not.

"Maud will be here soon to make up the bed," she said. "Tea will be served in the drawing room in half an hour, if you wish to join me."

She left too and I stood there like a statue, watching her walk stiffly away.

Half an hour later I joined her in the drawing room. Tea had already been served. She poured a cup and handed it to me. She did not ask me how I'd been or anything that a good hostess usually asked her newly arrived guest. Sylvia may not be an experienced hostess, but she wasn't usually a rude one. It would seem I had much work to do to win back her good opinion.

To my own surprise, I found myself eager to resume our friendship. She may have been silly and exasperating at times, but I liked her. This new awkwardness between us didn't sit well with me at all.

"How are you?" I asked.

"In good health. Thank you."

"It must be terribly worrying with the demon still on the loose."

"It is, but we're managing. Indeed, we've grown quite accustomed to demons around here."

"And your uncle?"

"He's well, too," she said, her tone short, clipped.

"Does he progress with his experiments?"

"I don't know. He doesn't discuss his work with me." She sipped her tea and did not meet my gaze.

"And Tommy?" I ventured. "He looks tired."

She set the cup down in the saucer with a clatter. "Dawson has performed his duties as admirably as he always does. I suspect if he was too tired I'd be told."

"That's not what I meant."

She merely shrugged.

I sighed. The conversation was tortuous, but I needed to clear the air or I couldn't remain at Frakingham. "I know you're upset with him for…keeping you at a distance."

"I don't know what you mean."

"And I know you're angry at me for advising him to do so."

Her eyebrows rose, nearly shooting right off her forehead. "That's not why I'm angry. Indeed, I didn't know you'd advised him. I should have guessed, I suppose."

I frowned. If she didn't know I'd told Tommy to stop flirting with her, then why was she angry with me? The glare she'd bestowed on me in my room had been full of icy fury, yet all I'd done was reassure Tommy—

Ah. Now I understood. She'd seen me touching him. The gesture had been a friendly one, but it could have been mistaken for something else. Something more.

"Sylvia," I began in earnest, "I don't like Tommy in that way. I never have. Nor does he think of me as a potential paramour."

She turned her cheek to me and sipped.

I drew in a breath as well as some patience. "We've been friends for years. If we liked one another beyond friendship, then we would have acted on those feelings long ago. We haven't. Be angry with me for advising him, but not for capturing his attentions. You could not be more wrong."

She lowered her cup to the saucer in her lap and bent her head. "I am angry with you for advising him too. Now."

At least we were getting somewhere. "Very well. I am sorry that we cannot be friends again. I'll miss your laughter. I don't have too many female friends and I was hoping to count you among their number."

Her lip wobbled. She bit it and looked up at me through watery eyes. "Oh, Charity. You're right. I do wish to be your friend."

"Then let's not let a man come between us again."

"I'll try not to."

"It will take some time to feel like yourself once more," I told her. "But you will recover from this."

"I hope so. I don't like the hollowness inside my chest. I wish it would go away."

I set down my cup and joined her on the sofa. "It will."

We sat for a few moments together, neither speaking, until she suddenly seemed to shrug off her melancholy with a toss of her head. "I have missed you. How have you been?"

"Well," I said. "I went to the funeral of Mr. Gladstone."

She gasped and almost dropped her teacup. "Charity! Was that wise?"

"I'm not sure."

"Did you see Samuel? Is he all right?" She sighed. "I do miss him."

"He seemed fine to me." I didn't elaborate on my reasons for going, or share my doubts about Samuel. She considered him a friend and probably wouldn't entertain negative opinions of him.

"I miss Jack and Hannah too," she said.

"Have you heard from them?"

"I received a letter yesterday." She proceeded to give me a list of all the places they'd visited on the continent. I listened, glad she was back to her old cheerful self.

She was giving me a detailed account of their third day in Paris when August Langley wheeled into the drawing room, pushed by Bollard.

"Welcome back, Charity," he said. "We thought we'd lost you."

"I decided it was safer here, for now." Whether he believed me or not, I couldn't tell. His face gave nothing away. Although he didn't have a happy, open countenance, it wasn't unfriendly either.

"Sylvia will be pleased to have you at Frakingham again."

"I am," she said. "I do starve for female company and I miss Hannah terribly."

I suspected if Hannah were still in residence I wouldn't be considered good company for Sylvia, not only by herself, but by her uncle too. It was a humbling thought. My position was a precarious one and I needed to remember my proper place or risk being tossed out. That meant no meeting Tommy alone again, no matter how innocent our motives.

Did it also mean not asking Langley about his work? If it did, I was about to walk on a very thin line, but it was a walk I felt I had to take nevertheless.

"Mr. Langley," I began, "I'm going to be honest with you and admit that my return here isn't simply to get away from London."

"Oh?" He leaned forward a little.

"I want to know more about the experiment you're conducting in your laboratory."

"I told you, I don't discuss my work before it's ready."

I ignored the sharp edge in his tone and forged on. "I believe you're inventing a device that can read minds."

Sylvia's gasp sliced through the dense silence of the drawing room. She covered her mouth with her hand and her gaze darted between her uncle and me. Bollard straightened to a towering height. His gaze bore into me.

Langley, on the other hand, went quite still. "Who told you that?" he snapped. "Samuel?"

"No." I did not want Samuel to get into trouble, particularly when he was innocent. Innocent of breaking a confidence, that is. He certainly wasn't innocent of much else.

"Myer?"

"No."

The air around us crackled with energy. Langley's face darkened. His brows crashed together. "It was Mrs. Gladstone, wasn't it?" His voice was low, quiet. Too quiet.

I said nothing. Lying to him now seemed foolish after I'd started down this track, yet I didn't want to cause problems between them. I'd not considered how my question would lead to his interrogation. I'd been selfishly focused on only one thing—Samuel's involvement.

"Tell me, Charity," he went on, "did you not stop to ask yourself how she knows? Or why she cares? Because I assure you, those are the first two questions that spring to my mind."

I wasn't sure what concerned me the most. The fact that he was right and I should have stopped to consider those questions, or the fact that he didn't refute Mrs. Gladstone's claim.

CHAPTER 10

"I assume Mrs. Gladstone cares because her son is involved in your experiment," I said. I didn't answer Langley's other question about how she could know about the device. I didn't think Samuel had told her, considering the fractious nature of their relationship. Perhaps it had been Myer. Or perhaps she'd crept into Langley's laboratory when she'd been staying at Frakingham. The very thought of the upright Mrs. Gladstone sneaking about like a thief was absurd, yet I was in no mood to giggle.

"Uncle," Sylvia said, her voice small. "Is this true? You're creating a mind reading instrument?"

"Don't judge what you don't know," he growled.

I jumped at his tone. My tea rippled in the cup grasped in my shaking hand. My initial instinct led me to mumble an apology and lower my head as Sylvia did. My second instinct was to become angry with myself for being meek and afraid. Langley wasn't dangerous. Jack trusted him, and so I should too. But I found it difficult to fight against the urge to run to my room and shut myself away.

That was the old Charity reacting to a scolding from a man. The old Charity tried to avoid whippings for impertinence at all costs. The new Charity needed to

125

remember that the master was dead, his spirit far away in London. August Langley wasn't going to beat me for asking a few challenging questions.

I drew in a deep breath and forged on. "I am simply concerned that your invention could be dangerous."

"It will only be as dangerous as the person controlling it."

"Precisely! Imagine the harm that could be inflicted."

"Not every man wishes to harm others, Charity." The guttural growl of his tone had vanished, replaced by a quieter, more sympathetic one. "Even you must concede that."

I swallowed hard and tried not to think about the master and my time trapped in his house. "No," I said, matching his soft tone. "But there are many who want to control, and this would make controlling people very easy indeed."

"I beg to differ. I say it will make people understand one another better. Anyway," he said with a dismissive wave of his hand, "there will be mechanisms in place to ensure no one but me can operate it."

"What sort of mechanisms?"

"Your inquisitive mind will have to wait for the answer to that. When the device is complete, all will be revealed. I promise you will be among the first to be given a demonstration."

"No, thank you. I'd rather be far away when that thing is in operation."

"As you wish, but I assure you, there will be nothing to fear from it. Indeed, you might find it benefits you."

"How could a machine that reads minds be of benefit to me?"

"Wait and see, Charity, wait and see." He made a twirling motion with his finger. "Turn me about, Bollard. We've work to do."

"Wait," I said and Bollard stopped. "Is Samuel helping you because he wants to?"

"He isn't being coerced, if that's what you mean," Langley said.

"So you're not forcing him to help in exchange for him living here?"

"Samuel is welcome to stay at Frakingham as long as he wants."

"And what about Myer?"

"When I first wrote to him asking for his assistance, he wrote back and insisted his involvement came with a price."

"That price being access to the ruins."

"Precisely. Whether you think I manipulated him or he me, it doesn't matter. The fact is, the agreement is to our mutual benefit. He has certainly never expressed any qualms. Neither has Samuel." He turned away. "Onward, Bollard."

I watched them go, frustrated with his lack of concern. At least I now knew what he was doing, but it worried me that he thought it a worthwhile invention. It worried me even more that Samuel did too.

"Do not stir up Uncle's ire like that, Charity," Sylvia said, once more sipping her tea. "He's a good man. If he believes his invention is good, then we should too."

"Your trust in him is admirable." Yet misguided. No woman should trust a man without questioning his motives. Even if that man was a relative.

***

The demon didn't approach the house, although I was quite sure I saw a naked figure running through the woods at dusk on the second night of my return. The light had been too poor to determine if it was human or not and besides, I wasn't particularly sure what a demon looked like. According to Sylvia it was too horrid to even attempt to describe and Tommy refused to tell me anything about it.

I realized on the morning of the third day of my stay that the demon's absence was due to Tommy leaving food at the edge of the woods. The wagon driver who'd delivered me from the station had also brought supplies of meat with him. Not just a few cuts either, but entire carcasses of sheep from a farm on the other side of the village. The farm had been struck by a disease that killed some of the flock and rendered the meat inedible. His misfortune had turned around when Tommy heard of it and offered to pay full price for the dead animals. So far, the demon had been satisfied with its meals and not needed to hunt further afield.

But supplies had run out and Tommy had told Mrs. Moore that he was going to the farm to see if more animals could be procured. Worried about his safety, she'd come to inform Sylvia of his plan.

I was rather glad of the interruption. Sylvia and I sat side by side on the piano stool in the music room. She'd been teaching me a simple piece to pass the time. I wasn't very good, not having had lessons, and she wasn't the most patient teacher. Every time I hit the wrong key she wrapped my knuckles with a closed fan.

"It's a foolish idea," Sylvia said to the housekeeper. "Send Dawson in to see me."

Mrs. Moore went to fetch Tommy and Sylvia played alone while we waited. She pounded the keys with such fury that her hair came loose from its arrangement. Her face had lost the innocent sweetness and was a picture of tempestuous concentration. I inched aside to get out of the way of her frenzied playing.

"You summoned me, Miss Langley?" Tommy said from the doorway.

Sylvia did not immediately look up, but finished her piece with a violent flourish that almost knocked me entirely off the stool. When the last note faded completely, she took a deep breath and looked coolly at Tommy.

"I forbid you to leave the house," she said.

"We need to feed the demon," he said. "Otherwise it will come closer."

"Or it will retreat into the woods and hunt there."

"We don't know that for sure."

"No one is to leave the house unless absolutely necessary."

"This is necessary."

"I disagree."

He waited, his hands behind his back, his chin thrust out. If he were a regular footman, he'd be in trouble for his open defiance. But he was Jack's friend. The usual rules didn't apply.

"Am I understood?" Sylvia demanded.

"Perfectly, Miss Langley," he said. "But someone has to fetch more food for it."

"Send the stable lad."

"No!" he and I both cried.

"Sylvia," I said, "if you refuse to allow Tommy to go, you cannot send anyone else out. Tommy is the strongest and fittest. He should be the one who fetches the meat."

"I also have the most experience with demons," he said. "And I know how to use a knife better than any soft lad from the stables. Jack's blade will be in my hand the entire time."

"There," I assured Sylvia. "He'll be quite safe."

She gave an emphatic shake of her head. "No. He's not leaving the house. No one is. It's too dangerous."

Tommy clicked his tongue. I thought he would say something back to her, but he simply spun around and stalked out of the music room before being dismissed.

Sylvia stood and strode to the door. "Come back here, Dawson!"

He didn't return.

She stamped her foot. "Dawson!"

A pounding on the front door interrupted her tantrum. Her anger dissolved and she shot a worried glance at me. "Who could that be?" she whispered.

I took her hand and squeezed. "It's probably not the demon. I'm quite sure they don't knock."

Her shudder rippled through our linked hands. "Not the uncontrolled ones, no, but if its summoner is here…"

"Shall we go and see?"

"I suppose we must."

We reached the entrance hall just in time to see Samuel pass his coat and hat to Tommy. The handle of a pistol peeped out of the inside pocket of the coat.

"Samuel!" Sylvia let go of my hand and raced to him. She clutched him by the arms and he embraced her briefly. "We weren't expecting you back so soon."

He glanced at me, as I slowly approached. His jaw dropped and his eyes widened. "What are you doing here?"

"I decided to come after all." I tried not to cast my eye over him, but I couldn't help it. He was quite an impressive sight with his windblown cheeks and unkempt hair. And was that the beginning of a beard on his jaw? It made him look rather wild. If it weren't for his neat clothing I'd have thought he'd lost all sense of propriety. "Are you sure you should be away from your family so soon after the funeral?"

He grunted. "I thought you'd be a little more pleased to see me. I must say that I'm pleased to see you. Very pleased." His heated gaze raked over me, lighting a fire in my belly. I blushed fiercely and turned my face away.

"We *are* happy to see you," Sylvia said, clasping his hand. "We're glad that you're here. Come into the drawing room. Tommy, fetch some tea. I mean, Dawson." She cleared her throat and resumed her earlier haughty pose of nose in the air. "Now that Samuel's back there will be no more discussion of going to the farm alone, will there? Will there?" she repeated when he didn't answer.

"If that's what you want," Tommy said, sullen.

"What farm?" Samuel asked.

"We'll explain in the drawing room," Sylvia said cheerfully. "You need some tea first."

She led him into the drawing room. I shared a grim smirk with Tommy before he left to prepare the tea, then followed Samuel and Sylvia. I felt a little like the moth drawn to the flame, unable to keep away from him even though I knew I should.

"I had to return," Samuel said, standing by the window and looking out to the lawn. "I couldn't allow you to defend yourselves against the demon alone. I need to send it back."

"You don't think Tommy can do it alone?" I asked.

"I don't want Tommy to *attempt* it on his own," he said without turning to face us. "That demon is my responsibility."

I somehow managed to swallow my gasp before it burst out of my mouth. *His* responsibility?

"Wh...what do you mean?" Sylvia asked, breathless.

He turned around. The fathomless depths of his blue eyes swirled. "I mean it killed my father. I want to be the one to return it."

She swallowed audibly and tucked a stray strand of her hair behind her ear. "Of course."

He frowned at me. "Charity? What's wrong?"

"Nothing," I said.

"You didn't want me to come."

I bit the inside of my cheek until I tasted blood. Of course I hadn't wanted him to come. And yet some deep place inside me had leapt for joy upon seeing him. It would seem I was still conflicted where Samuel was concerned, despite the stark reminder that he wasn't the gentle soul I used to think him to be. Perhaps a few more days in each other's company would hammer that home once and for all.

"I assumed you wouldn't return for some time," I said. "Your family needs you."

"Bert can cope without me."

"Surely he needs to lean on your strength at a time like this," Sylvia protested.

"He's perfectly strong of mind. It's only his body that fails him."

"And what of your mother?" I asked. "I'm sure she wants you near."

"Mother is more capable than she looks." He turned back to the view. "Despite what she says, she doesn't need me. Besides, my presence only gives her hope that I'll remain longer. She needs to grow used to not having me around again."

I didn't particularly blame him for leaving. His mother was quite the devious dragon and I wouldn't want to live with her. No doubt she was also trying to throw Ebony into his path once more. It must be frustrating to continually fend off both women.

Tommy arrived with tea and the men fell into discussing the plan to kill the demon. I listened intently, eager to help if I could. Sylvia, on the other hand, picked up her sewing basket and seemed to tune out of the discussion altogether.

***

Samuel and Tommy left Frakingham that afternoon, heavily armed and with the fastest, strongest horses harnessed to the cart. Sylvia and I watched them go from the tower window.

"I'm glad he's back," she said, reclining on the chaise once they disappeared from sight. She tucked her feet up under her skirts and yawned. "His assistance is sorely needed."

"Tommy hasn't coped on his own?"

She closed her eyes and sighed. "Tommy doesn't seem his usual self lately."

I sat on the edge of the chaise near her feet. "You've been worried about him?"

She opened her eyes and frowned. "Yes. I suppose I have. Are you happy to see Samuel, Charity?"

"I don't know. I'm glad he's here to help Tommy. I'm not so glad that he's here to be of service to help Langley with his mind reading contraption."

"We don't know for certain if it's a bad invention," she said. "Let's give Uncle the benefit of the doubt. I'm sure he knows what he's doing. And anyway, you haven't said whether *you're* glad that Samuel is back."

I turned to the window and stared out at the lake and ruins in the distance. I didn't answer her. I wasn't at all sure if I was glad to see Samuel or not. Having him nearby, in all his handsome glory, was suddenly the worst scenario imaginable.

***

I couldn't settle while Tommy and Samuel were out. Sylvia snoozed on the chaise in the tower room, but I felt too restless to sit by idly and wait. I ventured downstairs with the intention of walking the length of the house to get some exercise when I came across Mrs. Moore standing in the entrance hall, hands on hips, glaring at a large valise and a small wooden casket.

"Do those belong to Mr. Gladstone?" I asked.

"Aye," she said. "Tommy was meant to take them up, but he and Mr. Gladstone left in a hurry so they haven't moved."

"Are you taking them up instead?"

"The valise is too heavy for my bad back," she said.

"Is there no one else who can do it for you? What about the stable boy or one of the other men?"

She wrinkled her nose in horror. "I can't let one of the outdoor servants touch Mr. Gladstone's things! Or wander about the house! They'll get airs."

"Oh, of course. Quite right."

"I know things are done differently where you come from, Miss Evans, but here at Frakingham we like to maintain standards." She stared at the valise again as if it were a naughty child in her way. "A man of Mr. Gladstone's ilk should have a valet. I don't know why he doesn't."

"Would you like me to help you?" I asked.

"Now that wouldn't be proper. You're a guest."

"Of sorts," I said, appealing to her snobbery. "Besides, I'm strong. I could carry the valise up to Mr. Gladstone's room and you can take the casket."

She twisted her mouth from side to side and gave the items another accusatory glare. Finally, with a huff, she nodded. "Very well. If you insist."

"I do."

"Then follow me."

The valise was indeed heavy, but I managed to get it to Samuel's bedroom without needing to set it down in the interim. I placed it beside the bed and was about to leave when the casket toppled off the desk where Mrs. Moore had set it. The contents scattered across the rug.

"I'm such a clumsy fool!" She knelt awkwardly and gathered up a notebook and inkwell that had fallen out of the casket. "I do hope nothing is broken."

I knelt too and helped her pick up Samuel's belongings, despite her protest that I'd done enough. Fortunately everything seemed intact, including the glass bottle of ink. Aside from the inkwell, pen and notebook, there were also two books. Both had landed upside down and open. One was a slender tome on the study of phrenology and the thicker one was titled *An Introduction to Chemistry*. I picked them both up and a necklace fell out of the chemistry book. I flipped the book right side up and was surprised to see that it wasn't a book at all, but a box. The book's front cover formed the lid and the sides had been very carefully painted to look like pages. How clever.

I picked up the necklace to return it to the book-box, but something struck me about the wooden disc dangling from the slim leather strap. The carvings on the disc's face were startlingly familiar. The swirling pattern was the same as the one on the handle of Jack's knife. He'd carried that knife with him everywhere for as long as I could remember. It had also turned out to be a weapon that could kill demons. He'd left it in Samuel and Tommy's care while he was away.

How were the disc and knife connected?

And why had Samuel hidden the disc in the box?

Mrs. Moore packed the things back into Samuel's casket and set it once more on his desk, a little further away from the edge. "Thank you, Miss Evans," she said as we left together. "I hope you won't mention this to Miss Langley or Mr. Gladstone. There's no need to trouble them about my bad back."

"I'm sure they would be sympathetic," I said. "Perhaps if they knew they would employ another maid to assist you."

"There's no one else who'll work up here," she said on a sigh. "Frakingham is a dangerous place, what with wild dogs roaming about, off and on."

She bustled away down the hall. I didn't leave immediately. I stood outside Samuel's room and stared at his closed door. That disc had shaken me. The more I thought about it, the more uneasy I felt. Jack's knife was connected to the slaying of demons, so it stood to reason that the disc—with its identical motif—did too. Or perhaps not slaying, but something else; after all, it didn't look like a weapon. I knew little about demons and decided it was time to learn more.

I headed up to the tower room and found Sylvia still dozing on the chaise. I coughed to get her attention and waited while she awoke.

"Oh," she said, sitting up and rubbing her eyes. "It's you. Are Tommy and Samuel back?"

"Not yet." I sat on the edge of the chaise near her feet. "Sylvia, what do you know about demons?"

She blinked sleepily at me. "Why do you ask?"

"Because if I am to stay here while there is a demon on the loose, I think I should know everything there is to know about the creatures."

"Understand your enemy?"

"Something like that."

"Well, it's not often I get to be teacher, but I'll try my best. Demons live in another realm but can arrive in ours either through being summoned by someone here, or can be sent by their own people. Nobody seems to know much about the latter method, but the former has happened a few times. Once here, they must be controlled by their summoner, using special chants, or they'll run wild. Oh, and they're hungry when they first arrive. Horribly hungry," she mumbled, pulling a face. "That's when they're most…violent."

"And Jack's knife is the only way to kill them?"

"Kill, yes, but they can be sent back to their own realm, too."

"How?"

"By chanting an incantation while the amulet is held near the demon. The chanter and amulet holder do not need to be one and the same person, but they do need to be very close."

"I've heard you speak of an amulet before," I said, hardly breathing.

"It's the same device used by the summoner to bring the demon here."

"What does it look like?"

"Like, well, like an amulet of course. A basic piece of jewelry with a pattern carved into it."

I nodded, numb. There was no doubt in my mind that the disc in Samuel's possession was an amulet. The question was, had it been the one used to summon the demon now terrorizing Frakingham?

It must have been. The coincidence of it appearing now, hardly a week after the demon first appeared, was too great for it to be otherwise.

"How common are these amulets to come by?" I asked.

"I think they're extremely rare. Mr. Culvert, the demonologist, seems to think he knows of all the ones in existence."

Oh God. A wave of nausea slammed into me. I pressed my hand to my stomach and concentrated on controlling my breathing. It came in short, sharp gasps, keeping apace with the rapid beat of my heart.

"Charity?" Sylvia prompted, peering into my face. "Are you all right? You've gone quite pale."

"I…I'm fine."

"Did you hear my question?"

"I, uh, no. I'm sorry, what did you say?"

"I asked if that was at all helpful."

"Yes, thank you." I tried to speak normally so as not to alarm her, but still my voice quivered.

Thankfully she didn't seem to notice. "Who'd have thought I knew all of that?" she said, sounding pleased. "I suppose I was listening when Mr. Culvert came to visit a few months ago, after all."

"Excuse me," I said, rising.

"Your nerves again?" she asked.

I nodded.

"Would you like me to help you? Or get you something? How about a soothing cup of tea?"

"No, thank you."

She gave me a sympathetic look. "It's all this demon talk, isn't it? I find it unsettling as well."

"It is rather overwhelming. I just need to rest awhile." I left before she could ask more questions. I wasn't up to answering them.

I hurried to my room and closed the door. I lay on the bed and stared up at the canopy. My stomach still rolled as if I were on a boat, and my mind was a jumble of thoughts. I tried to pick each one apart and sift through all the possible scenarios that could explain why Samuel was in possession of an amulet. But, no matter how hard I tried, I couldn't disregard the most obvious one.

Samuel had used the amulet to summon the demon that killed his father.

CHAPTER 11

I tried to tell myself that my logic was flawed, the notion absurd. Samuel was a good man.

Yet the logic *wasn't* flawed and the notion not absurd at all. He was not the same man he had been mere weeks ago. He had changed almost beyond recognition since he saw my memories. The new Samuel Gladstone was troubled to the point of madness, and a madman was capable of acting on dark emotions. The question remained whether he was capable of murdering his own father.

I did not go downstairs for the rest of the day, even when I saw Samuel and Tommy return from my window. Nor when Sylvia came to see why I hid away.

I told her I didn't feel up to joining the rest of the household for dinner. She accepted my excuse of a headache without question.

Samuel did not.

I opened the door to his knock, thinking it was the maid come to collect my dinner tray. I fell back a step upon seeing him standing there in shirt and trousers, his tie askew and his eyes as dark as night. The light from the small gas lamp on the wall behind him burnished his hair and outlined him with a devilish glow.

"Are you all right?" he asked. "Sylvia said you were unwell."

"I have a headache."

"Can I get you anything?"

"No, thank you." I went to shut the door, but he put his hand out to stop it.

"I want to talk to you," he said.

I waited, even though my heart hammered out a warning in my chest. Even though every piece of me wanted to shut the door and lock it.

It was a long time before he spoke again. He seemed to be warring with himself, or choosing his words carefully. "You're avoiding me," he eventually said. It wasn't a question. This man knew me so well it was frightening.

I shook my head rapidly. "I have a headache."

He frowned. "Something's wrong. You've changed since I went out."

Be calm, Charity, don't let him see your fear. Don't let him know what you're thinking. "Have I?"

"You've not even asked if we managed to procure any more food for the demon."

Everything inside me tightened, preparing to spring back out of the way if necessary. "Did you?"

"Only two lambs. Not enough to satisfy it for long. We'll visit another farm tomorrow and buy more, even if the animals aren't diseased." He ran his hand through his hair, messing it up. "I don't know how long a few sheep will satisfy it, but it seems like the best choice until it can be killed."

I waited, hoping he would mention the amulet and how he'd found it somewhere by chance. But he didn't. He let me continue to think our only chances of defeating the demon lay in Jack's knife.

Part of me wanted to confront him, but that part was easily drowned out by the terrified girl inside, screaming silently in fear.

He leaned against the doorframe and looked past me into my room. Then he suddenly straightened. "Your bag is packed. You're leaving?"

I said nothing. I didn't dare lie, not to a madman who could read me like a book. But I didn't dare tell the truth either; he would only try to stop me going.

I folded my arms to hide my shaking and eyed him closely for any sudden lunges in my direction.

"Charity?" He stared at me and I felt like I was falling into his eyes, drowning in their dark intensity. "Are you leaving because of me?"

I dared not speak in case I said the wrong thing, so I simply gave my head a little shake.

"Don't go," he murmured. "I don't want you to leave."

I remained silent.

"Say something!" he snapped. "Talk to me."

I inched closer to the door, to put a barrier between us if necessary. All I could think about, all I wanted to do, was get away from this madman who could get me to do whatever he wanted with a few words.

His frown deepened. He pressed a hand to the doorframe at shoulder height as if he were propping himself up. His fingers curled into a fist against the wood. I kept my gaze on it.

"Why are you suddenly so afraid of me?" His voice had risen, but he wasn't quite shouting. He didn't need to shout to show his anger. It vibrated off him and slammed into me with the force of a tidal wave against the shore.

A trickle of sweat trailed down my spine, but I felt cold, my hands clammy as if I were in a fever. I swallowed and swallowed again, but the lump in my throat would not go away.

He suddenly thumped the doorframe with his palm. "Why, Charity?"

I jumped. My heart felt like it would leap out of my chest. I stepped back from the door, staring at him. That violent reaction right there was why, I wanted to tell him. But I couldn't. I couldn't speak aloud, couldn't form sentences. My fear was too consuming.

His face suddenly softened. The flushed angry color drained away, his eyes widened. There was fear in them too, but I couldn't fathom what *he* had to be afraid of.

"Charity." The ache in that single moaned word tugged at my heart. "Charity, please. I won't hurt you."

He stepped into my room. I stepped back.

He winced as if in pain. "I can't bear it if you're afraid of me."

Still I said nothing. He wasn't asking a direct question, and I'd learned the hard way not to speak unless specifically questioned.

"Charity, there's no need to fear me." His voice changed. The plea disappeared, replaced by a smoother, richer tone that had my head feeling light and dizzy. "I would never do anything to harm you. You *must* believe that." His words slipped over my skin and chased away the chill that had settled into my bones.

"I do," I said, taking an involuntary step closer to him. "I believe every word you say." My heartbeat quickened, not in fear, but something just as primal. Desire. I lifted my arms and circled them around his neck. I skimmed my lips across his throat, drawing the delicious masculine scent of him deep into my lungs. I lightly kissed his shoulder through his shirt. The muscles flexed. I pressed my palm against his chest and relished the rapid beat of his heart. It pounded like that for me. All for me.

"Charity?" he said on a groan.

"Don't talk."

A small sigh escaped his lips. "I'm going to regret this, but...stop!"

Awareness breezed through my mind, blowing away the dizziness. I gasped and stumbled backward until my legs hit the bed. I scrambled across the bedcovers to the far side and grabbed the pillow. I put it in front of me as if it could protect me.

"Charity...I'm sorry." He ran his hands over his face, behind his neck and then finally stared at them as if he'd wondered how they'd got there. "I don't know how that happened. I don't know..." He shook his head and closed his eyes. "Forgive me."

I clenched my jaw to stop my teeth chattering.

He opened his eyes. They were shadowy, haunted orbs. "You *must* know that I didn't do that on purpose."

I knew he hadn't, but it didn't make it any easier to bear. I nodded in the hope it would encourage him to stop talking and leave.

"Something seems to happen when I...when my emotions..." He swore softly and lowered his head. Jagged ends of his hair hung over his forehead and obscured his eyes. "I hate that you're afraid of me," he muttered. "I hate that you won't even talk to me now. I hate that you want to be far away from me." He lifted his head, but I still could not see his eyes through his hair. "I'll go now. But please don't leave Frakingham. You're safer here than in London while the master's ghost is there. I promise not to come near you, even though it'll kill me to stay away. You have nothing to fear from me, Charity, and I'm going to prove it to you, even if it takes me a lifetime."

His words clawed at my heart. I wanted to go to him, hold him, kiss him, and not because I was hypnotized but because I *wanted* to. Yet the frightened girl in me forbade it. She didn't trust him, especially now after finding the amulet. And she always won.

He pushed the hair off his forehead and settled his soft gaze on me. With a sigh, he shut the door. His footsteps retreated down the hall and finally faded altogether.

I climbed off the bed and raced to the door. I turned the key in the lock. It wasn't until that moment that I realized I'd been holding my breath. I let it out slowly and returned to the bed. I lay on top of the covers and fought back tears.

When would it ever end? When could I go home to London and away from this place and that man? The sooner

I put some distance between us, the sooner I could forget him, and forget the fact that I wanted to be with him, even now, knowing that he had such power over me. And knowing that he had most likely summoned the demon that killed his father.

***

I prepared to leave early the following morning. I had my valise packed and my gloves on. Unfortunately, I needed someone to drive me to the station. With the demon about, that meant one driver and at least another armed man to keep watch.

Tommy refused. "You can't leave now," he said when I approached him, early, in the kitchen.

I stood near the door, out of the way of the staff as they prepared breakfast for the household. The smells of bacon and sausages made my stomach growl. I tried not to hanker for the delicious morsels as they were piled onto platters, but I failed miserably.

"I have to," I told him as he placed the domed lid on one of the platters. I hadn't wanted to talk to him in front of everyone, but he'd given me no choice. He refused to stop work to speak to me alone and instead I'd had to beg him in front of the cook, her assistant, Maud and Mrs. Moore. It was all hands on deck for mealtimes.

He was too intent on balancing a second platter on his other hand to answer me. I doubted he'd even heard me. He headed toward the door. I stepped in front of him, blocking his exit.

"Move aside, Charity," he said, glaring at me. "I've got work to do."

"Not until you promise to accompany the driver."

He huffed out a breath and rolled his eyes to the ceiling.

"Go! Go!" the cook cried, shooing him with her apron. "Mr. Langley likes his sausages hot."

Tommy side-stepped around me. "I'll take you to the station if Miss Langley and Mr. Gladstone agree to it," he tossed over his shoulder.

I sighed. They wouldn't agree to it. I had to find another way. After breakfast. "May I have a tray of bacon, sausages and a piece of toast, please," I said to the cook. "I'll take it up to my room myself."

Maud bustled past me carrying a teapot. The cook muttered to herself as she organized my food on a tray. She handed the tray to me, but did not let go when I took it.

"It's dangerous out there," she said, her eyes alert beneath fat eyelids. "You shouldn't put yourself at risk, nor Tommy and Fray neither. You shouldn't ask that of them."

I nodded quickly and she let go of the tray and returned to her stove. I blinked back hot tears and turned to go. She was right and I thoroughly deserved that rebuke.

I took the service stairs up to my room to avoid seeing anyone. Or, more specifically, avoid Samuel. I ate my breakfast alone, something I thought I wanted. But it was lonely. I was used to the childish chatter of my charges in the mornings, not this smothering silence.

I was finishing off my tea when Sylvia knocked on my door. "It's me," she called out.

I opened the door and she swept into my room like a blustering wind. "You're not leaving," she said with all the majesty of a queen. "It's too dangerous."

"I know. I've decided to stay a while longer."

Her bluster vanished and she smiled. "Oh. Good. I am pleased. You had me worried for a moment. You've done nothing but hide away in here since yesterday and then all this talk of leaving... I must say you've been terribly selfish to deny us your company."

"I'm sure you hardly noticed my absence."

"Tosh. Of course we did. Uncle commented on it himself. Even Bollard asked why you weren't at breakfast. Samuel too."

"Samuel asked after me?"

"No, I mean he wasn't at breakfast. He ate in his rooms, Tommy said. Bollard was asking why you were both absent."

Samuel must have deliberately kept to his rooms so that I could join the family at breakfast and not be upset by his presence. It was just like him to be considerate. I bit the inside of my lip and regretted my harsh thoughts about him. Then I recalled *why* I'd thought them and stopped regretting.

"Shall we resume our piano lessons this morning?" Sylvia asked.

"We might as well. There's little else to do. When are Tommy and Samuel going out to see the farmers?" I asked idly.

"Soon. They're with Fray now, in the stables, preparing the cart and horses."

"Then let's go now, shall we?"

She clapped her hands. "Excellent. I'll meet you in the music room in ten minutes."

Ten minutes later I made my way down to the music room. I was intercepted by Bollard and Langley before I reached it. The servant wheeled his master out of the shadowy corner into my path. It was as if they'd been waiting for me.

"Good morning, Charity," Langley said. "May we have a word?"

We? I wasn't sure how he expected Bollard to 'have a word' with me. "Of course," I said, feigning enthusiasm. "What about?"

"Come into the music room."

I walked ahead and waited for Bollard to wheel Langley in after me. The mute servant then stood behind his master, his hands behind his back, looking every inch like a thug I knew from my days on the streets.

"I believe you no longer plan to leave Frakingham today," Langley said.

"That is correct. I changed my mind." How did he know I'd been planning to stay? Had Sylvia told him after she'd come to see me? Or had he used some other method? Sometimes Langley seemed omniscient, and at other times he was blissfully unaware of everything except his experiments. I was yet to understand him.

"Good," he said. "It's safer here."

"So everybody keeps telling me," I muttered.

Bollard's gaze shifted to mine. His blank face didn't change. He was completely unreadable, yet that simple movement of his eyes unnerved me. The big, silent man was no fool.

"You may be wondering why I wanted to speak to you now," Langley said.

"I am curious," I said. "I hope I've done nothing wrong."

"Not that I know of." His lips curled in what almost resembled a smile. Bollard cleared his throat and Langley's mouth flattened again. "I'm talking to you now because you can't understand sign language."

Was Langley implying that it was actually his *servant* who wished to speak to me? How odd. The men had a most unusual relationship if the servant could have the master communicate on his behalf.

Langley breathed in deeply and puffed out his chest as if he were fortifying himself. "You need to stop letting your fears conquer you," he told me. "It's time you learned to conquer them."

I waited for him to say something more, but that was it. He seemed to think there was nothing more to be said. "That's rather profound," I said before he could order Bollard to wheel him away. "But I can assure you, you're quite wrong."

"No, I don't think so."

His casual disregard for my struggle irritated me. What did this pampered, rich *man* know about my fears? "You're entitled to your opinion," I said with far more nonchalance than I felt.

"I once called you a coward for not wanting to remember your past. Do you remember that?"

I nodded. "You told me that our fears are what kept us safe."

"True, and they do. But they can also stop us from living a full life."

"I believe I noted that at the time."

"It's a fine line," he went on.

"One which I'm trying my best to navigate."

"Navigate or avoid altogether?"

I crossed my arms. "I don't think you're in any position to lecture me on avoidance, Mr. Langley, locked away as you are in your laboratory most of the time."

Bollard's eyes widened and I suddenly felt sick. Why couldn't I have kept my mouth shut? Why had I spoken out of turn like that, to August Langley of all people? He would surely throw me out now, or scold me, or...

"It would seem you're not afraid of speaking your mind to *all* men, then," Langley said, lightly.

I lowered my head, but peered up at him, wary. "I...I'm sorry."

"Don't be. I like your forthrightness."

My only response was to blink. I didn't want to say the wrong thing again.

He pressed his lips together in a fleshy pout as he regarded me. Behind him, Bollard did too, his face once more a blank mask. "Are you truly afraid of me, Charity? Of any of us? Or is your fear merely an excuse to hide behind?"

"An excuse!"

My outburst brought a smile to his face and I wondered if his provocative words had been a tactic to get me to speak. "Go on," he said.

"My fears are grounded in facts, sir." My confidence grew with every word. I *could* trust this man, and Bollard too. Neither had shown violent tendencies. Unlike Samuel. "There are reasons for those fears."

"Of course. No one is denying that, or expecting you to cast them aside as if they never existed. We know that's not possible. But you *need* to face up to what happened to you, so you can move on."

I hadn't been entirely referring to my past with the master. The facts surrounding Samuel and the discovery of the amulet in his belongings still played on my mind.

Bollard suddenly moved, as if he'd been wound up and let go. He pointed to his chest and formed rapid signals with his nimble fingers.

"What is he saying?" I asked.

Langley twisted in his chair and watched his man repeat the motions then he turned back to me. "He wants you to know that he agrees with me."

Bollard cleared his throat.

Langley rolled his eyes and sighed. "He says you need to come to terms with your past so that you can love again."

My pulse throbbed in my veins and my face heated. I wanted to tell these men that they knew nothing about love, or about me. How could they? Neither was married. If Langley loved his niece, he didn't show it. He seemed to merely accept her presence in his household. I'd never seen him show her any affection.

Without a word from his master, Bollard turned the wheelchair around and wheeled Langley out of the room. I drew in several deep breaths, until I was certain my emotions were under control, then sat at the piano. I began to play the tune Sylvia had taught me. I had to concentrate to get it right. I was determined to get it right. Determined for it to be perfect. After a few stumbles, the notes and rhythm filled my head, expelling all other thoughts and obliterating my conversation with Langley entirely.

I finished the piece to a round of applause. "Beautiful playing," Sylvia said, coming up alongside me.

I shifted over on the seat to accommodate her more voluminous skirt. "How much did you hear?"

"A little," she said, evasive. I hazarded a guess that she'd heard some, if not all, of my conversation with her uncle. "Now that you've thoroughly mastered that piece, let's find another." She flicked through the music book, humming as she did so.

A loud thump made her stop. We both twisted around, looking for the source.

"Did something just fall?" I asked.

"It was probably one of the servants," she said, returning to the book. "I do hope nothing's broken."

Another thump, louder, then another and another.

"It's coming from outside," I said.

Sylvia rose, but I grabbed her arm and jerked her back down to the seat. She stared wide-eyed at me. "The demon," she whispered.

"You may be right."

"What do we do?"

"Alert the servants and then we all move upstairs to your uncle's laboratory," I said, eyeing the window. The music room was on the ground floor, as was the service area. The demon could break one of the windows and enter the house. We couldn't watch them all.

I stood and clasped her hand, just as a large, dark object was flung at the window. The glass cracked but didn't break.

Sylvia screamed.

The object moved into view outside. I could just make out two eyes amid a hairy, distorted face. It had no nose or ears and didn't resemble either man or dog. Its tongue lolled out of the gash for its mouth, as if it saw a tasty feast.

But it didn't attack. It drew back from the window.

Sylvia stopped screaming. "Is it leaving?" she whispered, voice cracking.

The creature paused. Its lash-less yellow eyes blinked, as if it were considering what to do next. Then it bared jagged, crooked teeth in a snarl and ran right at us. It bore down on the weakened window like a train under full steam.

Sylvia opened her mouth and screamed again.

CHAPTER 12

I pulled the derringer pistol out of my skirt pocket, aimed and fired. Glass shattered, spraying shards in all directions and over the demon itself. The creature jerked and bucked, then slammed into the window frame instead of diving through. It whimpered like a wounded dog.

Then it disappeared from sight.

I kept the gun level, but my hand shook so much my aim wouldn't be true if I had to fire again.

Seconds passed. Nothing happened. Sylvia stopped screaming and an unnatural silence descended on us for what felt like an age. She clutched my arm and I clutched hers. We both trembled. I could feel her pulse racing, the rhythm matching my own.

Pounding footsteps from within the house preceded Bollard bursting through the door, his face etched with concern. His gaze took in both of us and the broken window.

"It was here," Sylvia said, voice quivering. "The demon. Charity shot it."

I stared at the little gun in my hand. Mrs. Peeble had given it to me to keep me safe. It had not failed me yet. "I didn't kill it," I said, rather stupidly. Of course I hadn't killed it. Only Jack's knife could do that. But I had frightened it away. For now.

Mrs. Moore, Maud and the stable boy entered the music room. The lanky youth carried a long kitchen knife and looked as if he'd gladly use it on a wild dog. Maud began to cry.

"Hush, girl," Mrs. Moore scolded. "You're all right." She put her arm around the young maid's shoulders and clucked over her.

"Everyone's all right," Sylvia said with a determined tone as if she could convince us. "It's gone."

"If only Tommy and Mr. Gladstone were here," Mrs. Moore muttered as she steered Maud out of the room.

"They'll be back soon," the lad said. He headed toward the window, but Bollard grabbed him by the collar and hauled him toward the door. "All right," the lad said. "I'm going."

"Bollard?" Langley shouted from somewhere deeper in the house. "Bollard?"

"I'll speak to him," Sylvia said and left too.

"The window needs to be boarded up," I told Bollard. "Until then, we ought to shut off this room. If the...creature returns this way, it'll get no further."

I went to follow Sylvia, but Bollard stopped me with a hand on my shoulder. He arched his brows in question.

"I'm all right," I said. "A little shaken."

He glanced down at the gun in my hand. I'd forgotten I was still holding it. I flexed my fingers around the handle. They felt stiff and achy from gripping it so tightly. It was a good thing that I still carried the weapon. The attack was a timely lesson in not becoming complacent.

Bollard fetched the key for the music room door from Mrs. Moore while I kept watch on the window, pistol in hand. Fortunately the demon didn't return and we locked the door. Bollard dragged a marble-topped table in front of it. The table wasn't large but it must have been heavy because the big man struggled.

We were admiring his handiwork when we heard the crunch of wheels on gravel outside. Jack and Tommy had returned.

Sylvia barreled down the stairs like an out of control boulder. "They're back! Quick, we must alert them to the danger."

"They have Jack's knife," I said. And the amulet. "They're safer than we were."

"They need to know."

Bollard and I followed her to the service area and we exited the house at the cobbled courtyard. The cart drove past the arched entrance and headed toward the stable block. We raced after it and caught up with them as they pulled the horses to a stop.

"Get back inside," Samuel growled upon seeing us. "It's not safe for you out here."

"You don't need to tell us!" Sylvia said in between her deep breaths. "We've come to warn you. There was an attack just a few minutes ago. It almost broke through the music room window."

"Bloody hell!" Tommy focused on Sylvia and half-rose from the seat. "Are you hurt, Miss Langley?"

"No, thank goodness, but it gave Charity and me an awful fright. We were playing the piano at the time."

Samuel jumped down, completely letting go of the reins. He came to me, as silent as Bollard, and rested his hands on my shoulders. They were solid, capable, reassuring hands. His thumbs brushed the underside of my jaw. He dipped his head to peer into my face and I was sucked into the endless depths of his eyes.

Hot tears threatened to spill. My chest tightened, making it hard to breathe. No man had ever looked at me with quite so much concern and relief all mixed together.

A small voice begged me to move away, but it was drowned out by my thumping heartbeat. It was as if my fear of him had been numbed, suppressed. Perhaps Samuel had hypnotized me again. Yet he couldn't have; he'd not said a word.

"Are you all right?" he finally asked in a hoarse rasp.

His voice snapped me out of my stupor, having the opposite effect to what it usually did. I stepped back, out of his reach. My skin prickled. A cold shiver washed over me. The fear hadn't entirely gone, it would seem. It had just been lurking, waiting for the right moment to return and conquer.

He lowered his hands to his sides. "I'm sorry," he whispered, so quietly that no one else could have heard. "I'm sorry I wasn't here for you."

I wanted to tell him that he couldn't be everywhere or that I was perfectly capable of taking care of myself, but my voice failed me. I tore my gaze away from his. I didn't want to know what he was feeling. I was too much of a coward to face that.

"Quickly, come inside," Sylvia said, beckoning us.

Tommy climbed down and slapped Samuel's shoulder the way men who'd faced battle together did. I'd never seen them so friendly and comfortable with one another. "We'll lock the horses up first," he said. "Can't leave the poor creatures out here to get eaten."

They removed some crates from the back of the cart while Sylvia and I kept watch. The putrid smell of dead meat burned my nostrils and the back of my throat. The demon would have something to eat tonight, at least.

The men unhitched the cart and led the horses into their stalls, then they carried one of the crates between them, to the edge of the woods. They would not let us come, but we kept watch until they rejoined us and together we four returned to the house.

Langley met us at the door to the locked music room. "You've returned," he said to the men. "Were you successful?"

Samuel nodded. "We took some food down to the woods. It should be satisfied for a little longer."

"We hope," Sylvia muttered.

Bollard unlocked the music room door and Samuel entered first. "Bloody hell," he said upon seeing the broken window. "How many times did it hit the glass?"

"Just once," Sylvia said. "It was going to try again, but Charity shot it."

Tommy swung round to face me. He looked rather impressed. Samuel didn't turn. He went very still. His fists closed at his sides. His shoulders squared as if he were about to pound an opponent in the boxing ring.

"We need to board it up," Langley said. "Dawson, search of some supplies. Everyone else, out. We'll keep the door locked until this thing is gone. Hopefully it won't try again now it has something to eat, but I want to be safe."

Everyone except Samuel followed him out. He stood with his back to us, his shoulders rising and falling with his deep breathing.

"Samuel," Sylvia called to him. "What are you doing?"

He dug in his pocket and pulled out Jack's knife. "It has to go," he muttered as he joined us. "And it has to go now."

Langley grabbed his arm. "We need a plan first. And you're doing it alone."

"I'll help him, sir," Tommy said.

Langley nodded at Samuel. "Have you gotten any more information out of Myer about who may have summoned it?"

"Bloody Myer," Samuel growled, watching Bollard lock the door to the music room. "He came to my father's funeral. I questioned him, but he's still claiming it wasn't him."

Langley drummed his fingers on the arm of his wheelchair. "Do you believe him?"

"The man is a liar and a snake."

Samuel's vehemence surprised me. I knew he disliked Myer, but that dislike seemed to have deepened into hatred. What had Myer said or done at the funeral to incur Samuel's wrath?

Langley grunted. "We must find out who brought it here and why. We can't have that thing causing havoc. The household has been disrupted enough. The servants are nervous and my tests have fallen behind." His drumming fingers stilled. He blinked up at Bollard. "Perhaps that's the intention. Perhaps someone wanted to sabotage my experiments and sent the demon to bring chaos."

Sylvia gasped. "Why would anyone go to such elaborate lengths to do such a thing? Surely there are easier ways."

"I agree," I said, daring to speak up. There was no better time to confront Samuel than in front of everybody. It was safer and there was too much at stake to keep quiet. "If the creature was summoned by someone to interfere then they would be here directing it now. Yet the demon seems to be unsupervised."

"True, true," Langley muttered, thoughtful. "The next logical question is *why* was it brought here? To kill your father on purpose?" he asked Samuel.

"It's a possibility," was all Samuel said. He did not look shocked by the suggestion, nor particularly upset that someone had wanted to murder his father.

"Good lord!" Sylvia pressed her hand to her stomach. "If it were Myer, what reason could he have to do such a thing to Mr. Gladstone?"

Nobody answered. Perhaps nobody dared share what was on their mind—that it might not have been Myer at all, but one of the Gladstone family. I'd wager that I was the only one who suspected Samuel, however.

"It could have been a stranger," she went on. "Even someone from the village."

"If only we could find the amulet," I said, watching Samuel out of the corner of my eye.

He flinched but said nothing. He didn't look at me. If he suspected that I knew he had it in his possession, he didn't show it. He certainly wasn't about to confess.

"Let's not discount Myer yet." Langley pushed the wheels of his chair forward and rolled across the tiles. "We'll be upstairs if needed."

Bollard took over and pushed the wheelchair to the staircase. He then picked his master up in his arms and carried him up the stairs.

Langley and Bollard's departure took my resolve with them. My nerves jangled. I didn't dare tell Samuel I knew about the amulet now. Sylvia walked off without warning and I made to head up the stairs too, but Samuel called after me. He kept his distance, however, and did not come too close. He was being true to his word that he would avoid me when possible.

"It doesn't belong to me," he said in a quiet voice. "Nor did I use it to summon the demon."

"How…?" My question dissolved on my tongue.

"How did I know that you knew? I guessed from your statement just now. Did Mrs. Moore show it to you?"

I backed up the stairs, slowly so as not to draw attention to myself. Blood throbbed in my veins, but I managed to keep my pace deliberate, careful. I couldn't outrun him unless I had a head start.

He put up his hands. "I don't mind that you know. In fact I'm relieved. It's been a burden to carry it around when all I wanted to do was tell you." He pinched the bridge of his nose. "I didn't because I was afraid it would give you reason to fear me more than you already do."

He was right on that score.

"Say something, Charity. Ask me the questions I know you have, or just tell me I'm a fool for not owning up in front of everyone. Just say *something*."

There was a long silence in which he watched me and I tried to pretend I didn't notice. I knew this trick. He was hoping the silence would force me to talk. I pressed my lips together, determined not to crack.

"I was afraid," he said. "That's why I said nothing. If they know I have the amulet, they'll think I used it to summon the demon. They'll think I killed my father. They'll think less of me, perhaps even fear me." His gaze locked with mine. "Just like you do."

Why was he telling me these things and not anyone else? Was it because he trusted only me? Because he wanted to inveigle himself back into my good graces? Or for some other reason?

"I don't think you summoned it," I lied.

"Why not? It's the first assumption I'd make if I found the amulet in someone's belongings."

"Where did you get it?"

He shook his head. "That's the one question I won't answer. Not even for you. I'm sorry, Charity."

"You don't need to apologize to me."

He grunted a humorless laugh. "You couldn't be more wrong. I feel like I must apologize all the time, lately."

"I wish you wouldn't," I said, turning to go. "You owe me nothing."

"Then why do I feel so bloody guilty all the time?" The black despair in his voice surrounded me, enthralled me. I didn't want him to feel guilty. I *wanted* to trust him.

But I could not. I wasn't ready. I picked up my skirts and hurried up the stairs. When I turned to look down at him from the half landing, he was gone.

***

Of all the things Samuel had said—and not said—since his return from his father's funeral, it was his fierce hatred of Everett Myer that intrigued me the most. Perhaps the amulet had come from him. It made sense. He was known to have summoned a demon before and he seemed quite without morals. Had he willingly given the amulet to Samuel or had Samuel taken it? But if Samuel had been the one to actually use it, why was he angry with Myer? Perhaps Myer had used the amulet and Samuel had taken possession of it afterward.

I sat in my room and tried to think of a reason why Myer would summon a demon to Frakingham. He'd done it the last time to test the strength of the abbey ruins' supernatural powers. Perhaps that explained this latest summoning.

Or perhaps he'd wanted to kill Mr. Gladstone. But why? Because of whatever linked them in the past? The more I thought about it, the more certain I became that Samuel hadn't summoned the demon. He didn't dabble in the supernatural beyond his hypnosis and he was no murderer. Besides, he had no reason to do it. If he had found it in Myer's things, and Myer had been the one to summon the demon, then it wasn't a surprise that Samuel now despised the man.

I tried to settle and think of other things, but I couldn't rest. There were too many unanswered questions. I scooted off the bed and went in search of Sylvia's frivolous company. A conversation with her ought to stop me thinking about Samuel, the demon and all manner of troubling things.

I found her in her own room, a collection of letters in her lap. "You've received post?" I asked.

"These are old ones of Uncle's." She lowered the letter she was reading to her lap. "He asked me to go through them and discard any irrelevant ones. They're cluttering up his workspace, so he said." She held out the letter to me. "This one's from Mr. Myer. In fact, a whole bunch of them are from him."

I took the letter and read it. In it Myer stated all manner of reasons he needed access to the abbey ruins. He wanted to study their formation, structure and composition. He listed his credentials and appealed to Langley's scientific mind.

I'm sure you wish to find answers to the same questions as me. As one scientist to another, you must allow me access to study my subject matter.

But it wasn't his words that had me re-reading the letter. It was his penmanship. The distinctive scrawl looked familiar.

"You've got an odd look on your face," Sylvia said. "What is it?"

"I know this hand. I've seen it before." I frowned at the paper and tried to recollect. "Have you got another from Myer?"

She rifled through the stack of letters and handed me a single sheet. Like the first, it was an appeal to allow Myer access to the ruins. It was briefer than the first and appeared to be hastily written. More bells clanged in my head.

I flicked the paper with my finger. "I've got it! Thank you, Sylvia." I kissed the top of her head and handed back the letter.

"You do say the oddest things, Charity. Whatever are you talking about?"

"Samuel found an anonymous note in the fireplace of his father's room the morning after his death. It was partially burned but was still legible nevertheless. I now know that it was Myer who wrote it. More importantly, when Samuel asked him at the time if he'd written it, Myer denied it."

She stared down at the letter. "Are you quite certain? Because that means he lied to your face. It's quite an accusation to make of a gentleman."

"That man is not a gentleman. Not in the true sense of the word."

"What did the note say?"

"'I know what you did.'"

Sylvia expelled a little breath. "It sounds ominous. I wonder what he was referring to."

"If he were here, we could ask him."

"I wonder if he's still at Samuel's parents' house. His brother's house, I mean. I suppose Bert owns it all, now. How fortunate that he has the opportunity to manage the estate while he's still alive."

"He could hardly inherit if he were dead," I said.

"You know what I mean."

Yes. Yes, I did. Bert was fortunate to have inherited while he was still healthy enough. He'd not been expected to outlive his father, hence their reason for wanting Samuel to return home. Yet all of that had changed with the death of Mr. Gladstone.

The thought that accompanied that sickened me. Surely Bert wasn't capable of killing his own father just so he could inherit? Though I knew he was no angel. It was possible that he was cruel enough to do it. Being a weakling himself meant he would need someone—or something—stronger to do it.

"Are you going to tell Samuel?" Sylvia asked, shaking Myer's letters at me.

"Can't you?"

"I've got to see Cook to discuss the week's menu. Besides, it was your discovery. You deserve his gratitude, not me."

"I'm not sure he'll be grateful. That note implied that Myer knew something that Mr. Gladstone did in his past. I doubt it was something virtuous or he wouldn't have written it. Samuel may not want to have his father cast in a poor light."

"I think he already thinks poorly of his father." She touched my arm. "You won't be adding any further burdens to his plate, Charity. Go and speak to him. There's no need to fear him."

I hesitated. "He's looking a little wild lately. A little…mad."

"That doesn't mean he's dangerous or that you need to be afraid. It simply means he's troubled. Indeed, he needs a friend to talk to." The look she gave me implied she expected me to be that friend.

"He has Tommy."

"Tommy is just a servant," she said, rising. "He may be Jack's friend, but he will never be Samuel's."

"Then, by the same token, neither can Samuel be mine."

She shoved the bundle of letters back in a small writing box and slammed the lid down. "How you do twist things."

"You're very sweet to overlook my past," I said. "But you can't overlook mine and not Tommy's. That's not fair."

She simply sniffed, her nose in the air, but did not argue the point further. I suspected that was because she knew she was wrong, yet I doubted she'd ever admit it. Sylvia liked elevating me beyond my status because she wanted a companion. It suited her needs. It did not suit her needs to see Tommy as more than a footman. She would never raise him up.

She gave a silvery laugh and toyed with the amethyst pendant on her necklace. "How Hannah would find it amusing to hear me giving advice. Usually I'm the one in need of it."

We parted ways outside her door and I went in search of Samuel. Instead I found Tommy emerging from one of the wall panels that hid the service stairs. He had shed his jacket and tie and rolled his sleeves up to his elbows. He held a hammer in one hand and small box of nails in the other.

"You startled me," I said, pressing my hand to my rapidly beating heart.

"Sorry. I'm on my way up to the attic to return these." He held up the hammer and box.

"Is the music room secured?"

"Aye. The window now has boards across it and Samuel is locking the door as we speak. Are you looking for him?"

I bit my lip. "I wanted to have a word. I thought you two were together."

"I'm glad you found me and not him." He lowered his voice and glanced up and down the corridor. "There's something I wanted to show you. Something that concerns Gladstone."

"Then why not show him?"

"Because of the nature of it." He jerked his head toward the stairs. "Come with me to the attic."

We traipsed up to the topmost level. The attic was one single, large expanse housed beneath thick black beams. The curtains covering the three windows had been opened to let in the light. The spectacular views reached all the way to the hills in the distance.

161

I stood in the doorway and gawped at the sheer volume of odds and ends stored in trunks and chests or simply lying loose. There seemed to be no particular organization of items, with old tools scattered amid clothes, scientific equipment grouped with dollhouses, and journals, books and toys were littered about as if they were of no use.

I picked up a miniature wingback chair and placed it inside the nearest dollhouse, a fully furnished mansion in the Georgian style. Someone had spent a great deal of effort making each individual piece to suit the period of the house, right down to the cat sleeping on a velvet cushion.

"My children would love these toys," I said on a breath. Indeed, *I* would love the dollhouse. I'd never so much as had a doll as a child. Not unless the strip of leather I'd once found in the gutter when I was six counted. I'd tied a knot in one end and pretended it was my little sister for months. My mother had taken it from me when she discovered it and used it to tie up her shoe.

"I'm sure Mr. Langley would donate them to the school if you asked," Tommy said, stepping over a sheet covering goodness knew what.

I closed the dollhouse doors and looked around. Dust and cobwebs covered everything. Poor overworked Mrs. Moore, with her bad back, couldn't even begin to keep it clean let alone go through all of it. "You ought to catalog these things and clean up. I'm sure much of it could be donated to the poor in the village if Mr. Langley can part with it."

"An admirable suggestion, except we don't have enough staff for such a monumental task."

"You need another footman or maid."

He sighed. "And where will we find such a person willing to come to Frakingham? Growing on a tree? It's hard enough keeping Maud and I can't tell you how many stable lads we've lost in recent months. Every time an owl hoots in the night they run off back to the village, scared out of their wits, convinced something will snatch them from their beds."

"You're very brave for sticking it out."

"I've got good reason to stay. It'll take more than a hooting owl or a demon to scare me away from here."

"Yes, of course. You've got Jack."

His gaze slid to me then away. "Yes, Jack."

"So what is it you wanted to show me?"

He set down the hammer and box of nails on a table and picked up another larger box. He opened the lid and pulled out a stack of daguerreotypes. "I found these when I was searching for a hammer. There's one in the stables, but we wanted to avoid going outside." He handed the top daguerreotype to me. "Recognize anyone?"

The picture was faded and the corners curled. I held it closer to the window for better light. "It's taken here at Frakingham," I said. "Down by the ruins." A group of six people stood amid large stones scattered through the grass, a low, broken wall behind them. Going by the clothing of the two women in the group, it was taken some time ago, perhaps in the late sixties or early seventies. Having a daguerreotype taken back then would have been an expensive and cumbersome exercise indeed.

"Look at the man on the far right," he said.

The man he indicated was tall and thin with a regal tilt to his chin. "Myer," I said on a breath. "He looks younger, but it's definitely him. He was studying the ruins even back then. I assume Lord Frakingham owned this place at the time."

"He did. But that's not the interesting part. Look at the woman in the center. Do you recognize her?"

The woman he indicated was small next to her male companions, her waist tiny. She wore a broad-brimmed hat that cast a shadow over part of her face. It was a face I knew, although it had grown sharper with age.

"Mrs. Gladstone! Good lord. So she *did* know Myer all the way back then. But where is *Mr.* Gladstone?"

"He's not in the picture."

"Perhaps he was taking it. Did he have an interest in the art?"

"I don't know. I don't want to ask either. I'm not sure how to broach the subject with Samuel. He seems particularly angry with Myer lately, and presenting him with evidence of Myer's friendship with his mother might fuel that anger."

"I agree," I said. "Samuel shouldn't see this. Not until we've learned the significance of it."

"What shouldn't I see?" came Samuel's growl from the attic doorway. He stood with his arms crossed over his chest, his sleeves rolled up, exposing his muscular forearms. "What are you two trying to hide from me?"

CHAPTER 13

I dropped the daguerreotype and shrank against Tommy. I felt him tense. It was no comfort to know that he feared Samuel's wrath just as much as I did.

"We were, uh, just looking through some things we found in here," Tommy said.

Samuel sized him up. His handsome blond looks used to make him seem boyish, but that had changed when his madness set in. The dimples didn't appear anymore because he never smiled. His eyes never danced with merriment either, but darted back and forth beneath hooded lids, always watching.

He bent and snatched up the daguerreotype. I expected him to tear it or scrunch it, but he simply handed it to me. "I already knew they were acquainted."

"I thought Myer knew your father," Tommy said carefully. "Not your mother."

"It would seem he knew both of them."

"Your father's not in that picture."

"Thank you for your keen observation."

"Were your parents married at the time this was taken?"

"The daguerreotype's not dated," Samuel snapped. "Any other questions?"

"Many, but I don't think you're going to answer them." Tommy seemed to have recovered from his shock at being overheard. He didn't flinch away from Samuel. "You have a few family secrets you don't wish to discuss. Charity and me, we have no family. We don't know what it's like to have secrets that could tear it apart."

Samuel stepped back as if Tommy had shoved him. He looked to me, his lips parted.

"That was unfair, Tommy," I scolded. "Samuel's father died under terrible circumstances. He doesn't have to tell us anything if he doesn't want to. His family is none of our affair and we have no right to ask about matters that don't concern us."

Silence filled the attic, heavy and full, like a rain cloud. Rain clouds always burst eventually. Waiting for this one to do so was excruciating indeed.

Samuel shifted his weight and the floor beneath his foot creaked. He blinked slowly and drew in a deep breath, as if he had made up his mind to do something he didn't want to do. He pointed to the daguerreotype in my hand.

"Do you recognize any of these other people?" he asked.

Tommy seemed as surprised as me that he'd taken up the discussion again as if there'd been no argument. He took a moment to answer. "I, er, no."

"Do you think Mrs. Moore will?" I asked. "How long has she been housekeeper here?"

"Not long enough, but she's lived in Harborough her entire life. She might know who they are."

"Wait a moment." Samuel pointed at the only man sitting. He perched on the corner of a ruined column, one hand on his hip. "This one looks familiar." He headed further into the attic where covered furniture loomed like ghostly figures in the dim light. He muttered to himself as he peered behind chairs and rifled through what appeared to be framed paintings. "Here it is!" He pulled out an unframed canvas and made his way back to us.

The painting was a small portrait of a stiff-backed gentleman of middle age, with high cheekbones and an unsmiling mouth. He stood in the foreground, a large hunting dog at his feet, with Frakingham House in the distance.

"That's him," Tommy said, holding the daguerreotype up to the portrait. It was indeed the same man, although the gentleman in the portrait looked older than the one in the daguerreotype.

"It's not finished," I said.

"That explains why Lord Frakingham didn't take it with him when he left," Samuel said.

"How do you know it's him? It could be a portrait of anyone." Tommy asked. "Have you met him?"

"It says so on the back here." He turned the portrait around for us to see. The artist's name and the year 1877 were written on the back of the canvas just beneath the words *Cromwell Malborough, 7th Earl of Frakingham.* "I came across this and the other paintings a little while ago when searching up here for something."

"So this is Lord Frakingham," I said, looking at the daguerreotype once more. "Do you think the other lady is his wife?"

"Could be," Tommy said, peering over my shoulder. "Are there any more portraits back there?"

"Only of dogs and horses. This was the only one of a person." Samuel set it down on the floor and leaned it against a table leg.

"It would seem Frakingham was friends with your mother and Myer," Tommy said.

"Myer admits to knowing my father, too," Samuel said. "There's no great mystery here. They could have all been friends years ago and had a falling out. It happens."

"Were your parents members of the Society For Supernatural Activity?" Tommy asked.

I held my breath. It was the question I'd wanted to ask, but hadn't dared.

But Samuel didn't answer with anger in his voice. He merely shrugged. "I don't know. If they were, they never spoke about it. The name hasn't even been mentioned."

I cleared my throat. I wasn't at all sure I wanted to speak up, but I forced myself to. "Your mother has heard of the society."

"How do you know?" Samuel asked.

"She thought I belonged to it. She seemed quite disturbed by the mere mention of it."

"Did you have this conversation when they were here at Frakingham?"

"No. She visited me in the Stag and Huntsman after your father's funeral."

"She did *what*!"

I bit my lip and inched closer to Tommy again.

Samuel swore and thumped his first on the table. The portrait toppled over and landed face down on the floor. "My apologies," he said, flexing his fingers. "Go on."

"I told her I had an interest in the supernatural and she assumed I was a member of the society. She seemed disturbed, as I said. Afraid, even. Whatever her experience is with the society, I don't think it's been a good one."

Samuel blew out a breath and sat on the edge of the table. "If my parents were members then that solves the mystery of how Myer knew them. I'd been wondering about a link. She wouldn't give me any clues."

"I'd been wondering too," I said.

He looked up sharply. "You've been thinking of me...of my family?"

The plea in his voice made my heart lurch. I had to forge on and not be sucked in by it. "There's something more. Do you recall that letter you found in the fireplace of your father's room, after his death?"

"'I know what you did,'" he recited.

"I think Myer wrote it."

"Bloody hell," Tommy murmured. "How did you draw that conclusion?"

"Sylvia was going through his letters to August Langley. She showed them to me and I recognized the handwriting. It matched the writing on the burned note."

"Myer lied," Samuel said, his jaw as rigid as stone. "He told us he didn't write it."

"Do you think the note was referring to something that happened years ago?" I indicated the daguerreotype I still held. "Or something more recent?"

"We may never know. My mother has proven to be a closed book about the past."

"Myer might tell us," I said, my enthusiasm pushing me to speak my mind. I was feeling more comfortable in Samuel's presence than I had ever since finding the amulet in his possession. "We could ask him."

The corner of Samuel's mouth unexpectedly quirked up. "We will."

"Of course, it's none of my affair," I added quickly. "You ought to speak to him alone."

"Nonsense. It's very much your affair. It has been all along. Besides, I want you involved."

I wanted to ask him why, but I dared not. Part of me was surprised I'd gotten so far, yet I was immensely relieved that I had. For one thing, it felt like a burden had lifted off my chest. For another, Samuel gave no sign of being angry with me for poking my nose into his family's business.

Tommy took the daguerreotype from me. "What's this?" he asked, pointing to some stones in the foreground.

"Just part of the wall that's fallen down," I said.

"They make a pattern."

I looked closer. The stones weren't particularly large, though they looked very similar to the ones in the ruins. They were arranged in various simple shapes, one inside the other. The outermost shape was a circle. Within it was a triangle, with all three points touching the stones that made up the outer circle. In the center of the triangle was a square. One side of the square shared the stones that made up the base of the triangle, and inside the square was another circle.

"It's some sort of symbol," I said, turning the daguerreotype around.

Samuel moved closer on my other side, distracting me from the picture. His chest brushed my shoulder and his breath warmed my cheek. My awareness of him sharpened, like a blurry image suddenly snapping into focus. He felt so large next to me, so solid and masculine. The tiny hairs on the back of my neck rose and a little shiver rippled down my spine. The urge to move away was strong, yet just as strong was another emotion. One that had my blood pounding through my veins and my heart beating for entirely different reasons.

"Do you recognize it?" Tommy's voice called me back to the daguerreotype. I was about to answer him when he added, "Gladstone? Did you hear me?"

Samuel cleared his throat and moved away. The loss of his closeness didn't untangle my emotions, but only served to confuse them further. I wanted him near, and yet I didn't. Would my feelings for Samuel always be so opposed to one another?

"It's not familiar to me," Samuel said. "It appears mathematical in nature. Or perhaps religious. Charity and I will ask Myer."

I wasn't sure whether to be delighted or worried that he wanted me to help. "We cannot speak to him until he returns," I said. "Unless you plan on traveling back to London, and I can assure you, I don't want to go there just yet."

"You won't," he said. "We'll wait for Myer to come back here."

"That could take some time. First the demon must be killed and then we must wait for a letter to reach him."

"The demon will be killed today," he said, his gaze connecting with Tommy's. "But there's no particular need to speak to Myer now. Learning how he knew my parents doesn't change anything. My father is dead."

"It might tell you who killed him," Tommy said. "Or who summoned the demon that killed him. You might even learn that it was Myer himself."

"And so? What will discovering that do? We cannot go to the police and tell them an otherworldly creature has been summoned and ate my father."

"He's right," I said to Tommy, before Samuel's temper could rise further. "Besides, we don't even know if Mr. Gladstone's death was intentional or not." I didn't want Samuel to think I suspected one of his family was responsible, yet he must suspect that I was thinking it. There was no other logical conclusion to jump to, once one considered the fact that Samuel was protecting someone. He would *not* protect Myer.

Tommy threw up his hands and let them slap against his thighs. "Very well. But I'd feel safer with some answers, whether we can go to the police with those answers or not. Wouldn't you?"

I would indeed, but I didn't say so. I didn't look to Samuel either, to see if he agreed. I didn't want to know if he did not.

***

An unexpected and unwelcome visitor arrived late afternoon, in the form of Mrs. Gladstone. She and her maid were ushered into the house while Samuel, Tommy and Fray escorted her coachman and horses to the stables. I didn't want to see her so I retreated to my rooms without greeting her.

"*Please* come downstairs," Sylvia begged me after she had spent half an hour alone in Mrs. Gladstone's company. "I don't know what to say to her or how to act or anything! She makes me feel like a child who shouldn't be dining with the adults. And Samuel's no help at all. He's made himself scarce and it's him she came to see! I'd like to wring his neck for leaving me alone with her."

"To be fair, he and Tommy are keeping watch for the demon."

They had organized their plan to capture it after we'd left the attic. They agreed to attack at night, when it came looking for another meal. Sylvia had protested that it was too dangerous, but I hadn't seen any other option. The demon had to be killed or sent back, and there was no one else to do it.

"Can't your uncle join you?" I said, setting aside the book I'd been reading. The light had begun to fade anyway, as dark clouds crowded into the sky.

"He's avoiding her too. Bollard came down to see who had called then promptly returned upstairs. I haven't seen hide nor hair of either of them since. Charity, please come and join me."

"She loathes me, Sylvia. She thinks me too far beneath her to breathe the same air. I'm in no mood to exchange barbs with someone who can't stand the sight of me."

"She won't be cruel with me there. Besides, she seems rather subdued today. Perhaps Mr. Gladstone's death has changed her."

"I doubt it."

"Or perhaps she's too worried about Samuel and the demon to pick a fight." There was a ring of truth to that. "Pleeeeaaaase, Charity."

I sighed, defeated. "All right. I'll come." As much as I would have liked answers to the questions we'd had about the daguerreotype and Mrs. Gladstone's association with Myer, I didn't want to be the one to ask them. She was Samuel's mother and the task ought to fall to him.

I placed the book on the table beside my chair and stood. "Very well. I'll sit with you both until it's time to change for dinner, or until she forgets her manners and calls me something colorful."

Sylvia embraced me. "Thank you."

"Don't thank me yet. I doubt we'll have anything to talk about. You may have to carry the entire conversation."

We strolled slowly to the door, arm in arm. "I can do that if you're there," she said, squeezing my arm. "If she doesn't join in then you and I can simply converse on whatever takes our fancy."

"It should be something to draw her into the conversation. Something that won't be controversial, or make her think about her husband."

She brightened. "We can discuss the latest fashions from Paris. I'll have the newest edition of the *Young Ladies Journal* on hand."

"She's in widow's weeds," I protested.

"One can still be fashionable in black."

"Still, I think we should have another topic or two handy in case that one falls flat."

We tossed ideas around quietly, lest we be overheard as we descended the stairs. We approached the drawing room, where Mrs. Gladstone was apparently waiting to be entertained by our sparkling conversation.

We were mistaken. She may have been in the drawing room, but she wasn't counting the seconds for us to join her. She was speaking to Samuel. Or begging him, to be more precise.

"Please return home with me," she was saying as Sylvia and I came to a halt near the drawing room door.

I held my arm out, blocking her path. She signaled that we should continue and announce our presence, but I shook my head. I wanted to listen in. If Samuel asked her anything important, I wanted to hear her answer. If I overheard her call me cruel things, then so be it. I'd heard it all before, anyway.

"You shouldn't have come," Samuel said. He sounded agitated, impatient to get away. "I'm not returning with you."

"Because of *her*."

"She has a name, Mother."

She sniffed.

"It's not Charity's fault that I came here in the first place," he said. "I didn't even know she was here. I came back because I couldn't allow that...thing to roam around the estate, terrorizing innocent people."

"So you thought to endanger yourself too! And so soon after your father's death, and with your brother's health in such a fragile state. It's terribly irresponsible, Samuel. You're the heir now. You will inherit one day. Act accordingly."

He heaved a sigh. "That conversation is growing tired. Shall we talk about *you* not acting responsibly, instead? You came here with only the driver for protection. Was he even armed?"

I was pleased to hear Samuel admonish her. It meant he wanted her to be safe, that he cared. It surprised me that I *wanted* him to care. I suppose it stemmed from my not having a family. However horrible his mother could be to me at times, she obviously loved her sons and only wanted to protect them. I envied Samuel. He didn't know how fortunate he was. Or perhaps he did, or he wouldn't be lecturing her.

Sylvia pushed me gently. *Go in*, she mouthed.

I shook my head and pressed my finger to my lips to keep her quiet. I didn't want her interrupting until the conversation required it.

"I have to go," he said.

What? That was it? He wasn't going to question her about her association with Myer? About the daguerreotype? Perhaps I'd missed that part of the conversation.

Or perhaps he was avoiding asking altogether.

"Stay with me," she begged. "I want to speak to my darling son and not that frivolous Langley girl. She makes my head ache."

Sylvia thrust her hands on her hips and poked her tongue out. I tried not to smile.

"We have nothing to discuss," Samuel said. "If you don't wish to talk to anyone, go to your room. Otherwise, I'd appreciate some civility toward my friends. You came here of your own accord. Nobody forced you."

"*You* forced me." Her voice was a slender thread that barely reached us in the corridor. "I *had* to come and bring you home where you belong. This is no place for...sane people."

"Perhaps that's why I like living here."

"It's not a joke, Samuel. This place is dangerous with that...thing on the loose. You said so yourself. Come home, where it's safe."

"Enough." The guttural grate of that single word had as much effect as a gunshot. My heart leapt into my throat and beat at a rapid rate. The air seemed to thicken around us. Sylvia's fingers tightened on my arm. She did not try to pull me away, but seemed as riveted to the spot as me.

"Enough talk of the danger here and keeping me safe," he ground out. "I will not leave when innocent lives are at stake."

"But you are Bert's heir." Mrs. Gladstone sounded as if she was crying. I felt some sympathy for her, mostly because I doubted her tears would soften Samuel's heart. "You have a responsibility to the Gladstone name."

"I have a responsibility to keep everyone here safe and rid this realm of that monster. Since you refuse to do it, then it's up to me to undo *your* work."

CHAPTER 14

Sylvia and I stared at one another. She clutched my arm and I clutched hers, as if we were holding each other steady. I couldn't believe what I'd heard.

'Your work,' Samuel had said.

Mrs. Gladstone had summoned the demon.

Samuel's mother had killed his father. It was a wonder that discovery hadn't sent him over the edge into complete madness already. The question remained, however: had she done it on purpose?

I was still in a stupor when Sylvia dragged me away from the drawing room door. Fortunately, Samuel strode off in the other direction or he would have spotted us. Sylvia and I weren't all that good at keeping our thoughts to ourselves. I could see the disturbance the news had caused written all over her pretty face.

"I was convinced it was Myer," she whispered.

And I'd thought it may have been Samuel at one time, but I was immensely glad that I'd been wrong. I ought to tell him so. I ought to apologize, even though I'd not accused him to his face. The only reason I hadn't was because I'd been too scared. I was still afraid of him for other reasons, but I would force myself to speak to him about it. It was only fair.

My apology would have to wait, however. He had raced off, no doubt to see Tommy and prepare to face the demon, and Sylvia was leading me toward the drawing room.

"Wait a moment," I said, extricating myself from her grip. "I'll be back in the blink of an eye."

"Charity," she hissed. "Don't leave me alone with her."

I walked quickly in the same direction as Samuel and up to the attic without meeting anyone. I found what I was looking for and returned to the drawing room. Sylvia was sitting on the sofa, her feet together and her hands clasped tightly in her lap. She had a strained smile on her face and was chattering on about a white ermine muff she wanted to purchase before next winter. Mrs. Gladstone seemed not to be listening. Her unfocused gaze was turned toward the window.

"Charity!" Sylvia cried with undisguised relief. "You're here."

Mrs. Gladstone twisted to see me. Her gaze sharpened as if my presence honed it to a lethal point. "Miss Evans," she said, through pursed lips.

I nodded a greeting. "Mrs. Gladstone. What an unexpected pleasure to see you again."

She made a miffed sound through her nose. Perhaps calling it a 'pleasure' was a little too thick, but good manners were hard to break, especially when they'd been drilled into me with a belt across my back.

"Sit down and have some tea," Sylvia urged me. "Maud brought a fresh pot."

"Thank you, but I don't feel like tea. I'd like Mrs. Gladstone's opinion on a daguerreotype."

"What daguerreotype?" both she and Mrs. Gladstone asked.

"Tommy found it in the attic earlier," I told them. "He's our footman," I said to Mrs. Gladstone. "You may have heard him called Dawson, but I prefer to use his given name. We've known each other a long time."

It was rather satisfying to see her mouth turn down and her nose wrinkle up. I did feel a little bad for embarrassing Sylvia with my poor manners, but only a little. She would recover.

"Honestly, Charity," she muttered.

I handed the daguerreotype to her first to distract her. "Recognize anyone, Sylvia?"

"Only Mr. Myer." She gave the daguerreotype back to me and I passed it to Mrs. Gladstone. She took it reluctantly, but did not study it straight away.

"What about you, Mrs. Gladstone?" I prompted. "Do you recognize anyone aside from Mr. Myer?"

She tossed the picture onto the table beside her where it skidded into the vase of roses. "This is absurd. I have no wish to play your silly parlor games. I am not a child."

"And this is no nursery story," I said. "It's real."

She got up to leave. I was going to lose what might turn out to be my one opportunity to speak to her without Samuel present.

"It's you, Mrs. Gladstone," I said quickly. "You, Mr. Myer, Lord and Lady Frakingham,"

She stopped at the door, her back to us. She stood there for a long time, then slowly turned. Her smooth brow remained unlined, but a keen observer would notice the pinched mouth, the slightly flared nostrils.

"Can you tell me how you know Myer and the Frakinghams?" I said.

"Charity," Sylvia hissed. "Is this wise considering…?"

I put my hand up to silence her. "Otherwise I may jump to the wrong conclusions and I might share those conclusions with Samuel," I said to Mrs. Gladstone. "I'm sure you wouldn't want that."

"You nasty little *whelp*." She spat each word, as if they tasted foul in her mouth.

I pushed on, despite Sylvia's distressed look of appeal. "You knew Mr. Myer back then. Indeed, I'd wager that all of you in this daguerreotype were friends."

"We were never friends with Myer. Never." She tilted her chin at the picture on the table. "That gathering was held here at Lord Frakingham's insistence. I'd never met Myer until that day."

"What about your husband? Did he know Myer before that?"

"I don't know."

I didn't quite believe her, but didn't press the point. "What was the gathering for?"

"Miss Evans," she bit off, "I don't have to answer your questions. My friendships are none of your affair."

"Of course," I said, surrendering the line of questioning. There were more important things to ask. Mrs. Gladstone turned to go again so I had no time to think of a more politic way of broaching my next question. "Where did you get the amulet?"

Sylvia's whimper of defeat was the only sound in the room. I would have to make it up to her, somehow. The poor girl probably thought her life was over now that one of her guests had thoroughly offended another more socially powerful one. Mrs. Gladstone didn't make any sound, but she didn't walk off, either.

"From Mr. Myer?" I persisted. "Or have you had it in your possession for a very long time? Since you belonged to the society, when that daguerreotype—"

"You're a fool, Miss Evans," Mrs. Gladstone said. "An ignorant fool. It's fortunate that you're beautiful, otherwise there'd be nothing to recommend you."

Her words stung me more than I liked to admit. I'd been prepared for her to try and bludgeon me with blunt accusations and had resolved to let everything she said wash over me. Yet they did not. Not entirely.

It was clear that she wasn't going to answer me. I was a little surprised that *she* wasn't surprised that I knew about the amulet. She must have realized Sylvia and I had overheard her conversation with Samuel.

"Why did you summon it?" I persisted.

Her chuckle grated on my taut nerves. I clenched my hands together and tried to stop my intense frustration from boiling over. "Good day, ladies. Miss Langley, I'll be dining in my room this evening. I feel a headache blooming."

Sylvia made a gurgling sound of acknowledgement as Mrs. Gladstone picked up her skirts. I was not prepared to let her go just yet.

"Did Mr. Myer write that note to *you*?" I asked.

She arched her brow. "What note?"

"A note written by his hand was found in your husband's room the morning after his death. 'I know what you did,' it said. Myer must have been referring to you summoning the demon. Is that because he knew you had an amulet at your disposal?"

"Once again, Miss Evans, you prove yourself to be not very bright. If the note you speak of was in my husband's room, then it must have been intended for him, not me. How you do leap to conclusions."

"Charity," Sylvia whispered. "Enough."

I bit my tongue. She was right. I'd gone too far. Mrs. Gladstone was not going to give me the answers I sought. My ire would only grow if I continued our fruitless conversation and my blood boiled enough as it was.

"Good day, Mrs. Gladstone," I said with a curt nod. "I hope your headache eases before you leave us. How long are you intending to stay?"

"As long as necessary." She strode out of the room with a swish of her heavy skirt. The *tap tap* of her shoes finally faded and I slumped against the sofa back. Sparring with dragons was exhausting.

"Thank goodness that's over," Sylvia murmured. "You ought not to rile her like that, Charity."

"Why not? She thoroughly deserved that interrogation, particularly now that we know she summoned the demon."

"Yes, but she is still a grand lady."

"She's just a woman, like any other, capable of doing great good or great harm if she chooses." I only hoped she didn't attempt to control the demon and set it on me. I'd thought of that much too late. I poured myself a cup of tea. I needed one quite badly.

"She is Samuel's mother," Sylvia said as if that explained everything.

"And?"

"And he is your friend. You ought not drive a wedge between them."

"Not only did she bring her own wedge, but she has firmly shoved it in the crack and is the one leveraging it, not me." I left the 'friend' part of her comment alone. I wasn't sure what category Samuel fit into, anymore.

She lowered her cup to her saucer. "Charity, you and I both know what it's like to be motherless. Don't wish that on Samuel, too."

Sometimes I thought being motherless was preferable to having a dragon for a parent, but I didn't say so. I suspected Sylvia wouldn't agree with me. Sometimes I forgot that she too lacked first-hand knowledge of the bond between mother and child.

"I'm sorry, Sylvia. I behaved appallingly just now to your guest. I hope you can forgive me."

"Hmmm. I think I can, as long as you promise not to do it again."

She sipped her tea and didn't seem to notice that I didn't acquiesce. I could make no such promise where Mrs. Gladstone was concerned. Not now that I knew she was responsible for her husband's death.

***

Dinner was a tense affair. Not because of my conversation with Mrs. Gladstone—true to her word, she didn't join us—but because Tommy, Samuel and even Bollard were poised to lay siege to the demon. Langley, Sylvia and I could hardly concentrate on our food, so anxious were we. We jumped at every footstep and ate hardly a thing.

The creature had consumed its fill of the food the men had supplied and was due to return for more. According to Tommy, it usually looked for another helping after dusk. This time, however, nothing had been left for it. They wanted it hungry and hunting, so that it would come close enough for them to kill it. Kill it, not send it back. Samuel had not told anyone about the amulet. Neither Sylvia nor I mentioned it either, or Mrs. Gladstone's involvement in summoning the demon in the first place.

I was surprised by Sylvia's silence on the matter. She wasn't known for discretion. I suppose it had more to do with her fear of the lady than a change of character. It was understandable, considering what Mrs. Gladstone had done.

After dinner I went in search of Samuel. I found him with Tommy in the tower room, standing by the window, the room in darkness to eliminate the reflection on the glass. They did not look around when I entered and continued to scan the countryside. Bollard was preparing weapons in the gun room.

"Is it wise to do this at night?" I asked them. "Shouldn't you wait for the morning?"

"No time like the present," Tommy said without taking his gaze off the window. "If it doesn't come out then we'll try again in the morning."

"Samuel," I said, "may we speak?"

He swung around. "You wish to speak to me?" He finger brushed his hair as if to make himself more presentable. It was an endearing trait that almost had me smiling. But then I remembered what I needed to say to him and what I had to admit to overhearing.

I swallowed heavily and hoped he would forgive my eavesdropping.

He indicated I should go ahead of him out of the room, but I wanted to remain near Tommy. "In here is suitable," I said. If we stood near the door and spoke softly, Tommy might not hear us. If he did, then so be it. I wasn't going to risk Samuel's wrath alone.

"I have a confession to make," I said, steeling myself.

Samuel leaned against the wall near the door and crossed his arms. It was too dark to make out much of his face, but I could feel his intense gaze on me as surely as if I could see his eyes.

"I overheard your conversation with your mother in the drawing room today," I said, keeping my voice low, even though Tommy gave no indication that he could hear. "I know the amulet belonged to her."

"I see," he murmured. It was impossible to tell from those two words what he thought of my behavior.

"Sylvia was with me," I added. "We didn't intend to listen in, it just happened. I'm sorry. I hope you can forgive us."

I hadn't noticed that I'd submissively lowered my head until he lifted my chin with his finger. His touch was gentle and he pulled back almost immediately as if he'd just realized what he'd done. "There's nothing to forgive," he said. "It saves me from telling you myself." He crossed his arms and tucked his hands high up under his armpits, as if he were trying to stop himself from touching me again. "I meant to," he added. "Several times I've almost sought you out to tell you."

"Why didn't you?" I ventured.

"I suppose I didn't want you to think any worse of her than you already do."

I couldn't think why. Liking her was an impossibility now. Not that it was very likely before.

"I wanted to apologize for accusing you," I said. "When I found the amulet in your things, I thought *you'd* used it to summon the demon. I shouldn't have assumed the worst. I'm sorry."

"You don't need to apologize. It was a logical conclusion to make. And I should have told you then and there that it was my mother's. I found it in her things at home, just like you found it in my things here." He shook his head. "I couldn't believe it when I saw it just lying on her dressing table, as if it were a piece of jewelry she'd just removed. It knocked the wind out of me."

"I'm sure it did. It's quite shocking."

He snorted softly. "That's an understatement."

"Have you asked her why she did it?"

He turned his face into profile, but I couldn't make out his eyes anyway in the dark. "You mean whether she did it to kill my father on purpose or not?" He sounded strung out, stretched thin, as if he were barely holding himself together.

"Yes," I whispered.

"She claims it was an accident."

"Do you believe her?"

"I think so." He suddenly turned back to face me. His eyes glistened in the darkness. "I want to, very much. The whole thing…it's overwhelming, Charity. I feel like I'm drowning in mud. It's sucking me down and I can't get out. I can't breathe."

My hand twitched, aching to touch him, but I held it in check at my side. There was nothing to say to ease his pain, and I didn't want to give him the wrong idea by comforting him physically. I simply stood there and waited for him to say something more.

"I have to live with the knowledge that my mother killed my father," he said.

"But if it was an accident…"

He simply grunted.

"What did she want to bring a demon here for in the first place?"

"To study the supernatural. She claims to have an interest in the science."

Like Myer. "Did you know about this interest?"

"It's news to me."

I couldn't tell if he believed his mother or not. The darkness hid his face too well. I certainly didn't believe her, based on those answers. Why would she suddenly show an interest in demons *now*? Why summon one *now*? There were too many unanswered questions to satisfy me.

"Why did she summon the demon then let it roam about uncontrolled?" I asked. "Surely she knew how dangerous that would be. Why didn't she try to send it back after it…did its worst?"

His broad shoulders slumped. "I asked her that and she said it couldn't be controlled."

"Why not?"

He shrugged. "I wish I knew."

"Where do you think she got the amulet?"

"Myer." His voice was a low growl deep within his chest. It had Tommy turning to look at us before once more keeping watch out the window.

"Do you know that for sure?"

"Suspicion only, but I must be right. They've known each other for years and he's mad enough to supply her with one in his possession. Perhaps he did it for old times' sake."

"That sounds rather cavalier," I said cautiously. He seemed determined to blame Myer and I wasn't sure if trying to prove otherwise was going to turn his ire in my direction.

"The man has few morals and he likes to experiment with the supernatural. This way he gets to see the results of an experiment without taking the blame for it himself."

If it had been almost anyone else who'd said that, I would have reminded them that handing someone a gun does not force them to pull the trigger. Even if Myer had given her the amulet, Mrs. Gladstone was responsible for using it. But I didn't have enough trust in Samuel to tell him that. Besides, he seemed to need to think his mother not altogether blameworthy.

"Could it have been anyone else who gave it to her?" I asked. "Perhaps another member of the society? Someone from that daguerreotype, perhaps?"

He shook his head. "The note I found in my father's fireplace would suggest that it was Myer, since he authored it. I think he must have sent it to her instead of Father, after his death, and she put it there so it couldn't be found in her possession."

"I asked her about it and she claimed not to know of its existence."

"You spoke to her?"

I nodded. "After we learned the amulet belonged to her. I...I meant to tell you earlier. I'm sorry, I got distracted."

"Charity," he purred. "Don't fret. It's all right. Tell me, did you receive any answers to your questions?"

"None. She claimed not to know anything about a note from Myer, however. She suggested that it must have been sent to your father, since it was found in his fireplace."

He stroked his chin in thought. "She could be lying. She's committed so many sins, why not add that one to the ledger?"

I wasn't entirely convinced. She'd not answered all my other questions, yet she'd answered that one. Why? "Could it be possible that Myer sent the note to your father, but was referring to something else? Something Mr. Gladstone did in the past. Something that your mother learned of just recently and disapproves of highly."

I felt his gaze boring into me, even through the veil of darkness. "You mean she had the demon kill Father deliberately as...revenge for this past crime?"

"Yes," I whispered, suddenly wishing I hadn't told him my theory. He was too volatile at the moment, too unpredictable. Too violent.

"It's a possibility," he said. "But one I find difficult to entertain. She and my father cared for one another. It made them unusual, in their set. She certainly has her faults, but I cannot imagine Mother *murdering* Father. That's why I think it was an accident. As to him having done something wrong, that is likely. He was no saint."

"What did your mother say when you discovered she killed your father?"

"She was upset, to say the least. She pleaded for my forgiveness and begged me not to tell Bert, or anyone else.

It's why I'm doubly glad that I can share the burden with you. I...need to speak about it with somebody or I'll go completely mad."

I folded my arms against a chill creeping across my skin. I didn't want to be the one thing standing between Samuel and madness. It was too much of a burden, particularly when I wanted nothing to do with him. I would return to London and be far away from him, as soon as the master's ghost crossed over.

"Thank you," he murmured in those deep, rich tones that had me tensing and instinctively moving away.

"What for?" I whispered.

"For being on speaking terms with me again."

I relaxed. His voice was normal once more, perhaps because he sensed my unease.

"And thank you for apologizing," he said. "Even though it was unnecessary. Charity...does this mean you're no longer afraid of me?"

I shook my head, but wasn't sure if he would have seen it in the darkness. "I always will be. I'm sorry, Samuel. It's just the way it is. Nothing can change that."

"Because of my hypnosis?"

"Yes." I didn't add that it was also because of the reason he'd been sent to Newgate. The reason his family had all but abandoned him during that time, and why the older members were still hesitant to allow their daughters near him.

There were some things that could not be voiced, particularly to a man already standing on the brink of an abyss.

"It's here!" Tommy's shout reverberated off the walls and shattered my nerves. He ran between us and out the door. "Come on, Gladstone! Stop flirting, and come with me."

Samuel grasped my shoulders and bent his head to my level. My heart leapt into my throat, but he did not hurt me. "Stay inside, Charity. Lock the doors and keep away from the windows. If we don't return, fetch the amulet from my room."

"*Now*, Gladstone!" Tommy shouted as he barreled down the stairs.

Samuel let me go and raced after him.

CHAPTER 15

I trailed some distance behind Tommy and Samuel, thanks to my petticoats and skirt almost tripping me up as I ran down the stairs. I heard their progress well enough. Their shouts for "Bollard!" caused the entire household to materialize as if from the woodwork, servants and all. Even Mr. Langley wheeled himself to the foot of the staircase. I caught up to them there, Mrs. Gladstone at my heels.

"Don't do this," she ordered. "It's madness."

"I am already mad, Mother." Samuel accepted a shotgun from Bollard. "Have you not noticed?"

She grasped his arm above the elbow with both hands. "Please, Samuel. Don't go out there. It's not safe."

He shook her off as if she were a troublesome insect.

"Samuel, please." She clasped her hands in front of her and hovered at his side. "You are my son. If you're harmed...or worse..."

"I have to do this, Mother. You of all people ought to understand why." The wretchedness in his eyes was equal to her own, but for different reasons.

"No. You don't. Let someone else do it. You're too important."

He cut his icy gaze to her. "Pardon?"

She let out a single sob. "Too important to *me*," she whispered. "Please, I'm begging you. Don't go out there. Your family needs you. *I* need you."

He turned his back on her. Her face crumpled, but she made no sound. She lowered her veil and her shoulders silently shook.

Sylvia wrung her hands and blinked at Tommy as if she too wished to grasp him and beg him to stay. She had more sense than Mrs. Gladstone, however, and refrained.

"Jack's knife?" Tommy said to Samuel.

"Strapped to my forearm," Samuel replied. "Ready?"

Tommy hoisted up his shotgun. "Ready. Bollard?"

The big mute gave his master a quick glance. Langley responded with a grim smile. Bollard picked up the lantern glowing on the nearby table and, pistol in his other hand, headed for the front door.

"Can't I come, sir?" the stable lad appealed.

"No," Samuel said without pausing. "Lock the door after us, Syl." And then he and the other men disappeared into the darkness.

Sylvia remained rooted to the spot so I slammed the bolt home, locking them outside.

Mrs. Gladstone flew at the door and scrabbled at the iron bolt. "Open it! What if they need to return? Open it at once!"

"No, Mrs. Gladstone." Mr. Langley's stern order invited no dispute.

Even so, she disputed. "That's my *son*. My boy." I caught her arm and Sylvia her other. She tried to shake us off, but we held firm. She was a slight woman and perhaps her grief made her weak. We were able to hold her back.

"We can watch them from an upstairs window," Sylvia soothed. "I have opera glasses."

I didn't know if watching them would achieve much satisfaction, but I thought it a good idea to placate the distraught woman. I was in two minds regarding her. On the one hand, I felt sorry for her. On the other, the demon was only present because of her. She'd brought this problem down on the estate, and now she must deal with the consequences. Samuel felt responsible, thanks to her. He wanted to be the one to kill it, and rightly so.

"Keep away from the windows," Langley directed the staff. "Try to remain calm. It'll all be over soon."

"I hate this place," Maud muttered. She pressed her apron hem to her mouth to stifle her sobs. Mrs. Moore clicked her tongue and directed her and Mrs. Gladstone's trembling maid away from us.

Langley rolled himself off, while Mrs. Gladstone allowed Sylvia to lead her up the stairs. I followed behind and stared at the slumped shoulders of the woman I'd pegged as stiff, uncompromising and, more recently, foolish for summoning a demon. She cared for her sons. That had never been in question, but after viewing her hysterical display as Samuel prepared to leave, I believed I understood better what it meant for a mother to love her children. She would do anything to keep them safe. Knowing they were near danger made her sick with worry and behave irrationally.

So why would she introduce something that could harm them? She'd summoned the demon with both sons in residence at Frakingham. Even if she thought she could control it, she must have known how dangerous such a thing could be.

Sylvia directed us into her private sitting room and deposited her lamp on a table, tucked between two armchairs near the windows. The large arched windows overlooked the lawn, ruins and lake during the daytime. It was a cloudy night, with nothing but inky blackness punctuated by Bollard's swaying lantern, off to our left, near the woods.

"Where are they?" Sylvia muttered as she rifled through a drawer on her dressing table. With a click of her tongue, she slammed it shut and opened another. "Aha!" She pulled out a pair of mother of pearl opera glasses, rimmed with gold.

She handed them to Mrs. Gladstone, already seated at the window.

The older lady hesitated, as if she'd not expected the kindness. "Thank you," she whispered and lifted her veil. Her face was mottled, her eyes and nose red. She turned her attention to the window and held the opera glasses in place.

Just at that moment the clouds parted and the full moon bathed the estate in its glow. It was as if Mrs. Gladstone herself had ordered the light.

"What can you see?" Sylvia asked, settling in the other armchair. I came to stand beside her and rested my hip against the window frame near the curtain. Thanks to the moon, I could now see the shapes of the three men and that of the demon, only a few feet away from them.

I swallowed and prayed as hard as I'd ever prayed.

"It's there," Mrs. Gladstone whispered. She leaned closer to the window. "Good god. It's..."

"Hideous," I finished for her.

She pressed her fingertips to her lips, but it didn't stop her little gasp from escaping. Sylvia met my gaze and put out her hand. I held it firmly and tried to lend her what strength I still possessed. But it was hard. So very hard to watch from a safe distance and know that I could do nothing to help. I wasn't accustomed to feeling so useless. Only when I'd been in the master's grasp had I ever felt like that. Not even as a child, under the so-called care of my mother, had I felt so pathetically inadequate.

"Ow." Sylvia tugged at my hand. "Charity, you're hurting me."

I loosened my grip. "Sorry," I muttered, without turning away from the window.

"It's all right. You're worried. We all are."

Mrs. Gladstone lowered the opera glasses to look at me. Her watery eyes unnerved me, but there was no malice in them for once, only extreme distress. She'd aged in the few minutes since the men had left. She was no longer the redoubtable matriarch of a powerful family, but simply a mother worried about her son.

A gunshot pierced the night. We all jumped.

"They're moving!" Sylvia pointed to the lantern now bobbing like a drunken glow worm away from the woods. "The glasses, Mrs. Gladstone!"

Mrs. Gladstone put up the opera glasses and peered through the window again. "Oh God!" She dropped them and leapt up.

I grabbed her arm. She tried to pull away from me, but I held on as Sylvia picked up the opera glasses.

"What is it?" I snapped. "What did you see?"

Mrs. Gladstone turned sightless, frightened eyes on me. "He's dead. My son is dead."

Bile rose to my throat. *No. Please, God, no.* My stomach rolled. My legs weakened. If I collapsed on the floor would I ever be able to get up again?

"Not dead," Sylvia said, her voice a high squeak. "Just knocked flat to the ground. He's up again and running after the lantern. I'm not sure, but I think the creature is chasing them, not the other way around. Look."

Mrs. Gladstone did not look. She jerked free and ran for the door as fast as her age would allow. I followed her. We were of the same mind—the time for inertia was over. We had to act.

Except we were not of the same mind. While I made for Samuel's room, she continued down the stairs. His door was unlocked, thankfully, and I barged in. It was dark and I stumbled about until I managed to throw open the curtains and let in the moonlight. I found the amulet in a drawer of his desk and rushed to catch up to the others.

Sylvia was at the front door with Mrs. Gladstone. The latter held a pistol. Bollard must have left it nearby. I remembered my derringer and felt for it in my pocket.

"How good is your aim, Mrs. Gladstone?" I asked.

She didn't hear me. She was trying to open the bolt on the door with one hand.

"We know yours is quite accurate," Sylvia said to me. She frowned and pointed at the dangling amulet. "You're bringing that?"

"Of course."

"Do you know an incantation to send it back?"

"No, but Mrs. Gladstone must."

At the mention of her name, Mrs. Gladstone stopped trying to unlock the door and blinked at me. Her eyes still bore the marks of her crying, but she seemed more alert now that she had something to do. "I don't," she said simply, and turned back to the door.

I grabbed her shoulder with the hand that held the amulet and swung her round to face me. I wanted to see her eyes when she answered me. I wanted to know if she lied.

"The time for falsehoods is over," I snapped. "Their lives depend on you now. *Samuel's* life depends on you. You *must* send it back."

"Don't you think I know that?" Her voice was not her own, but harsher. "Don't you think I would send it back if I could?"

I shook my head, over and over. "How could you bring that thing here and not know how to control it or return it?"

"I know one," Sylvia said. At my arched brows, she added, "I know an incantation to send back demons. We all memorized one at Christmas, the last time we had a demon here. I haven't forgotten it."

"Bloody hell, Sylvia, why didn't you say so?"

"I just did! And Charity, please mind your language."

I handed her my pistol and strapped the amulet around my neck. I used both hands to slide back the bolt then grabbed my pistol in one hand, and her hand in my other, and together we ran outside. Mrs. Gladstone was directly behind us.

The clouds had once more shut away the moon and its light. The night air felt cool and damp from drizzling rain. The grass squelched under our shoes and our breath ballooned in silvery puffs as it left our mouths. The amulet tapped against my chest, a solid reminder of what needed to be done. It was a comfort; my only one.

We ran toward the lantern in the distance. Mrs. Gladstone fell behind, and Sylvia and I waited for her to catch up. We ought to keep together.

"No," Mrs. Gladstone gasped between heavy breaths. "Go!"

We did. The lantern was down at the ruins and had become still. This worried me more than the sight of it bobbing along at a fast clip.

We slowed down as we drew closer. The broken arches of the ruined abbey erupted from the ground like ice crystals, their pale stones ghostly in the darkness. It was quiet. Too quiet. The lantern sat on top of a low wall. It glowed preternaturally, casting its pathetic light in a small circle. There was nobody about.

Mrs. Gladstone caught up to us and we three approached the ruins carefully together. Every nerve ending was drawn as taut as a bow, every sense tuned in to our surroundings. I would hear the slightest sound, smell even a whiff of foulness. I felt the magic all around.

A cold whispering breeze washed over me. The hairs on the back of my neck rose and my warmed cheeks cooled. It was an unnatural cold. Dry, not damp, and penetrating. It wrapped icy tendrils around my bones and did not let go.

Beside me, Sylvia shivered. Mrs. Gladstone drew closer. If I had a spare hand I would have taken hers for comfort. As it was, I could feel her body shaking uncontrollably. She was as terrified as Sylvia and me.

"Where are they?" she whispered.

I shushed her.

Something snorted and snuffled to our right. Sylvia tensed. Her grip became bruising. Mrs. Gladstone sidled closer again, until we were all huddled in trembling silence.

"Get back," someone hissed. It wasn't one of us three. "Get back to the house."

"Tommy," Sylvia whispered. "Tommy, where are you?"

"Samuel?" Mrs. Gladstone pulled away and headed toward Tommy's voice.

The snorting and snuffling stopped. An unearthly silence fell over the ruins. No owls hooted in the woods, no insects chirruped. Nothing.

Then came labored breathing. And a footfall. Another and another. It was coming our way.

"Here," came Samuel's voice near Tommy's. It sounded thin, however, but gritty as if he were clenching his teeth. "It's too late to leave. Come over here."

My relief at hearing him almost overwhelmed me to the point of not responding. Not so Mrs. Gladstone. She ran toward his voice. It came from behind one of the more intact walls of the ancient abbey. The wall was quite long, and came to about waist height. It was a serviceable hiding spot, but offered little protection once discovered.

Sylvia tugged me and together we raced to the wall. I dropped to my knees beside Bollard. I scanned the faces of each man, but it was impossible to see expressions in the dark. "What's happened?" I asked. "Why is the lantern over there?"

"It attracts the beast," Tommy said. He reached up to take Sylvia's hand as she joined us. She settled on her knees beside him, far too close for a proper lady.

"Isn't that what you want?" I asked. "To attract it and kill it?"

"That was the plan," Samuel said. There was that gritting of his teeth again. And he appeared to be clutching his leg.

"You're hurt," his mother hissed as I noticed it too. She pushed his hair from his face. He jerked away from her touch. "Let me see."

"Not now," he growled.

I gripped the pistol handle harder and managed to remain where I was, despite every piece of me wanting to go to him and do exactly what his mother had just done.

"The plan went awry," Tommy said. "The demon was too quick and dodged the knife. It attacked Samuel and knocked it out of his hand."

"Where is it?" I asked.

"Lying in the grass, somewhere near the woods." Even in the darkness, I could see Tommy's gaze meet mine. "We have to get back over there and search for it."

"No," I said. "We don't."

"The amulet." Samuel grunted in pain. "Clever girl. I know the incantation."

"So do I," Sylvia said.

"And I," Tommy chimed in.

Bollard shifted beside me. His fingers dug into the soft earth. Perhaps he felt inadequate for not being able to speak, poor man.

"Time to call over our friend," Samuel said. "Do not, under any circumstances, shoot."

"Unless it attacks someone," Sylvia cut in.

"We don't want to frighten it off."

"We don't want anyone to die, either."

Samuel hauled himself to his feet. His grunt of pain had me wincing and his mother begging him to sit down again.

"Let the others fight," she pleaded with him.

Samuel had no chance to respond. The demon emerged from the darkness like a ship through fog. It bore down on us, snuffling and snorting like a wild pig.

Sylvia screamed. Tommy shoved her behind him and she fell onto her side, silenced. Mrs. Gladstone's scream took up where Sylvia's left off. She grasped both Samuel's arms and tried to drag him away, but he shook her off.

"Tommy!" he ordered.

Tommy stood beside him and began to chant as the demon came at us. Bollard joined them and the three men formed a blockade in front of us. They were an imposing group, tall and powerfully built.

The demon barreled through as if they were mere children.

We three women scattered. Sylvia screamed and ran off to another wall. Mrs. Gladstone hid behind a column base. I was conscious of remaining nearby and stayed. I had the amulet around my neck and it was vital to our success.

Tommy, bless him, continued his chant. The demon swung around as if the chant were a siren song that it couldn't escape. Its yellow eyes glowed in the dark. It stank like raw meat left out in the sun too long.

"Charity!" Samuel cried. "Give me the amulet."

"No." I stepped a little away from him lest he grab it off me. "You're injured."

"It will come for you! Give it to me. I can fight it."

"No, Samuel, you can't. You can barely walk."

"I can use my fists," he growled. "Christ, Charity, do as I say!"

I stepped closer to Tommy. Not out of fear of Samuel's rising temper, but because being near the person chanting was necessary. Besides, the demon was eying both Tommy and me now. It knew we were the danger, not Samuel, or Sylvia, or Mrs. Gladstone, or Bollard.

Samuel swore colorfully and loudly. The demon was coming again, gathering speed. I could hear its snorting grunts and the *whap whap* of its paws on soft earth. Then I saw the yellow of its eyes, directed on me. It must have picked me out as the weaker of the two. I clutched the amulet, willing Tommy to hurry up and end the chant.

The beast loomed out of the darkness, a monstrous thing covered in fur with a massive head on gigantic shoulders. Its face was a collection of bulging muscle with a slit for a mouth and those penetrating yellow eyes. It was exactly as I imagined a hound from hell to look like. The lipless mouth widened and it bared its pointed teeth as it drove straight for me. The ground beneath my feet rumbled with its pounding steps.

I willed my heart to calm, but it only beat harder against my ribs. Instinct almost had me ruining everything and jumping to the side too soon, but I fought against it and won. I braced myself for impact.

Sylvia's scream shattered the air just at the same moment that Samuel stepped between the demon and me. He punched and ducked, punched and ducked, each jab smacking the demon around the body and head. They say a madman can fight with the strength of ten men. Watching Samuel made me believe it.

But the demon was stronger. It was inevitable that Samuel would lose. It was just a matter of time. Bollard came to help, but he was easily dashed aside by a huge paw. The demon used its superior strength to crash into Samuel. They hit the ground with a bone-crunching thud.

My scream lodged in my throat along with my tears. No one had ever fought for me before, not even Jack. I'd gotten away from the master the first time, on my own, and I'd defeated him when he was in ghostly form too. Watching someone defend me with fists and brute strength was as new to me as the terror filling me.

Not terror for my own life. Terror for Samuel's.

"Samuel!" I cried through my sob. He would die if Tommy didn't finish the chant soon. I couldn't stand by and let that happen.

My pistol. Where was my pistol? I must have returned it to my pocket. I fished inside and my fingers gripped the hard metal. I drew it out and aimed, but it was impossible to get in a good shot. They rolled together, their limbs tangled. I couldn't get in a clear shot of the demon. Damn, damn and hell!

Samuel grunted in pain and I felt sick to my stomach. *Hurry, Tommy!*

The demon managed to wrestle Samuel flat to the ground. Finally, a clear shot! I used two hands to hold the pistol steady and aimed.

The demon suddenly reared back to reveal Samuel lying beneath it, his eyes closed, his body still. He didn't move.

CHAPTER 16

NO! Please, Samuel, get up!

He did not.

The demon stood on thickly muscled hind legs and fixed its eyes on me. Tears turned my vision blurry, but I pulled the trigger anyway. The shot rang out, quickly followed by a second, barely a blink later. The demon fell back with a groan, stunned, thank God.

Still Samuel did not get up.

I swung around. Through my tears I saw Mrs. Gladstone standing near the column, gripping her pistol with both hands like me. She stared wide-eyed at her son's prone form. Then she ran to him. I went to step in the way, to stop her getting too close to the demon, but I need not have worried. Tommy's chant stopped. The demon began to disintegrate and within moments it was nothing more than a pile of dust.

Sylvia came out of seemingly nowhere and embraced me fiercely. She then let me go and fell to her knees near Samuel. He hadn't moved, not even when his mother wept over him. His shredded shirt sleeves and waistcoat revealed the bloodied skin underneath. So much blood.

My heart plunged and my stomach with it. I approached him and his sobbing mother on legs of jelly. His eyes were still closed and his face was as pale as the moon. My throat closed and my tears streamed down my cheeks in a waterfall. Someone circled an arm around my shoulders. Tommy, I thought. But no, it was Bollard's face that I peered into.

I clung to his jacket lapels in the hope it would steady me when all I wanted to do was collapse beside Samuel. "Is he...?"

"He breathes!" Sylvia cried.

I pulled away from Bollard and sank to the ground. I wanted to cradle Samuel's head in my hands and gently push the damp hair from his forehead, but his mother did that. I had to kneel there and watch, wait.

He opened his eyes and blinked at me. "Samuel?" I whispered.

His mother echoed my question. She turned his face to look at her with what I thought a little too much force. "Say something," she whispered.

I touched his hand. His fingers curled around mine. His grip was strong. Pure relief flooded me. I started to cry again.

"I'm all right," he rasped. "But I have a pounding headache."

He drew my hand up to his lips and kissed the knuckles. His mother reared back and fixed our linked hands with a look of distaste. I quickly withdrew mine and tucked it into my skirt folds.

He opened his mouth to say something, but Mrs. Gladstone cut in. "Can you sit?"

He sat up with assistance, but swayed. He closed his eyes and put his hands to his temple. "I think my brain is going to explode."

"You need rest," Sylvia said in a crisp, no-nonsense voice. "Can you walk back to the house?"

Tommy and Bollard helped him up and assisted Samuel to limp across the lawn. Sylvia marched ahead, Mrs. Gladstone hovered alongside, and I fell back to the rear. Nobody took any notice of me there. I could cry in peace.

Mrs. Moore opened the door for us. She must have watched our progress from a window because nobody needed to knock. Mr. Langley sat in his wheelchair behind her. Sylvia ran to him and threw her arms around his shoulders. He patted her back awkwardly.

"You're wet," was all he said.

"It's gone," she spluttered through her tears.

"I know. Samuel?"

"A little bruised," Samuel said. It was quite the understatement. Standing beneath the blazing chandelier his injuries could be better inspected. His chest was scratched and deep gashes striped his leg. His clothing could not be salvaged.

"Tommy, go into the village and fetch Dr. Gowan," Mr. Langley ordered.

Sylvia drew back. "Hasn't Tommy done enough tonight?"

"I'll go," Tommy said. "As soon as we get Gladstone upstairs."

I half expected Mrs. Gladstone to admonish him for his informal address of her son, but she did not. She was too intent on Samuel's comfort and probably hadn't even heard the conversation. She brushed grass and mud off Samuel's back and eyed his bloodied leg with concern.

Samuel and his entourage slowly climbed the stairs. The gawping servants finally returned to their work or their beds, and Mr. Langley wheeled himself off. I slipped back outside, down to the ruins, with the intention of retrieving the lamp. Instead I sat on a low column nearby and stared out to the lake.

It was restful in the dark, despite the horrific scene that had just played out not far away. I didn't cry. My heart was no longer heavy, but uplifted and light. We'd been so fortunate to come through relatively unscathed. Samuel would recover from his injuries soon enough. His mother would probably take him back home, where she could keep her eye on him, and normal life at Frakingham would resume.

I closed my hand around the amulet still strung around my neck. I frowned. So strange that she would summon the thing in the first place with her sons near.

The rumble of wheels down the drive signaled Tommy's departure to fetch the doctor. The light from the coach lamps jostled as the horses moved swiftly, yet not too fast, in the dark. It began to rain again. I was already soaked so I made my way toward the dark mass of the woods instead of back to the house. I searched for Jack's knife, finally finding it only moments before the lamp extinguished.

Back inside the house, I returned the lamp to the deserted kitchen and retrieved a candle instead. I was heading for the stairs when Sylvia called my name.

"There you are!" she said, bustling up to me. She hadn't changed. Her hair fell down around her shoulders in a tangle, but at least it had dried. Mine dripped down my neck. "Where have you been? I've looked everywhere for you."

"Getting the lamp and knife." I opened my palm to reveal the small weapon. "Do you want to give it back to Samuel?"

"Why don't you? He's asking for you."

It made my heart sing to hear it, but I shook my head. "He has enough nurses."

"Not the one he wants."

"I'm sure Mrs. Gladstone is able to care for him well enough."

She snorted. "Hen peck him to death, you mean. Or to madness."

"I suppose that's what mothers do." Caring ones, anyway.

She sighed. "You're right. Of course they do." She tucked her hair behind her ear. "Still, I think seeing you will improve his spirits. He's not in a very good mood."

"Is he ever, lately?"

She tossed out a weak smile. "He has a lot on his mind."

"At least there is now one less burden."

"Thank goodness," she said on a breath. "Are you sure you're determined not to go to him?"

"I'm sure."

"Perhaps in the morning." She hooked her arm through mine. "You're shivering. Come on, let's go upstairs and light the fires in our bedrooms. I'm too tired to draw a bath and Maud and Mrs. Moore have retired for the evening. It will have to wait until the morning."

I let her lead me to my room and sat on the rug before the hearth as she lit a fire. She didn't retire to her own room straight away, but sat alongside me. We stared into the dancing flames for a long time in silence.

"She's a horrid woman," Sylvia suddenly said.

"Mrs. Gladstone?"

She nodded. "I hope she's satisfied now that her son is injured. Why did she want to bring a demon here, anyway?"

"She told Samuel she wanted to study it."

She clicked her tongue. "Another one. When will they ever learn to leave well enough alone? Her curiosity almost killed her own son!"

I said nothing. I couldn't blame her because I was quite sure she didn't do it. What I wanted to know was, why had she claimed responsibility? Who was she protecting?

***

Samuel asked for me again the next day. I didn't go to see him, although I heard about his recovery from Sylvia and Tommy. Sylvia in particular gave me a detailed account of his health and demeanor.

"His wounds appear to be healing without any sign of infection, but his temper has gotten fouler," she said two days after the incident. "Won't you go and see him, Charity? It'll cheer him up immensely."

"No." I gave her no reason, so she could pass none on to him. I thought it was obvious, however. Sitting beside him would only encourage him and give him hope that I might change my mind. I wasn't prepared to open that particular book. Best to leave it shut and deal with his moodiness instead.

Besides, his mother may not have let me into his room. She hardly left his side. She ate her meals in there and didn't return to her own room until late each night—according to Maud, who kept me informed. I preferred to think that it was Mrs. Gladstone's constant presence that caused Samuel's foul temper and not my absence.

He arose from his sickbed on the third day. I and the other members of the household were alerted to this event before we set eyes on him. His mother's stern order of "Get back to bed, now!" greeted our ears where we sat in the sitting room.

Samuel showed up a few moments later, dressed in a blue smoking jacket with a gold dragon embroidered on the sleeve. He must have borrowed it from Mr. Langley; it seemed like the sort of thing he would wear. His feet were bare and he winced with each step. His face lacked color, except where stubble roughened his jaw. I tended to agree with his mother. He did not look like a man who ought to be out of his sickbed.

"There you both are," he said upon seeing Sylvia and me. We'd chosen the sitting room because it was smaller and cozier than the more formal drawing room. We saw no reason for formality, with Mrs. Gladstone's absence. The lady, however, soon graced us with her presence.

"You shouldn't be up," she scolded her son. "The doctor ordered bed rest."

"Leave it alone, Mother," he growled. "I can't stand to be confined any longer."

"Perhaps Miss Langley can read to you."

"I'd rather be lanced with a thousand needles."

Sylvia gave him a withering glare. "That can be arranged."

"Or Dawson could fetch some cards," Mrs. Gladstone persisted. "We can have a game of Cribbage to pass the time."

Samuel sucked air between his teeth, but wisely refrained from answering. His gaze focused on me. "How are you, Charity?"

"Well, thank you. No ill effects from that night."

"Good. I'm glad to see you in good spirits."

"And you? Are your wounds healing?"

"Not fast enough." He limped further into the room, no longer wincing. I suspect it wasn't an easy thing to hide. He lowered himself into a chair with a long exhalation of breath.

"Mrs. Gladstone is right," I said. "You should be in bed."

To my surprise, she gave me a stiff nod of thanks.

"You've only got yourself to blame," Samuel said with a sparkle in his eye that reminded me of the old Samuel. "If you'd come to see me, I would have no reason to get up."

I lowered my head to hide my smile and bit my lip to make doubly sure. We were entering dangerous waters. Time to change the subject. "When will you be returning home?"

"I'm not."

"Tomorrow," Mrs. Gladstone said over the top of her son. "Since he's up and about, I don't see why he needs to remain any longer now the…creature has gone."

"Tomorrow seems a little too soon, " Sylvia hedged.

"I'm staying here," Samuel said again, with a roll of his eyes.

"Perhaps see what Dr. Gowan thinks." Sylvia sounded satisfied that her suggestion was the best one.

"I don't wish to cast aspersions on your doctor, Miss Langley," Mrs. Gladstone said, "but our family physician is vastly more experienced."

"Dr. Naigle is as ancient as the abbey ruins!" Samuel said. "And let me reiterate, since you both seem to not have heard me the first two times. I. Am. Not. Leaving."

Sylvia clicked her tongue. "There's no need to raise your voice. But I am pleased to hear that you've decided to stay. I do think you're not up to traveling yet and we enjoy your company. Most of the time."

He grunted and shot a glance in my direction. I said nothing and remained very still. His mother, however, huffed her displeasure and launched into all the reasons why he should return.

I made my excuses and left.

"Charity!" he called after me. "Charity, wait! I wish to speak to you. Blast this leg!"

I was gone before he managed to stand. There were some benefits to his injuries, at least.

***

Neither Samuel nor Mrs. Gladstone left the following day. I managed to avoid both of them, mostly because Samuel once more kept to his bedroom.

"He hasn't had a relapse, has he?" I asked Sylvia when I saw her. I may not wish to see him, but the thought of his condition worsening had me worried.

"No," she said on a sigh. "But I'm afraid if we don't get his mother away soon, he's going to unleash his temper."

"What can we do?"

"I could talk to her."

"Er, no. I don't think that would help. The only thing that would distract her from nursing her son back to health is another family crisis of greater magnitude."

"Bert!"

I smiled. "Precisely. Send him a letter begging him to write to her and request her to return home. We'll send it in today's post."

She clapped her hands. "Excellent! What a devious mind you have, Charity."

I only hoped it didn't backfire on us and bring Bert to our doorstep too. I could cope with a foul tempered Samuel, but not an oily Bert *and* his mother.

When a carriage drove up to the house the following day, my heart stopped. How could he have gotten here so quickly? Unless he'd left before he received Sylvia's letter. I prepared to dash up to my room and lock the door so I didn't have to see him, but stopped as I caught sight of the man alighting from the carriage. It wasn't Bert, but Myer.

"What's *he* doing here?" Sylvia asked, coming up alongside me.

"To see your uncle, perhaps," I said. "Or resume his studies down at the ruins. Perhaps Mrs. Butterworth informed him that our 'wild dog' problem had been resolved."

She flounced onto the sofa in a huff, a look of disgust on her face. "I hope he doesn't come in here. I don't wish to speak with him. Ever."

I, on the other hand, did. I went in search of him and found him handing his coat and hat to Tommy. Samuel was with them. My gasp of surprise had them all turning to look at me.

"Charity!" Samuel limped toward me and Myer followed. "I had been on my way to look for you when Myer arrived."

"Your mother's not here?"

"She's indisposed. I wanted to talk to you, but...I need to speak to Myer as well. Will you wait for me?"

"I had the same idea as you when I saw the carriage." I nodded a greeting to Myer. "Good morning, Mr. Myer. I wanted to ask you some questions, too."

Myer sighed and plucked the fingertips of his gloves to remove them. "It seems inevitable that you two would have the same questions. I might as well answer them together, if I can. Shall we adjourn somewhere more private?"

I hesitated and swallowed. He wanted me alone with him? Him and Samuel?

"I give you my word I won't hypnotize you, Miss Evans."

"You bloody well will not," Samuel ground out. "Not with me around."

I didn't tell him that I was just as afraid of him. I curled my hands into fists and dug my fingernails into my palms. The sting distracted me enough from my fear to continue. "The library is free. Tommy, will you bring in tea, please." I tried to convey with one glance that I wanted him to deliver the tea and check on me, but if he understood, he gave no indication.

The main library at Frakingham housed different books to the ones in Langley's laboratory. I liked to sit in the deep leather armchairs in the evening, and tuck my feet up beneath me, as I read a book plucked from one of the many shelves. When the lamps in the wall sconces were lit and the heavy brocade curtains pulled shut, it was easy to imagine oneself transported to the world between the pages. During the day, it was a little less magical but no less comfortable, although I was much too on edge to relax. I left the double doors wide open. Neither man objected.

"What a pleasant room," Myer said, drawing in a deep breath and seating himself in the largest armchair, positioned by the fireplace.

"Forget pleasantries, Myer," Samuel said. "I have only a few moments before my mother finds us and I wish to ask you some questions without her present. How do you know her?"

"You are nothing if not direct, Mr. Gladstone. But I believe I've answered that question before."

"I was hoping for the truth, this time."

Myer crossed one leg over the other and linked his fingers on his stomach. "She was a frequent visitor to this house when Lord Frakingham owned it. We met when I came to study the ruins."

"You told us you hardly knew Lord Frakingham."

His only response was an apologetic shrug.

"Why did my mother come here? Was she a member of the society? Was she married to my father at the time?" Samuel's questions were like bullets, direct and uncompromising.

"They were married. When I met her, your brother was born and she was in the early stages of carrying you. Indeed, I didn't even know she was with child, until afterwards."

"So it was 1867," I said, quickly calculating.

He nodded. "As to why she came here." He shrugged. "She wasn't a member of the society, but she was...searching for answers of a philosophical nature. Lord Frakingham had gatherings here, from time to time, with like-minded ladies and gentlemen."

"Enlighten me," Samuel said. "What do you mean by philosophical?"

Myer shifted in his chair. "I don't feel comfortable discussing this. It's none of my affair. You should ask Mrs. Gladstone."

"I'm asking you. And unless you want Langley to revoke his permission for you to study the ruins, you had better answer me."

Myer's thumbs tapped against one another in a quick beat. Then they suddenly stilled. "She was unhappy. She wanted answers to some very big questions and hoped Frakingham's philosophers, as they were known, could help."

"What questions?"

"Is there a god? And if there is, why does he allow a young boy to suffer?"

"My brother," Samuel murmured.

"He was ill," I said, thinking aloud.

"He was born sickly and she thought it unfair," Myer went on. "She wanted to know why her family had been dealt such a blow. That's all. Well, as far as I know, that's all. She didn't confide in me."

"Did my father join her here?" Samuel asked.

"Once, yes, but never again afterwards. Indeed, she stopped coming when it came time for her confinement. Perhaps the arrival of a healthy son restored her faith and she had no need for philosophy anymore."

"So her presence here had nothing to do with the ruins and the paranormal?"

He shrugged one shoulder. "The group were known to hold their gatherings down at the old abbey in good weather. The energy was stronger there, in those days. One could feel it as one entered the area. It's only natural that they would want to be closer to that energy source."

It still seemed unlikely that a philosophical group would have a need for that type of energy, but I didn't press the issue. "Why does Mrs. Gladstone not like you?" I asked.

He shrugged again. "I suspect I remind her of that uncertain, anxious time. I was often here when the philosophers were having their meetings."

"She disliked you so intensely that she wanted to frame *you* for the demon summoning."

"You should ask *her* about that. Only she can answer you."

"None of this explains why you and I can hypnotize," Samuel said.

"No, Gladstone, it does not. I have given up trying to find an explanation. My advice to you is to do the same. Now, if that's all, I'd like to continue my work with Langley. This demon business has put everything on hold long enough."

"I know you gave her the amulet," Samuel said. "The blame must lie partly at your feet."

"Me! I most certainly did not give it to her."

Samuel looked as if he wanted to thump Myer. Although I wouldn't have minded seeing Myer receive a pommelling, I did think it would be unfair if given for the wrong reason.

"Perhaps you didn't give it to *her*," I said. "But to someone else."

Both men turned to me, eyebrows arched in a twin expression of curiosity. "That note you wrote, Mr. Myer. The one we found in Mr. Gladstone's fireplace. You didn't write it to Mrs. Gladstone, did you?"

Samuel swiveled to face me fully. "Charity, what are you saying?"

"I'm saying that your mother took the blame for summoning the demon, but she didn't do it."

Samuel's brow thickened and his eyes darkened, but I didn't feel as if he was growing angry with me. Rather, he was trying to think back through all the clues and discussions.

"She cares for both you and Bert deeply. She is a wonderful mother, in that respect. Nobody can fault her love for her sons. She would never summon a demon here when you are near. Never. Couple that with the fact she didn't know how to control it and I cannot believe she would do such a dangerous thing."

Samuel looked as if the stuffing had been knocked out of him. His pale cheeks grew paler and his lashes lowered over his eyes, hiding the confusion I saw briefly in them.

"Bert," he said, weakly. "She's hiding the fact that it was Bert who summoned it."

I nodded but he wasn't looking at me. He lowered his head. His fingers scrunched through his hair. "Bloody, stupid clod!" he growled. "I can't believe he would do something so foolish, then run away home. I can't believe he would…kill our father. And for what? His damned inheritance?"

I wanted to cradle him as he fought the emotions he must be feeling. Wanted to tell him that he mustn't let his family's faults cause him grief. He was hurting—and I could do nothing except watch.

Myer cleared his throat and glanced at the doorway. I looked around, but there was nobody there. Not even Tommy entered with our tea yet.

"What I don't understand is why the note from you, Mr. Myer, was found in Mr. Gladstone's fireplace?" I said. "Why did Bert give it to his father? Or did Mr. Gladstone find it in Bert's possession? No," I said, answering my own question. "That can't be right. He was already dead when you wrote that note to Bert."

Once more Myer cleared his throat.

"My God. We have it wrong, don't we?" I whispered, as a few more pieces of the puzzle fell into place.

Samuel looked up. His stricken gaze tore strips off Myer as if he could peel back the lies to uncover the truth.

Myer flattened his tie and again glanced at the doorway. This time, someone entered: Mrs. Gladstone. She looked just as distraught as her son as she met his gaze with her own. She clutched the lace collar at her throat as if it were too tight.

"Don't blame your brother," she choked out. "It's not his fault. It's your father's."

Samuel held up his hands as if he were warding off the information as it assaulted him. "*Father* summoned the demon?"

She nodded. He looked to Myer and he nodded too. Then he looked to me. All I could do was blink back at him, even though I wanted to offer comfort.

"That's why no one could control it," I said. "*He* summoned the demon, but it killed him and the creature was left masterless."

"Why did he want to bring it here?" Samuel asked, his voice hollow.

Mrs. Gladstone's gaze flicked to Myer. Oh God. I think I knew why, but I would not say. I would not be the one to tell Samuel. That responsibility belonged to his mother. She'd created this mess and it was time she ended it.

Mrs. Gladstone stood with her back to the fireplace, her hands twisted into a knot in front of her. She looked small against the large mantel, her face bloodless against the polished black wood. "He wanted it to attack Mr. Myer," she said matter-of-factly.

Myer didn't flinch or look at all surprised by her accusation. He must already have known, or suspected.

"Why?" Samuel asked.

Mrs. Gladstone drew in a deep breath and her gaze fixed on a point a little to Samuel's left. "Because many years ago, when I used to join the Frakingham Philosophers for discussions and so forth, Mr. Myer here...encouraged me to set aside my marital vows."

I gaped at her. My breath left my body.

"What?" Samuel exploded. His face reddened and his eyes flashed. He suddenly launched out of his chair in complete disregard for his injuries and grabbed Myer by the collar. "I'll kill you," he snarled. "I'll bloody kill you."

CHAPTER 17

Myer's face turned mottled. His eyes bulged. His mouth opened and shut like that of a dying fish on the dock. Spittle collected in the corner and he scrabbled at Samuel's hand, clawing and dragging to no effect.

"Samuel! Stop it!" Mrs. Gladstone snapped from her position by the fire.

Samuel didn't let go and the color of Myer's face deepened to a dangerous purple. I went to him and stood very close where he couldn't fail to notice me. I rested my hand on his shoulder.

"Samuel," I said, firm but not loud. "Let him go. Come and sit with me."

My voice seemed to have an effect. The muscles beneath my hand shifted a little, relaxing. He loosed his grip and Myer gasped in a deep breath.

I took Samuel's other hand in mine and closed my fingers firmly around it. He let go of Myer completely and backed away with me to the sofa. We sat together, still holding hands. I wanted to let go...yet I didn't want to, either. Touching him felt important somehow, like I was his anchor in a raging storm. He needed me and, for now, I would be there for him.

He did not take his gaze off Myer, however, as Myer sat back down and adjusted his tie. His color had almost returned to normal, but he kept his wary gaze on Samuel as if he expected him to leap up again at any moment.

"If you had let me speak," he said in a dry, rasping voice, "you would have heard me say that nothing came of it. Mrs. Gladstone was...intent on finding answers to her eldest son's illness. She was also already with child. Her mind was occupied with other thoughts."

"You didn't hypnotize her?" I challenged.

He shook his head and since she didn't protest, I assumed he told the truth.

"Mr. Gladstone found out about this?" I asked. Samuel seemed incapable of speech, so I felt it was up to me to find out the truth. "Is that why he wanted Myer dead?"

Mrs. Gladstone gave a single, stiff nod. "I was reluctant to come to Frakingham again to retrieve Samuel. My memories of this place are troubled. My husband wanted to know why."

I felt Samuel's fingers twitch inside mine. I tightened my grip and received a wide-eyed blink in return.

"I didn't tell him at first, but he remembered my philosophical gatherings here all those years ago," she went on. "He continued to press me with questions because he seemed to know that something specific had troubled me. Eventually he hit on the right question to ask and I was unable to lie well enough for him to believe me. He blamed the wrong man at first. He thought Lord Frakingham tried to..." She turned her face away as if the thought disgusted her. "It wasn't until we arrived here and he saw my reaction to Mr. Myer that he put two and two together."

"Not that I tried to renew my attentions," Myer protested, his hands in the air.

Samuel bared his teeth and Myer snapped his mouth shut.

"Is that why he wrote to Mr. Butterworth?" I asked. "To discover more?"

Mrs. Gladstone nodded. "That was before I told him everything."

"There was nothing in the letter alluding to…that time," Myer said. "I suspect it was merely an attempt to form an acquaintance."

"But you found that letter and had Mrs. Butterworth destroy it for you," I said to Myer. "Then you hypnotized Mr. Butterworth so he couldn't recall its contents. Why, if it was innocent?"

"It linked me to Gladstone. After he summoned the demon, I wanted our connection to remain hidden. I knew what conclusions you would jump to."

Mrs. Gladstone cleared her throat. "Unbeknown to me, my husband paid Mr. Myer a visit in the village after we arrived and Mr. Myer gave him the amulet."

"You just *gave* it to him?" Samuel asked, incredulous.

"It wasn't like that," Myer said hotly. "He came to me at the Butterworths' and asked me about the supernatural. He seemed to have quite an interest in the topic. I can assure you, he had some rudimentary knowledge, particularly hypnosis, naturally. Not once did he accuse me of befriending his wife. I had no idea that he even knew. He was very jolly and asked me many questions about my work. Indeed, he was so interested that he requested some evidence of the supernatural. I showed him my readings from the ruins, my book of notes, et cetera. I produced the amulet too, since he became quite curious when I mentioned the demon problems you had at Christmas."

Samuel squeezed his forehead between his thumb and forefinger. "Fool," he muttered.

Myer cleared his throat. "Perhaps I was. In my defense, he was very convincing. I thought he might like to join the society, so I left him to fetch paper and writing implements to write down my address."

"He took the amulet," I said.

"And tore out a page of my notebook," Myer said with a click of his tongue. "The page with the summons written on it."

Samuel groaned and closed his eyes.

"I'm surprised the Butterworths didn't mention this visit," I said. "Did you place a memory block on them?"

"I couldn't have them knowing so much," Myer said. "Those two are not true believers. Not even Mrs. Butterworth. Talk of the supernatural would only alarm them."

Vile man. "Then, that evening, Mr. Gladstone summoned it in the hope it would attack you." I frowned. "But you weren't down at the ruins that night. Had you informed him that you would be and changed your mind at the last moment?"

Myer shook his head and would not meet my gaze.

"Then why did he summon it at all? Did he not know that it would manifest near *him* and not you?"

He looked to Mrs. Gladstone. She merely lowered her veil over her face and said nothing.

"Because he didn't *want* to kill Myer," Samuel said. He swore and rubbed his hand over his face. "He wanted to kill himself and have Myer blamed for it."

"We don't know that," Mrs. Gladstone said quickly.

"But it's possible," Samuel said. "That's why you didn't tell me any of this earlier. That's why you've asked Myer not to tell me about the meeting with Father. You've tried to protect me from the fact that you think he wanted to end his own life."

"It may not be true." She dabbed at her eyes through the veil with a black handkerchief. "It may have been an accident. We don't know for certain, but you're right. That's why I didn't want you to know that he summoned it himself. I didn't want you and Bert thinking it for even a moment."

Samuel merely grunted. It was impossible to know what he was thinking, although I could feel how rigid he was through our linked hands.

"Your father wasn't himself in those last few days," she went on. "He worried that you may never come home. He worried about Bert's health, and then the jealousy of finding out about..." She waved her hand. "I suspect it all became overwhelming. I prefer to think that he felt as if he had to act to remove one of those obstacles."

"Me," Myer said, stretching his neck out of his collar. It was still a little red from where Samuel had tried to strangle him. "Even if he didn't send it to kill me, he might have wanted to end his own life and lay the blame at my feet."

"I simply wanted to keep your memory of your father intact," Mrs. Gladstone told Samuel. "He was a good man. He loved you both."

"He had an odd way of showing it," Samuel bit off.

I could see how the building pressure from so many forces could make a man act irrationally. Particularly a man like Mr. Gladstone, who was used to being in control and wielding power over those around him. I suspected he'd begun to feel quite powerless and that must have frightened him. Finding out about Myer and his wife could have tipped him over the edge.

I looked at Samuel out of the corner of my eye. He lowered his head and seemed to be taking it all in. He still held my hand as if it were a natural thing to do. To my surprise, his mother said nothing about it. She seemed distracted, lost in her memories and worries.

"I found the amulet in the pocket of the waistcoat he was wearing that day," she went on. "I didn't know what it was, at the time. Indeed, not until you confronted me here, only a few days ago, Samuel. I thought it was a trinket he'd bought and hadn't gotten around to giving me, although it was quite an unusual looking piece."

And when Samuel had found it in her things, he'd never questioned her about it. Just assumed she'd been the one to use it.

"What about the note, Mr. Myer?" I asked. "Why did you write it and send it to Mr. Gladstone? When did you?"

"I realized a short time after he left the Butterworths' house that he'd taken the amulet. I hadn't noticed the missing page, so didn't realize he possessed all the tools to summon it. I thought he was harmless. A thief, but harmless. I wrote him that note and had it sent up here as a warning, of sorts. I hoped he would return the amulet under his own volition, without me confronting him. But then the worst happened after all, and he died before I could speak to him about it."

"And why didn't you tell us what he'd done immediately?"

"Mrs. Gladstone asked me not to, for the same reason she herself kept silent. Because she didn't want her sons thinking ill of their father and that he may have summoned it to end his own life. I can only apologize for misleading you all. I hope I can be forgiven." He looked to Samuel, but Samuel didn't respond. He continued to stare down at the rug.

"I don't think your research is under threat," I told him. "Perhaps, Mr. Myer, you and I should leave." I tried to unlink my fingers from Samuel's, but he wouldn't let go. "Samuel," I said gently. "You ought to speak to your mother alone."

He lifted his face and blinked weary, watery eyes at me. "Charity...thank you." He untangled his hand from mine and gave me a flat smile.

Myer and I left them alone and shut the library door.

***

I managed to avoid Samuel for the rest of the day. I warred with myself over whether I should go to him and talk to him about what his father had done, but decided not to. My feelings where he was concerned were mixed, confusing. Yet I worried about his state of mind, and so sent Sylvia up to his room to see him.

She returned and reported that he was the same as always—a little morose, quiet and sick of his mother's hovering. He didn't ask after me.

I sent Tommy up too. He returned and said the same things.

Good. I was glad Samuel didn't ask for me. Perhaps he was cured of his affection. Perhaps he was focusing on his recovery. I refused to feel put out by it. After all, I had no one but myself to blame, since it was exactly what I wanted.

The following day I weakened. I told myself I needed to see if he was coming to terms with all that his mother had told him. In truth, I just wanted to see him. I finally summoned enough courage around noon, just after a letter arrived for him from his brother.

"What do you think it said?" I asked Sylvia, not fifteen minutes after its arrival, as we completed another music lesson. Tommy had come in to tell us about the letter before taking it upstairs. I'd been on tenterhooks since.

"Go and ask," she said.

"I can't."

"Why not? You're not afraid of his mother, are you?"

"Certainly not."

"You're still afraid of him?"

I smoothed my skirt over my lap. "I…I don't want to encourage his affections by visiting him."

"Charity," she said on a sigh. "I've visited him and nobody thinks I'm encouraging his affections. Go on." She gave me a little shove in the arm. "Go and see him. I'd wager he needs a distraction."

I smothered a smile and did as I was told. Upstairs, Samuel's door was open and his mother hovered in the doorway, her back to the corridor. I remained several feet away, to see if she was coming or going. In truth, I wasn't sure if I wanted her there or not. On the one hand, I didn't want a confrontation with her, but on the other, nothing could happen with her present. Samuel could neither try to seduce me nor hypnotize me.

So I stood there, paralyzed.

"I'm not at all sure about this," Mrs. Gladstone said, her voice reaching me.

"Mother, he needs you more than I do now. I'm recovering while his health worsens. He says so, plain as can be."

I bit my lip. What would he do if he learned that Sylvia and I orchestrated the letter from Bert? Perhaps he would be pleased that we freed him from his mother, the dragon. I hoped.

"Very well," I heard her mutter. "But Samuel, I know there is the unspoken thing between us."

"Don't," he said.

"I have to."

I winced and wished I could walk away and not listen to them discuss his father's behavior again, or his mother's liaison with Myer. Yet I couldn't. I was rooted to the spot. I strained to listen to their voices.

"Don't do anything foolish with her," she said.

Her? Did she mean me? *I* was the unspoken thing between them?

"I said don't," he snapped. "I'm a grown man. Let me settle my own affairs."

"I will, yes. But let my sorry situation be a lesson to you. Her future husband and your future wife won't thank you if something happens now between you. Those sorts of…connections cannot be undone. It may come back to haunt you. Both of you. Think of that, Samuel, before you run headlong into an *affaire de coeur*. "

"You have it all wrong, Mother. I have no wish to have an *affaire*. I wish to marry her."

Oh Samuel. My heart sank. My throat closed. He sounded so determined too. Part of me wished things could be different and I wasn't so afraid of him. But the other part cowered in fear. How far would he go to make his assertion a reality?

Mrs. Gladstone sighed. "My darling boy. Be reasonable and think of her, for once, instead of your own selfish desires."

"I am!"

"She would be subject to ridicule and gossip, not only by your friends but by your family, too. You, of all people, know how important it is to maintain a certain face or be ravaged by their cruel tongues."

"I don't care for gossipers. Nor does she. We'll go away from here and London. I'll protect her."

My heart lurched in my chest. Tears burned the backs of my eyes. Oh Samuel....

"What makes you think she wants to leave her life? Her school? She seems rather settled there, by all accounts."

It was odd that a woman who could hardly stand to be in my presence knew me better than the man who professed to love me.

"Besides," she went on, "I've come to believe that even she knows that being with you is an uphill battle, and not worth fighting for."

"I beg to differ," he growled.

She didn't say anything further, but emerged fully from the doorway. She saw me and stopped, but did not give away my presence to Samuel. Instead, she closed his door and made her way toward me.

"You heard that," she said. It wasn't a question.

I nodded. "Thank you," I said in a shaky voice. "For putting it succinctly and without prejudice."

She inclined her head in a nod. There was no softness in her eyes, no gentle motherliness. She could have been speaking to a shop assistant or servant. Or a teacher, who'd once been little better than a whore. "I don't hate you, Miss Evans."

"Thank you," I said wryly.

"I see that you can be considerate and kind. I see that the Langleys like you. But that doesn't mean you can dig your claws into my son. There is no possible way there can be a union between the two of you."

"I know that. You even said yourself that I knew. I have no interest in marrying Samuel."

She gave another brief nod. "Then I wish to add one more thing. If you care for him at all, do not offer to…comfort him, after he's married."

I spluttered a protest then quickly glanced at Samuel's door. It remained shut. "Mrs. Gladstone, I can assure you, I don't wish to be anything to Samuel. Not even a friend. I hope all communication between us will be severed, as soon as possible. I believe that to be the only possible course of action, don't you?"

"Well. If you'll excuse me, I need to oversee my packing." She went to move around me, but I stopped her with a hand to her arm. She shook me off.

"I have some advice that I'd like you to pass on to Miss Carstairs," I said.

Shock rippled across her face, shedding her stony facade. "Ebony?"

"We discussed this before, Mrs. Gladstone, but I am in earnest now. Tell Miss Carstairs to cease any plans she has of a political career for Samuel. He doesn't want it and it's only pushing him away. If she is willing to forego her dreams then she has a much better chance of securing him. But she must tread slowly, and you should not try to throw them together. Let it come from her alone."

She frowned at me, the lines in her forehead deeper from her recent worries. "You are sincere," she said in wonder, as if she couldn't believe a woman *wouldn't* want to be with her son.

I nodded.

"I don't understand, Miss Evans. Why?"

I blinked at her and eventually she looked away.

"Oh," she murmured. That was it. One single word, but we understood one another. She knew that I knew what he'd done to get himself confined to Newgate. And she didn't blame me for wanting to stay away.

"He is a good man, Miss Evans. But he has done some foolish things."

"We all have."

"Some are unforgiveable."

"For me, that one is. I'm sure if he's honest with Miss Carstairs he might find that she's not quite so condemning." I inclined my head. "Good day, Mrs. Gladstone."

"Good day, Miss Evans." She trudged off, her footsteps heavy for such a slight woman.

I watched her go, my heart full, and headed for Samuel's room. I knocked before I changed my mind.

"Charity!" he said upon opening it. "I'm glad to see you. Come in."

I shook my head.

"I hoped you would come to visit me," he went on, unperturbed.

"You did?" I caught myself saying.

He gave me a fleeting smile. "Yes. And here you are." Another smile, this time more uncertain and awkward. It was endearing.

I steeled myself. "There's something I wanted to say before my courage failed me."

"Oh?"

I cleared my throat. "I seem to have a habit of listening in to conversations, lately. I heard you and your mother talking, just now."

His face clouded. "I'm sorry. I wish you hadn't."

"There's nothing to apologize for. Your mother is right. There can be nothing between us. Nor do I want there to be."

He pounded his fist against the doorframe and sucked in a deep breath. He screwed his eyes shut as if gripped by pain. "I may be mad, Charity, but I would never hurt you. Not ever. If that is your only objection…"

I backed away. There was nothing more to be said and my presence was only making things harder for both of us.

"Wait," he said and reached out to take my arm. He let his hand fall back to his side, however, before touching me. "Don't go," he whispered. "Stay. Talk to me."

"Samuel," I said on a sigh. "I can't."

"Because you don't trust me?"

I nodded and he rocked back on his heels. "You know why," I said.

"My hypnosis."

I folded my arms and stared down at my feet. I nodded.

"I know it happens involuntarily when I'm with you sometimes, but I would never do anything to you while you were under. Never. Why can you not believe me?"

Because of what you did to end up in Newgate.

It was time to learn once and for all if Bert had told me the truth about that. But I wanted to hear it from Samuel's lips, not his mother or brother's. I wanted to hear him tell me what happened in his own words. It seemed fair, and important.

"Can I ask you a very delicate question?" I ventured. My hands shook. My feet wanted to run away. But I forced myself to stay and push forward. Always forward.

"Go on."

"Why were you in Newgate?" I lifted my gaze to meet his wretched one. "What did you do?"

He pressed his lips together and blinked up at the ceiling. The muscles in his jaw bunched and relaxed, bunched and relaxed. "That is the one question I cannot answer, Charity. The one and only."

I stepped back a little. With his injuries, he couldn't move particularly fast. I could run off if need be. But I persisted. "Why not?"

He met my gaze with his own and as hard as I resisted, I sank into the swirling blue pools. Utterly lost. Forget running away; in that moment, I wanted to stay. He could have kissed me and I wouldn't have objected. Could have held me and had me, despite the fear still tapping at my chest. And he hadn't even hypnotized me. "I can't because you'll hate me even more."

"I don't hate you." I whispered, but my voice sounded loud in my head. My heart hammered even louder against my ribs, a wild, heady rhythm that throbbed through my body and set it alight.

"Maybe not, but you will become more afraid of me than you already are. And I cannot bear that, Charity. So please don't ask me about Newgate."

"If you won't tell me, how can I ever trust you?"

He said nothing. Silence weighed heavily around us, smothering, suffocating.

"I overheard you tell your mother that you *will* marry me, but Samuel, that cannot happen." I breathed deeply and met his gaze with my own direct one. "I want you to set aside your feelings for me and marry Ebony. She is better suited to you."

"Right," he sneered. "Because she's Lord Mellor's daughter. I don't care about any of that!"

"No. Not because she's a lady and I'm nobody. You should marry her because she's not afraid of you."

He reeled back as if my words had slapped me across the face. He took several deep breaths, composing himself, then he slowly took a step toward me. My heart beat even faster, begging me to flee, but I forced myself to stay. When he saw that I didn't move, he very slowly touched my cheek. He grazed his knuckles lightly down to my chin, stroking me as if I were a frightened animal.

"I'm going to prove to you that you *can* trust me." His voice wasn't mesmerizing, but it was low, deep and filled with promise. "Give me time, Charity, and I will show you that I'm worthy of you."

Him worthy of me? His mother would convulse in horror if she heard him say that.

I blinked back at him and willed myself to move away, out of his touch. But I couldn't. I was as thoroughly caught, as if he were holding me in his hands. He was so gentle, so soothing and calm. His touch was like a lure and I a fish on the end of a hook, powerless to get away.

So utterly powerless.

Panic seized my chest. A fist squeezed around my heart, locking it down. How could I trust him? How could I ever let a man with so much power over me get so close?

I shouldn't. I would be a fool to allow it.

I pulled away and ran off, but not before I saw the sorrow in his eyes and heard the plea die on his lips.

"Charity."

THE END

LOOK OUT FOR

Edge Of Darkness

The third book in the second FREAK HOUSE TRILOGY.

To be notified when C.J. has a new release, sign up to her newsletter. Send an email to cjarcher.writes@gmail.com

ABOUT THE AUTHOR

C.J. Archer has loved history and books for as long as she can remember. She worked as a librarian and technical writer until she was able to channel her twin loves by writing historical fiction. She has won and placed in numerous romance writing contests, including taking home RWAustralia's Emerald Award in 2008 for the manuscript that would become her novel *Honor Bound*. Under the name Carolyn Scott, she has published contemporary romantic mysteries, including *Finders Keepers Losers Die*, and *The Diamond Affair*. After spending her childhood surrounded by the dramatic beauty of outback Queensland, she lives today in suburban Melbourne, Australia, with her husband and their two children.

She loves to hear from readers. You can contact her in one of these ways:
Website: www.cjarcher.com
Email: cjarcher.writes@gmail.com
Facebook: www.facebook.com/CJArcherAuthorPage

Made in the USA
Lexington, KY
28 December 2017